The
Dain Curse

The
Dain Curse

DASHIELL HAMMETT

VINTAGE BOOKS

A Division of Random House
NEW YORK

Vintage Books Edition, October 1972

Originally published by Alfred A. Knopf, Inc., in 1929.
Library of Congress Cataloging in Publication Data
Hammett, Dashiell, 1894–1961.
The Dain curse.
I. Title
[PZ3.H1884Dai 16]   [PS3515.A4347]   813'.5'2   72–1755
ISBN 0-394-71827-5

Manufactured in the United States of America

Cover painting by Alan Reingold

To
Albert S. Samuels

The
Dain Curse

Part One: The Dains

I : EIGHT DIAMONDS

It was a diamond all right, shining in the grass half a dozen feet from the blue brick wall. It was small, not more than a quarter of a carat in weight, and unmounted. I put it in my pocket and began searching the lawn as closely as I could without going at it on all fours.

I had covered a couple of square yards of sod when the Leggetts' front door opened.

A woman came out on the broad stone top step and looked down at me with good-humored curiosity.

She was a woman of about my age, forty, with darkish blond hair, a pleasant plump face, and dimpled pink cheeks. She had on a lavender-flowered white housedress.

I stopped poking at the grass and went up to her, asking: "Is Mr. Leggett in?"

"Yes." Her voice was placid as her face. "You wish to see him?"

I said I did.

She smiled at me and at the lawn.

"You're another detective, aren't you?"

I admitted that.

She took me up to a green, orange, and chocolate room on the second floor, put me in a brocaded chair, and went to call her husband from his laboratory. While I waited, I looked around the room, deciding that the dull orange rug under my feet was probably both genuinely oriental and genuinely ancient, that the walnut furniture hadn't been ground out by machinery, and that the Japanese pictures on the wall hadn't been selected by a prude.

Edgar Leggett came in saying: "I'm sorry to have kept you waiting, but I couldn't break off till now. Have you learned something?"

His voice was unexpectedly harsh, rasping, though his manner was friendly enough. He was a dark-skinned erect man in his middle forties, muscularly slender and of medium height. He would have been handsome if his brown face hadn't been so deeply marked with sharp, hard lines across the forehead and from nostrils down across mouth-corners. Dark hair, worn rather long, curled above and around the broad, grooved forehead. Red-brown eyes were abnormally bright behind horn-rimmed spectacles. His nose was long, thin, and high-bridged. His lips were thin, sharp, nimble, over a small, bony chin. His black and white clothes were well made and cared for.

"Not yet," I said to his question. "I'm not a police detective—Continental Agency—for the insurance company —and I'm just starting."

"Insurance company?" He seemed surprised, raising dark eyebrows above the dark tops of his spectacles.

"Yeah. Didn't—?"

"Surely," he said, smiling, stopping my words with a small flourish of one hand. It was a long, narrow hand with over-developed finger-tips, ugly as most trained hands are. "Surely. They would have been insured. I hadn't thought of that. They weren't my diamonds, you know; they were Halstead's."

"Halstead and Beauchamp? I didn't get any details from the insurance company. You had the diamonds on approval?"

"No. I was using them experimentally. Halstead knew of my work with glass—coloring it, staining or dyeing it, after its manufacture—and he became interested in the possibility of the process being adapted to diamonds, particularly in improving off-color stones, removing yellowish and brownish tinges, emphasizing blues. He asked me to try it and five weeks ago gave me those diamonds to work on. There were eight of them, none especially valuable. The largest weighed only a trifle more than half a carat, some of the others only a quarter, and except for two they were all of poor color. They're the stones the burglar got."

"Then you hadn't succeeded?" I asked.

"Frankly," he said, "I hadn't made the slightest progress. This was a more delicate matter, and on more obdurate material."

"Where'd you keep them?"

"Usually they were left lying around in the open—always in the laboratory, of course—but for several days now they had been locked in the cabinet—since my last unsuccessful experiment."

"Who knew about the experiments?"

"Anyone, everyone—there was no occasion for secrecy."

"They were stolen from the cabinet?"

"Yes. This morning we found our front door open, the cabinet drawer forced, and the diamonds gone. The police found marks on the kitchen door. They say the burglar came in that way and left by the front door. We heard nothing last night. And nothing else was taken."

"The front door was ajar when I came downstairs this morning," Mrs. Leggett said from the doorway. "I went upstairs and awakened Edgar, and we searched the house and found the diamonds gone. The police think the man I saw must have been the burglar."

I asked about the man she had seen.

"It was last night, around midnight, when I opened the bedroom windows before going to bed. I saw a man standing upon the corner. I can't say, even now, that there was anything very suspicious-looking about him. He was standing there as if waiting for somebody. He was looking down this way, but not in a way to make me think he was watching this house. He was a man past forty, I should say, rather short and broad—somewhat of your build—but he had a bristly brown mustache and was pale. He wore a soft hat and overcoat—dark—I think they were brown. The police think that's the same man Gabrielle saw."

"Who?"

"My daughter Gabrielle," she said. "Coming home late one night—Saturday night, I think it was—she saw a man and thought he had come from our steps; but she wasn't sure and didn't think anything more of it until after the burglary."

"I'd like to talk to her. Is she home?"

Mrs. Leggett went out to get her.

I asked Leggett: "Were the diamonds loose?"

"They were unset, of course, and in small manila envelopes—Halstead and Beauchamp's—each in a separate envelope, with a number and the weight of the stone written in pencil. The envelopes are missing too."

Mrs. Leggett returned with her daughter, a girl of twenty or less in a sleeveless white silk dress. Of medium height, she looked more slender than she actually was. She had hair as curly as her father's, and no longer, but of a much lighter brown. She had a pointed chin and extremely white, smooth skin, and of her features only the green-brown eyes were large: forehead, mouth, and teeth were remarkably small. I stood up to be introduced to her, and asked about the man she had seen.

"I'm not positive that he came from the house," she said, "or even from the lawn." She was sullen, as if she didn't like being questioned. "I thought he might have, but I only saw him walking up the street."

"What sort of looking man was he?"

"I don't know. It was dark. I was in the car, he was walking up the street. I didn't examine him closely. He was about your size. It might have been you, for all I know."

"It wasn't. That was Saturday night?"

"Yes—that is, Sunday morning."

"What time?"

"Oh, three o'clock or after," she said impatiently.

"Were you alone?"

"Hardly."

I asked her who was with her and finally got a name: Eric Collinson had driven her home. I asked where I could find Eric Collinson. She frowned, hesitated, and said he was employed by Spear, Camp and Duffy, stockbrokers. She also said she had a putrid headache and she hoped I would excuse her now, as she knew I couldn't have any more questions to ask her. Then, without waiting for any reply I might have made to that, she turned and went out of the room. Her ears, I noticed when she turned, had no lobes, and were queerly pointed at the top.

"How about your servants?" I asked Mrs. Leggett.

"We've only one—Minnie Hershey, a Negress. She doesn't sleep here, and I'm sure she had nothing to do with it. She's been with us for nearly two years and I can vouch for her honesty."

I said I'd like to talk to Minnie, and Mrs. Leggett called her in. The servant was a small, wiry mulatto girl with the straight black hair and brown features of an Indian. She was very polite and very insistent that she had nothing to do with the theft of the diamonds and had known nothing about the burglary until she arrived at the house that morning. She gave me her home address, in San Francisco's darktown.

Leggett and his wife took me up to the laboratory, a large room that covered all but a small fifth of the third story. Charts hung between the windows on the white-washed wall. The wooden floor was uncovered. An X-ray machine—or something similar—four or five smaller machines, a forge, a wide sink, a large zinc table, some smaller porcelain ones, stands, racks of glassware, siphon-shaped metal tanks—that sort of stuff filled most of the room.

The cabinet the diamonds had been taken from was a green-painted steel affair with six drawers all locking together. The second drawer from the top—the one the diamonds had been in—was open. Its edge was dented where a jimmy or chisel had been forced between it and the frame. The other drawers were still locked. Leggett said the forcing of the diamond drawer had jammed the locking mechanism so that he would have to get a mechanic to open the others.

We went downstairs, through a room where the mulatto was walking around behind a vacuum cleaner, and into the kitchen. The back door and its frame were marked much as the cabinet was, apparently by the same tool.

When I had finished looking at the door, I took the diamond out of my pocket and showed it to the Leggetts, asking: "Is this one of them?"

Leggett picked it out of my palm with forefinger and thumb, held it up to the light, turned it from side to side, and said: "Yes. It has that cloudy spot down at the culet. Where did you get it?"

"Out front, in the grass."

"Ah, our burglar dropped some of his spoils in his haste."

I said I doubted it.

Leggett pulled his brows together behind his glasses, looked at me with smaller eyes, and asked sharply: "What do you think?"

"I think it was planted there. Your burglar knew too much. He knew which drawer to go to. He didn't waste time on anything else. Detectives always say: 'Inside job,' because it saves work if they can find a victim right on the scene; but I can't see anything else here."

Minnie came to the door, still holding the vacuum cleaner, and began to cry that she was an honest girl, and nobody had any right to accuse her of anything, and they could search her and her home if they wanted to, and just because she was a colored girl was no reason, and so on and so on; and not all of it could be made out, because the vacuum cleaner was still humming in her hand and she sobbed while she talked. Tears ran down her cheeks.

Mrs. Leggett went to her, patted her shoulder, and said: "There, there. Don't cry, Minnie. I know you hadn't anything to do with it, and so does everybody else. There, there." Presently she got the girl's tears turned off and sent her upstairs.

Leggett sat on a corner of the kitchen table and asked: "You suspect someone in this house?"

"Somebody who's been in it, yeah."

"Whom?"

"Nobody yet."

"That"—he smiled, showing white teeth almost as small as his daughter's—"means everybody—all of us?"

"Let's take a look at the lawn," I suggested. "If we find any more diamonds I'll say maybe I'm mistaken about the inside angle."

Half-way through the house, as we went towards the front door, we met Minnie Hershey in a tan coat and violet hat, coming to say good-bye to her mistress. She wouldn't, she said tearfully, work anywhere where anybody thought she had stolen anything. She was just as honest as anybody else, and more than some, and just as much entitled to respect, and if she couldn't get it one place she could another, because she knew places where people wouldn't accuse her of stealing things after she had worked for them for two long years without ever taking so much as a slice of bread.

Mrs. Leggett pleaded with her, reasoned with her, scolded her, and commanded her, but none of it was any good. The brown girl's mind was made up, and away she went.

Mrs. Leggett looked at me, making her pleasant face as severe as she could, and said reprovingly: "Now see what you've done."

I said I was sorry, and her husband and I went out to examine the lawn. We didn't find any more diamonds.

II : LONG-NOSE

I put in a couple of hours canvassing the neighborhood, trying to place the man Mrs. and Miss Leggett had seen. I didn't have any luck with that one, but I picked up news of another. A Mrs. Priestly—a pale semi-invalid who lived three doors below the Leggetts—gave me the first line on him.

Mrs. Priestly often sat at a front window at night when she couldn't sleep. On two of these nights she had seen the man. She said he was a tall man, and young, she thought, and he walked with his head thrust forward. The street was too poorly lighted for her to describe his coloring and clothes.

She had first seen him a week before. He had passed up and down on the other side of the street five or six times, at intervals of fifteen or twenty minutes, with his face turned as if watching something—or looking for something—on Mrs. Priestly's—and the Leggetts'—side of the street. She thought it was between eleven and twelve o'clock that she had seen him the first time that night, and around one o'clock the last. Several nights later—Saturday—she had seen him again, not walking this time, but standing on the corner below, looking up the street, at about midnight. He went away after half an hour, and she had not seen him again.

Mrs. Priestly knew the Leggetts by sight, but knew very little about them, except that the daughter was said to be a bit wild. They seemed to be nice people, but kept to themselves. He had moved into the house in 1921, alone except for the housekeeper—a Mrs. Begg, who, Mrs. Priestly understood, was now with a family named Freemander in Berkeley. Mrs. Leggett and Gabrielle had not come to live with Leggett until 1923.

Mrs. Priestly said she had not been at her window the previous night and therefore had not seen the man Mrs. Leggett had seen on the corner.

A man named Warren Daley, who lived on the opposite side of the street, down near the corner where Mrs. Priestly had seen her man, had, when locking up the house Sunday night, surprised a man—apparently the same man —in the vestibule. Daley was not at home when I called, but, after telling me this much, Mrs. Daley got him on the phone for me.

Daley said the man had been standing in the vestibule, either hiding from or watching someone up the street. As soon as Daley opened the door, the man ran away, down the street, paying no attention to Daley's "What are you doing there?" Daley said he was a man of thirty-two or three, fairly well dressed in dark clothes, and had a long, thin, and sharp nose.

That was all I could shake the neighborhood down for. I went to the Montgomery Street offices of Spear, Camp and Duffy and asked for Eric Collinson.

He was young, blond, tall, broad, sunburned, and dressy, with the good-looking unintelligent face of one who would know everything about polo, or shooting, or flying, or something of that sort—maybe even two things of that sort—but not much about anything else. We sat on a fatted leather seat in the customers' room, now, after market hours, empty except for a weedy boy juggling numbers on the board. I told Collinson about the burglary and asked him about the man he and Miss Leggett had seen Saturday night.

"He was an ordinary-looking chap, as far as I could see. It was dark. Short and chunky. You think he took them?"

"Did he come from the Leggett house?" I asked.

"From the lawn, at least. He seemed jumpy—that's

why I thought perhaps he'd been nosing around where he shouldn't. I suggested I go after him and ask him what he was up to, but Gaby wouldn't have it. Might have been a friend of her father's. Did you ask him? He goes in for odd eggs."

"Wasn't that late for a visitor to be leaving?"

He looked away from me, so I asked: "What time was it?"

"Midnight, I dare say."

"Midnight?"

"That's the word. The time when the graves give up their dead, and ghosts walk."

"Miss Leggett said it was after three o'clock."

"You see how it is!" he exclaimed, blandly triumphant, as if he had demonstrated something we had been arguing about. "She's half blind and won't wear glasses for fear of losing beauty. She's always making mistakes like that. Plays abominable bridge—takes deuces for aces. It was probably a quarter after twelve, and she looked at the clock and got the hands mixed."

I said: "That's too bad," and "Thanks," and went up to Halstead and Beauchamp's store in Geary Street.

Watt Halstead was a suave, pale, bald, fat man, with tired eyes and a too tight collar. I told him what I was doing and asked him how well he knew Leggett.

"I know him as a desirable customer and by reputation as a scientist. Why do you ask?"

"His burglary's sour—in spots anyway."

"Oh, you're mistaken. That is, you're mistaken if you think a man of his caliber would be mixed up in anything like that. A servant, of course; yes, that's possible: it often happens, doesn't it? But not Leggett. He is a scientist of some standing—he has done some remarkable work with color—and, unless our credit department has been misinformed, a man of more than moderate means. I don't mean that he is wealthy in the modern sense of the word, but too wealthy for a thing of that sort. And, confidentially, I happen to know that his present balance in the Seaman's National Bank is in excess of ten thousand dollars. Well—the eight diamonds were worth no more than a thousand or twelve or thirteen hundred dollars."

"At retail? Then they cost you five or six hundred?"

"Well," smiling, "seven fifty would be nearer."

"How'd you come to give him the diamonds?"

"He's a customer of ours, as I've told you, and when I learned what he had done with glass, I thought what a wonderful thing it would be if the same method could be applied to diamonds. Fitzstephan—it was largely through him that I learned of Leggett's work with glass—was skeptical, but I thought it worth trying—still think so—and persuaded Leggett to try."

Fitzstephan was a familiar name. I asked: "Which Fitzstephan was that?"

"Owen, the writer. You know him?"

"Yeah, but I didn't know he was on the coast. We used to drink out of the same bottle. Do you know his address?"

Halstead found it in the telephone book for me, a Nob Hill apartment.

From the jeweler's I went to the vicinity of Minnie Hershey's home. It was a Negro neighborhood, which made the getting of reasonably accurate information twice as unlikely as it always is.

What I managed to get added up to this: The girl had come to San Francisco from Winchester, Virginia, four or five years ago, and for the last half-year had been living with a Negro called Rhino Tingley. One told me Rhino's first name was Ed, another Bill, but they agreed that he was young, big, and black and could easily be recognized by the scar on his chin. I was also told that he depended for his living on Minnie and pool; that he was not bad except when he got mad—then he was supposed to be a holy terror; and that I could get a look at him the early part of almost any evening in either Bunny Mack's barber-shop or Big-foot Gerber's cigar-store.

I learned where these joints were and then went downtown again, to the police detective bureau in the Hall of

Justice. Nobody was in the pawnshop detail office. I crossed the corridor and asked Lieutenant Duff whether anybody had been put on the Leggett job.

He said: "See O'Gar."

I went into the assembly room, looking for O'Gar and wondering what he—a homicide detail detective-sergeant —had to do with my job. Neither O'Gar nor Pat Reddy, his partner, was in. I smoked a cigarette, tried to guess who had been killed, and decided to phone Leggett.

"Any police detectives been in since I left?" I asked when his harsh voice was in my ear.

"No, but the police called up a little while ago and asked my wife and daughter to come to a place in Golden Gate Avenue to see if they could identify a man there. They left a few minutes ago. I didn't accompany them, not having seen the supposed burglar."

"Whereabouts in Golden Gate Avenue?"

He didn't remember the number, but he knew the block —above Van Ness Avenue. I thanked him and went out there.

In the designated block I found a uniformed copper standing in the doorway of a small apartment house. I asked him if O'Gar was there.

"Up in three ten," he said.

I rode up in a rickety elevator. When I got out on the third floor, I came face to face with Mrs. Leggett and her daughter, leaving.

"Now I hope you're satisfied that Minnie had nothing to do with it," Mrs. Leggett said chidingly.

"The police found your man?"

"Yes."

I said to Gabrielle Leggett: "Eric Collinson says it was only midnight, or a few minutes later, that you got home Saturday night."

"Eric," she said irritably, passing me to enter the elevator, "is an ass."

Her mother, following her into the elevator, reprimanded her amiably: "Now, dear."

I walked down the hall to a doorway where Pat Reddy

stood talking to a couple of reporters, said hello, squeezed past them into a short passage-way, and went through that to a shabbily furnished room where a dead man lay on a wall bed.

Phels, of the police identification bureau, looked up from his magnifying glass to nod at me and then went on with his examination of a mission table's edge.

O'Gar pulled his head and shoulders in the open window and growled: "So we got to put up with you again?"

O'Gar was a burly, stolid man of fifty, who wore wide-brimmed black hats of the movie-sheriff sort. There was a lot of sense in his hard bullet-head, and he was comfortable to work with.

I looked at the corpse—a man of forty or so, with a heavy, pale face, short hair touched with gray, a scrubby, dark mustache, and stocky arms and legs. There was a bullet hole just over his navel, and another high on the left side of his chest.

"It's a man," O'Gar said as I put the blankets over him again. "He's dead."

"What else did somebody tell you?" I asked.

"Looks like him and another guy glaumed the ice, and then the other guy decided to take a one-way split. The envelopes are here"—O'Gar took them out of his pocket and ruffled them with a thumb—"but the diamonds ain't. They went down the fire-escape with the other guy a little while back. People spotted him making the sneak, but lost him when he cut through the alley. Tall guy with a long nose. This one"—he pointed the envelopes at the bed—"has been here a week. Name of Louis Upton, with New York labels. We don't know him. Nobody in the dump'll say they ever saw him with anybody else. Nobody'll say they know Long-nose."

Pat Reddy came in. He was a big, jovial youngster, with almost brains enough to make up for his lack of experience. I told him and O'Gar what I had turned up on the job so far.

"Long-nose and this bird taking turns watching Leggett's?" Reddy suggested.

"Maybe," I said, "but there's an inside angle. How many envelopes have you got there, O'Gar?"

"Seven."

"Then the one for the planted diamond is missing."

'How about the yellow girl?" Reddy asked.

"I'm going out for a look at her man tonight," I said. "You people trying New York on this Upton?"

"Uh-huh," O'Gar said.

III : SOMETHING BLACK

At the Nob Hill address Halstead had given me, I told my name to the boy at the switchboard and asked him to pass it on to Fitzstephan. I remembered Fitzstephan as a long, lean, sorrel-haired man of thirty-two, with sleepy gray eyes, a wide, humorous mouth, and carelessly worn clothes; a man who pretended to be lazier than he was, would rather talk than do anything else, and had a lot of what seemed to be accurate information and original ideas on any subject that happened to come up, as long as it was a little out of the ordinary.

I had met him five years before, in New York, where I was digging dirt on a chain of fake mediums who had taken a coal-and-ice dealer's widow for a hundred thousand dollars. Fitzstephan was plowing the same field for literary material. We became acquainted and pooled forces. I got more out of the combination than he did, since he knew the spook racket inside and out; and, with his help, I cleaned up my job in a couple of weeks. We were fairly chummy for a month or two after that, until I left New York.

"Mr. Fitzstephan says to come right up," the switch-board boy said.

His apartment was on the sixth floor. He was standing at its door when I got out of the elevator.

"By God," he said, holding out a lean hand, "it *is* you!"

"None other."

He hadn't changed any. We went into a room where half a dozen bookcases and four tables left little room for anything else. Magazines and books in various languages, papers, clippings, proof sheets, were scattered everywhere —all just as it used to be in his New York rooms.

We sat down, found places for our feet between table-legs, and accounted roughly for our lives since we had last seen one another. He had been in San Francisco for a little more than a year—except, he said, for week-ends, and two months hermiting in the country, finishing a novel. I had been there nearly five years. He liked San Francisco, he said, but wouldn't oppose any movement to give the West back to the Indians.

"How's the literary grift go?" I asked.

He looked at me sharply, demanding: "You haven't been reading me?"

"No. Where'd you get that funny idea?"

"There was something in your tone, something proprietary, as in the voice of one who has bought an author for a couple of dollars. I haven't met it often enough to be used to it. Good God! Remember once I offered you a set of my books as a present?" He had always liked to talk that way.

"Yeah. But I never blamed you. You were drunk."

"On sherry—Elsa Donne's sherry. Remember Elsa? She showed us a picture she had just finished, and you said it was pretty. Sweet God, wasn't she furious! You said it so vapidly and sincerely and as if you were so sure that she would like your saying it. Remember? She put us out, but we'd both already got plastered on her sherry. But you weren't tight enough to take the books."

"I was afraid I'd read them and understand them," I explained, "and then you'd have felt insulted."

A Chinese boy brought us cold white wine.

Fitzstephan said: "I suppose you're still hounding the unfortunate evil-doer?"

"Yeah. That's how I happened to locate you. Halstead tells me you know Edgar Leggett."

A gleam pushed through the sleepiness in his gray eyes, and he sat up a little in his chair, asking: "Leggett's been up to something?"

"Why do you say that?"

"I didn't say it. I asked it." He made himself limp in the chair again, but the gleam didn't go out of his eyes. "Come on, out with it. Don't try to be subtle with me, my son; that's not your style at all. Try it and you're sunk. Out with it: what's Leggett been up to?"

"We don't do it that way," I said. "You're a storywriter. I can't trust you not to build up on what I tell you. I'll save mine till after you've spoken your piece, so yours won't be twisted to fit mine. How long have you known him?"

"Since shortly after I came here. He's always interested me. There's something obscure in him, something dark and inviting. He is, for instance, physically ascetic—neither smoking or drinking, eating meagerly, sleeping, I'm told, only three or four hours a night—but mentally, or spiritually, sensual—does that mean anything to you?—to the point of decadence. You used to think I had an abnormal appetite for the fantastic. You should know him. His friends—no, he hasn't any—his choice companions are those who have the most outlandish ideas to offer: Marquard and his insane figures that aren't figures, but the boundaries of areas in space that are the figures; Denbar Curt and his algebraism; the Haldorns and their Holy Grail sect; crazy Laura Joines; Farnham—"

"And you," I put in, "with explanations and descriptions that explain and describe nothing. I hope you don't think any of what you've said means anything to me."

"I remember you now: you were always like that." He grinned at me, running thin fingers through his sorrel hair. "Tell me what's up while I try to find one-syllable words for you."

I asked him if he knew Eric Collinson. He said he did;

there was nothing to know about him except that he was engaged to Gabrielle Leggett, that his father was the lumber Collinson, and that Eric was Princeton, stocks and bonds, and hand-ball, a nice boy.

"Maybe," I said, "but he lied to me."

"Isn't that like a sleuth?" Fitzstephan shook his head, grinning. "You must have had the wrong fellow—somebody impersonating him. The Chevalier Bayard doesn't lie, and, besides, lying requires imagination. You've—or wait! Was a woman involved in your question?"

I nodded.

"You're correct, then," Fitzstephan assured me. "I apologize. The Chevalier Bayard always lies when a woman is involved, even if it's unnecessary and puts her to a lot of trouble. It's one of the conventions of Bayardism, something to do with guarding her honor or the like. Who was the woman?"

"Gabrielle Leggett," I said, and told him all I knew about the Leggetts, the diamonds, and the dead man in Golden Gate Avenue. Disappointment deepened in his face while I talked.

"That's trivial, dull," he complained when I had finished. "I've been thinking of Leggett in terms of Dumas, and you bring me a piece of gimcrackery out of O. Henry. You've let me down, you and your shabby diamonds. But" —his eyes brightened again—"this may lead to something. Leggett may or may not be criminal, but there's more to him than a two-penny insurance swindle."

"You mean," I asked, "that he's one of these master minds? So you read newspapers? What do you think he is? King of the bootleggers? Chief of an international crime syndicate? A white-slave magnate? Head of a dope ring? Or queen of the counterfeiters in disguise?"

"Don't be an idiot," he said. "But he's got brains, and there's something black in him. There's something he doesn't want to think about, but must not forget. I've told you that he's thirsty for all that's dizziest in thought, yet he's cold as a fish, but with a bitter-dry coldness. He's a neurotic who keeps his body fit and sensitive and ready—

for what?—while he drugs his mind with lunacies. Yet he's cold and sane. If a man has a past that he wants to forget, he can easiest drug his mind against memory through his body, with sensuality if not with narcotics. But suppose the past is not dead, and this man must keep himself fit to cope with it should it come into the present. Well, then he would be wisest to anæsthetize his mind directly, letting his body stay strong and ready."

"And this past?"

Fitzstephan shook his head, saying: "If I don't know— and I don't—it isn't my fault. Before you're through, you'll know how difficult it is to get information out of that family."

"Did you try?"

"Certainly. I'm a novelist. My business is with souls and what goes on in them. He's got one that attracts me, and I've always considered myself unjustly treated by his not turning himself inside out for me. You know, I doubt if Leggett's his name. He's French. He told me once he came from Atlanta, but he's French in outlook, in quality of mind, in everything except admission."

"What of the rest of the family?" I asked. "Gabrielle's cuckoo, isn't she?"

"I wonder." Fitzstephan looked curiously at me. "Are you saying that carelessly, or do you really think she's off?"

"I don't know. She's odd, an uncomfortable sort of person. And, then, she's got animal ears, hardly any forehead; and her eyes shift from green to brown and back without ever settling on one color. How much of her affairs have you turned up in your snooping around?"

"Are you—who make your living snooping—sneering at my curiosity about people and my attempts to satisfy it?"

"We're different," I said. "I do mine with the object of putting people in jail, and I get paid for it, though not as much as I should."

"That's not different," he said. "I do mine with the object of putting people in books, and I get paid for it, though not as much as I should."

"Yeah, but what good does that do?"

"God knows. What good does putting them in jail do?"

"Relieves congestion," I said. "Put enough people in jail, and cities wouldn't have traffic problems. What do you know about this Gabrielle?"

"She hates her father. He worships her."

"How come the hate?"

"I don't know; perhaps because he worships her."

"There's no sense to that," I complained. "You're just being literary. What about Mrs. Leggett?"

"You've never eaten one of her meals, I suppose? You'd have no doubts if you had. None but a serene, sane soul ever achieved such cooking. I've often wondered what she thinks of the weird creatures who are her husband and daughter, though I imagine she simply accepts them as they are without even being conscious of their weirdness."

"All this is well enough in its way," I said, "but you still haven't told me anything definite."

"No, I haven't," he replied, "and that, my boy, is it. I've told you what I know and what I imagine, and none of it is definite. That's the point—in a year of trying I've learned nothing definite about Leggett. Isn't that—remembering my curiosity and my usual skill in satisfying it—enough to convince you that the man is hiding something and knows how to hide it?"

"Is it? I don't know. But I know I've wasted enough time learning nothing that anybody can be jailed for. Dinner tomorrow night? Or the next?"

"The next. About seven o'clock?"

I said I would stop for him, and went out. It was then after five o'clock. Not having had any luncheon, I went up to Blanco's for food, and then to darktown for a look at Rhino Tingley.

I found him in Big-foot Gerber's cigar-store, rolling a fat cigar around in his mouth, telling something to the other Negroes—four of them—in the place.

". . . says to him: 'Nigger, you talking yourself out of skin,' and I reaches out my hand for him, and, 'fore God, there weren't none of him there excepting his footprints in the ce-ment pavement, eight feet apart and leading home."

Buying a package of cigarettes, I weighed him in while he talked. He was a chocolate man of less than thirty years, close to six feet tall and weighing two hundred pounds plus, with big yellow-balled pop eyes, a broad nose, a big blue-lipped and blue-gummed mouth, and a ragged black scar running from his lower lip down behind his blue and white striped collar. His clothes were new enough to look new, and he wore them sportily. His voice was a heavy bass that shook the glass of the showcases when he laughed with his audience.

I went out of the store while they were laughing, heard the laughter stop short behind me, resisted the temptation to look back, and moved down the street towards the building where he and Minnie lived. He came abreast of me when I was half a block from the flat.

I said nothing while we took seven steps side by side.

Then he said: "You the man that been inquiring around about me?"

The sour odor of Italian wine was thick enough to be seen.

I considered, and said: "Yeah."

"What you got to do with me?" he asked, not disagreeably, but as if he wanted to know.

Across the street Gabrielle Leggett, in brown coat and brown and yellow hat, came out of Minnie's building and walked south, not turning her face towards us. She walked swiftly and her lower lip was between her teeth.

I looked at the Negro. He was looking at me. There was nothing in his face to show that he had seen Gabrielle Leggett, or that the sight of her meant anything to him.

I said: "You've got nothing to hide, have you? What do you care who asks about you?"

"All the same, I'm the party to come to if you wants to know about me. You the man that got Minnie fired?"

"She wasn't fired. She quit."

"Minnie don't have to take nobody's lip. She—"

"Let's go over and talk to her," I suggested, leading the

way across the street. At the front door he went ahead, up a flight of stairs, down a dark hall to a door which he opened with one of the twenty or more keys on his ring.

Minnie Hershey, in a pink kimono trimmed with yellow ostrich feathers that looked like little dead ferns, came out of the bedroom to meet us in the living-room. Her eyes got big when she saw me.

Rhino said: "You know this gentleman, Minnie."

Minnie said: "Y-yes."

I said: "You shouldn't have left the Leggetts' that way. Nobody thinks you had anything to do with the diamonds. What did Miss Leggett want here?"

"There been no Miss Leggetts here," she told me. "I don't know what you talking about."

"She came out as we were coming in."

"Oh! *Miss* Leggett. I thought you said *Mrs.* Leggett. I beg your pardon. Yes, sir. Miss Gabrielle was sure enough here. She wanted to know if I wouldn't come back there. She thinks a powerful lot of me, Miss Gabrielle does."

"That," I said, "is what you ought to do. It was foolish, leaving like that."

Rhino took the cigar out of his mouth and pointed the red end at the girl.

"You away from them," he boomed, "and you stay away from them. You don't have to take nothing from nobody." He put a hand in his pants pocket, lugged out a thick bundle of paper money, thumped it down on the table, and rumbled: "What for you have to work for folks?"

He was talking to the girl, but looking at me, grinning, gold teeth shining against purplish mouth. The girl looked at him scornfully, said: "Lead him around, *vino*," and turned to me again, her brown face tense, anxious to be believed, saying earnestly: "Rhino got that money in a crap game, mister. Hope to die if he didn't."

Rhino said: "Ain't nobody's business where I got my money. I got it. I got—" He put his cigar on the edge of the table, picked up the money, wet a thumb as big as a heel on a tongue like a bath-mat, and counted his roll bill by bill down on the table. "Twenty—thirty—eighty—hundred—hundred and ten—two hundred and ten—three hundred and ten—three hundred and thirty—three hundred and thirty-five—four hundred and thirty-five—five hundred and thirty-five—five hundred and eighty-five—six hundred and five—six hundred and ten—six hundred and twenty—seven hundred and twenty—seven hundred and seventy—eight hundred and twenty—eight hundred and thirty—eight hundred and forty—nine hundred and forty—nine hundred and sixty—nine hundred and seventy—nine hundred and seventy-five—nine hundred and ninety-five—ten hundred and fifteen—ten hundred and twenty—eleven hundred and twenty—eleven hundred and seventy. Anybody want to know what I got, that's what I got—eleven hundred and seventy dollars. Anybody want to know where I get it, maybe I tell them, maybe I don't. Just depend on how I feel about it."

Minnie said: "He won it in a crap game, mister, up the Happy Day Social Club. Hope to die if he didn't."

"Maybe I did," Rhino said, still grinning widely at me. "But supposing I didn't?"

"I'm no good at riddles," I said, and, after again advising Minnie to return to the Leggetts, left the flat. Minnie closed the door behind me. As I went down the hall I could hear her voice scolding and Rhino's chesty bass laughter.

In a downtown Owl drug-store I turned to the Berkeley section of the telephone directory, found only one Freemander listed, and called the number. Mrs. Begg was there and consented to see me if I came over on the next ferry.

The Freemander house was set off a road that wound uphill towards the University of California.

Mrs. Begg was a scrawny, big-boned woman, with not much gray hair packed close around a bony skull, hard gray eyes, and hard, capable hands. She was sour and severe, but plain-spoken enough to let us talk turkey without a lot of preliminary hemming and hawing.

I told her about the burglary and my belief that the thief had been helped, at least with information, by somebody who knew the Leggett household, winding up: "Mrs.

Priestly told me you had been Leggett's housekeeper, and she thought you could help me."

Mrs. Begg said she doubted whether she could tell me anything that would pay me for my trip from the city, but she was willing to do what she could, being an honest woman and having nothing to conceal from anybody. Once started, she told me a great deal, damned near talking me earless. Throwing out the stuff that didn't interest me, I came away with this information:

Mrs. Begg had been hired by Leggett, through an employment agency, as housekeeper in the spring of 1921. At first she had a girl to help her, but there wasn't enough work for two, so, at Mrs. Begg's suggestion, they let the girl go. Leggett was a man of simple tastes and spent nearly all his time on the top floor, where he had his laboratory and a cubbyhole bedroom. He seldom used the rest of the house except when he had friends in for an evening. Mrs. Begg didn't like his friends, though she could say nothing against them except that the way they talked was a shame and a disgrace. Edgar Leggett was as nice a man as a person could want to know, she said, only so secretive that it made a person nervous. She was never allowed to go up on the third floor, and the door of the laboratory was always kept locked. Once a month a Jap would come in to clean it up under Leggett's supervision. Well, she supposed he had a lot of scientific secrets, and maybe dangerous chemicals, that he didn't want people poking into, but just the same it made a person uneasy. She didn't know anything about her employer's personal or family affairs and knew her place too well to ask him any questions.

In August 1923—it was a rainy morning, she remembered—a woman and a girl of fifteen, with a lot of suitcases, had come to the house. She let them in and the woman asked for Mr. Leggett. Mrs. Begg went up to the laboratory door and told him, and he came down. Never in all her born days had she seen such a surprised man as he was when he saw them. He turned absolutely white, and she thought he was going to fall down, he shook that bad. She didn't know what Leggett and the woman and the girl said to one another that morning, because they jabbered away in some foreign language, though the lot of them could talk English as good as anybody else, and better than most, especially that Gabrielle when she got to cursing. Mrs. Begg had left them and gone on about her business. Pretty soon Leggett came out to the kitchen and told her his visitors were a Mrs. Dain, his sister-in-law, and her daughter, neither of whom he had seen for ten years; and that they were going to stay there with him. Mrs. Dain later told Mrs. Begg that they were English, but had been living in New York for several years. Mrs. Begg said she liked Mrs. Dain, who was a sensible woman and a first-rate housewife, but that Gabrielle was a tartar. Mrs. Begg always spoke of the girl as "that Gabrielle."

With the Dains there, and with Mrs. Dain's ability as a housekeeper, there was no longer any place for Mrs. Begg. They had been very liberal, she said, helping her find a new place and giving her a generous bonus when she left. She hadn't seen any of them since, but, thanks to the careful watch she habitually kept on the marriage, death, and birth notices in the morning papers, she had learned, a week after she left, that a marriage license had been issued to Edgar Leggett and Alice Dain.

IV : THE VAGUE HARPERS

When I arrived at the agency at nine the next morning, Eric Collinson was sitting in the reception room. His sunburned face was dingy without pinkness, and he had forgotten to put stickum on his hair.

"Do you know anything about Miss Leggett?" he asked, jumping up and meeting me at the door. "She wasn't home last night, and she's not home yet. Her father wouldn't say he didn't know where she was, but I'm sure he didn't. He told me not to worry, but how can I help worrying? Do you know anything about it?"

I said I didn't and told him about seeing her leave Minnie Hershey's the previous evening. I gave him the mulatto's address and suggested that he ask her. He jammed his hat on his head and hurried off.

Getting O'Gar on the phone, I asked him if he had heard from New York yet.

"Uh-huh," he said. "Upton—that's his right name—was once one of you private dicks—had a agency of his own—till '23, when him and a guy named Harry Ruppert were sent over for trying to fix a jury. How'd you make out with the shine?"

"I don't know. This Rhino Tingley's carrying an eleven-hundred-case roll. Minnie says he got it with the rats and mice. Maybe he did: it's twice what he could have peddled Leggett's stuff for. Can you try to have it checked? He's supposed to have got it at the Happy Day Social Club."

O'Gar promised to do what he could and hung up.

I sent a wire to our New York branch, asking for more dope on Upton and Ruppert, and then went up to the county clerk's office in the municipal building, where I dug into the August and September 1923 marriage-license file. The application I wanted was dated August 26 and bore Edgar Leggett's statement that he was born in Atlanta, Georgia, on March 6, 1883, and that this was his second marriage; and Alice Dain's statement that she was born in London, England, on October 22, 1888, and that she had not been married before.

When I returned to the agency, Eric Collinson, his yellow hair still further disarranged, was again lying in wait for me.

"I saw Minnie," he said excitedly, "and she couldn't tell

me anything. She said Gaby was there last night to ask her to come back to work, but that's all she knew about her. But she—she's wearing an emerald ring that I'm positive is Gaby's."

"Did you ask her about it?"

"Who? Minnie? No. How could I? It would have been —you know."

"That's right," I agreed, thinking of Fitzstephan's Chevalier Bayard, "we must always be polite. Why did you lie to me about the time you and Miss Leggett got home the other night?"

Embarrassment made his face more attractive-looking and less intelligent.

"That was silly of me," he stammered, "but I didn't— you know—I thought you—I was afraid—"

He wasn't getting anywhere. I suggested: "You thought that was a late hour and didn't want me to get wrong notions about her?"

"Yes, that's it."

I shooed him out and went into the operatives' room, where Mickey Linehan—big, loose-hung, red-faced—and Al Mason—slim, dark, sleek—were swapping lies about the times they had been shot at, each trying to pretend he had been more frightened than the other. I told them who was who and what was what on the Leggett job—as far as my knowledge went, and it didn't go far when I came to putting it in words—and sent Al out to keep an eye on the Leggetts' house, Mickey to see how Minnie and Rhino behaved.

Mrs. Leggett, her pleasant face shadowed, opened the door when I rang the bell an hour later. We went into the green, orange, and chocolate room, where we were joined by her husband. I passed on to them the information about Upton that O'Gar had received from New York and told them I had wired for more dope on Ruppert.

"Some of your neighbors saw a man who was not Upton loitering around," I said, "and a man who fits the same description ran down the fire-escape from the room Upton was killed in. We'll see what Ruppert looks like."

I was watching Leggett's face. Nothing changed in it. His too bright red-brown eyes held interest and nothing else.

I asked: "Is Miss Leggett in?"

He said: "No."

"When will she be in?"

"Probably not for several days. She's gone out of town."

"Where can I find her?" I asked, turning to Mrs. Leggett. "I've some questions to ask her."

Mrs. Leggett avoided my gaze, looking at her husband.

His metallic voice answered my question: "We don't know, exactly. Friends of hers, a Mr. and Mrs. Harper, drove up from Los Angeles and asked her to go along on a trip up in the mountains. I don't know which route they intended taking, and doubt if they had any definite destination."

I asked questions about the Harpers. Leggett admitted knowing very little about them. Mrs. Harper's first name was Carmel, he said, and everybody called the man Bud, but Leggett wasn't sure whether his name was Frank or Walter. Nor did he know the Harpers' Los Angeles address. He thought they had a house somewhere in Pasadena, but wasn't sure, having, in fact, heard something about their selling the house, or perhaps only intending to. While he told me this nonsense, his wife sat staring at the floor, lifting her blue eyes twice to look swiftly, pleadingly, at her husband.

I asked her: "Don't you know anything more about them than that?"

"No," she said weakly, darting another glance at her husband's face, while he, paying no attention to her, stared levelly at me.

"When did they leave?" I asked.

"Early this morning," Leggett said. "They were staying at one of the hotels—I don't know which—and Gabrielle spent the night with them so they could start early."

I had enough of the Harpers. I asked: "Did either of you—any of you—know anything about Upton—have any dealings with him of any sort—before this affair?"

Leggett said: "No."

I had other questions, but the kind of replies I was drawing didn't mean anything, so I stood up to go. I was tempted to tell him what I thought of him, but there was no profit in that.

He got up too, smiling politely, and said: "I'm sorry to have caused the insurance company all this trouble through what was, after all, probably my carelessness. I should like to ask your opinion: do you really think I should accept responsibility for the loss of the diamonds and make it good?"

"The way it stands," I said, "I think you should; but that wouldn't stop the investigation."

Mrs. Leggett put her handkerchief to her mouth quickly.

Leggett said: "Thanks." His voice was casually polite. "I'll have to think it over."

On my way back to the agency I dropped in on Fitzstephan for half an hour. He was writing, he told me, an article for the *Psychopathological Review*—that's probably wrong, but it was something on that order—condemning the hypothesis of an unconscious or subconscious mind as a snare and a delusion, a pitfall for the unwary and a set of false whiskers for the charlatan, a gap in psychology's roof that made it impossible, or nearly, for the sound scholar to smoke out such faddists as, for example, the psychoanalyst and the behaviorist, or words to that effect. He went on like that for ten minutes or more, finally coming back to the United States with: "But how are you getting along with the problem of the elusive diamonds?"

"This way and that way," I said, and told him what I had learned and done so far.

"You've certainly," he congratulated me when I finished, "got it all as tangled and confused as possible."

"It'll be worse before it's better," I predicted. "I'd like to have ten minutes alone with Mrs. Leggett. Away from her husband, I imagine things could be done with her. Could you get anything out of her? I'd like to know why Gabrielle has gone, even if I can't learn where."

"I'll try," Fitzstephan said willingly. "Suppose I go out there tomorrow afternoon—to borrow a book. Waite's *Rosy Cross* will do it. They know I'm interested in that sort of stuff. He'll be working in the laboratory, and I'll refuse to disturb him. I'll have to go at it in an offhand way, but maybe I can get something out of her."

"Thanks," I said. "See you tomorrow night."

I spent most of the afternoon putting my findings and guesses on paper and trying to fit them together in some sort of order. Eric Collinson phoned twice to ask if I had any news of his Gabrielle. Neither Mickey Linehan nor Al Mason reported anything. At six o'clock I called it a day.

V : GABRIELLE

The next day brought happenings.

Early in the morning there was a telegram from our New York office. Decoded, it read:

LOUIS UPTON FORMER PROPRIETOR DETECTIVE AGENCY HERE STOP ARRESTED SEPTEMBER FIRST ONE NINE TWO THREE FOR BRIBING TWO JURORS IN SEXTON MURDER TRIAL STOP TRIED TO SAVE HIMSELF BY IMPLICATING HARRY RUPPERT OPERATIVE IN HIS EMPLOY STOP BOTH MEN CONVICTED STOP BOTH RELEASED FROM SING SING FEBRUARY SIX THIS YEAR STOP RUPPERT SAID TO HAVE THREATENED TO KILL UPTON STOP RUPPERT THIRTY TWO YEARS FIVE FEET ELEVEN INCHES HUNDRED FIFTY POUNDS BROWN HAIR

AND EYES SALLOW COMPLEXION THIN FACE LONG
THIN NOSE WALKS WITH STOOP AND CHIN OUT STOP
MAILING PHOTOGRAPHS

That placed Ruppert definitely enough as the man Mrs.
Priestly and Daley had seen and the man who had probably killed Upton.

O'Gar called me on the phone to tell me: "That dinge
of yours—Rhino Tingley—was picked up in a hock shop
last night trying to unload some jewelry. None of it was
loose diamonds. We haven't been able to crack him yet,
just got him identified. I sent a man out to Leggett's with
some of the stuff, thinking it might be theirs, but they said
no."

That didn't fit in anywhere. I suggested: "Try Halstead
and Beauchamp. Tell them you think the stuff is Leggett's.
Don't tell them he said it wasn't."

Half an hour later the detective-sergeant phoned me
again, from the jewelers', to tell me that Halstead had positively identified two pieces—a string of pearls and a topaz
brooch—as articles Leggett had purchased there for his
daughter.

"That's swell," I said. "Now will you do this? Go out
to Rhino's flat and put the screws on his woman, Minnie
Hershey. Frisk the joint, rough her up; the more you scare
her, the better. She may be wearing an emerald ring. If
she is, or if it—or any other jewelry that might be the Leggetts'—is there, you can take it away with you; but don't
stay too long and don't bother her afterwards. I've got her
covered. Just stir her up and beat it."

"I'll turn her white," O'Gar promised.

Dick Foley was in the operatives' room, writing his report on a warehouse robbery that had kept him up all
night. I chased him out to help Mickey with the mulatto.

"Both of you tail her if she leaves her joint after the
police are through," I said, "and as soon as you put her in
anywhere, one of you get to a phone and let me know."

I went back to my office and burned cigarettes. I was

ruining the third one when Eric Collinson phoned to ask if I had found his Gabrielle yet.

"Not quite, but I've got prospects. If you aren't busy, you might come over and go along with me—if it so happens that there turns out to be some place to go."

He said, very eagerly, that he would do that.

A few minutes later Mickey Linehan phoned: "The high yellow's gone visiting," and gave me a Pacific Avenue address.

The phone rang again before I got it out of my hand.

"This is Watt Halstead," a voice said. "Can you come down to see me for a minute or two?"

"Not now. What is it?"

"It's about Edgar Leggett, and it's quite puzzling. The police brought some jewelry in this morning, asking whether we knew whose it was. I recognized a string of pearls and a brooch that Edgar Leggett bought from us for his daughter last year—the brooch in the spring, the pearls at Christmas. After the police had gone, I, quite naturally, phoned Leggett; and he took the most peculiar attitude. He waited until I had told him about it, then said: 'I thank you very much for your interference in my affairs,' and hung up. What do you suppose is the matter with him?"

"God knows. Thanks. I've got to run now, but I'll stop in when I get a chance."

I hunted up Owen Fitzstephan's number, called it, and heard his drawled: "Hello."

"You'd better get busy on your book-borrowing if any good's to come of it," I said.

"Why? Are things taking place?"

"Things are."

"Such as?" he asked.

"This and that, but it's no time for anybody who wants to poke his nose into the Leggett mysteries to be dilly-dallying with pieces about unconscious minds."

"Right," he said: "I'm off to the front now."

Eric Collinson had come in while I was talking to the novelist.

"Come on," I said, leading the way out towards the elevators. "This might not be a false alarm."

"Where are we going?" he asked impatiently. "Have you found her? Is she all right?"

I replied to the only one of his questions that I had the answer to by giving him the Pacific Avenue address Mickey had given me. It meant something to Collinson. He said: "That's Joseph's place."

We were in the elevator with half a dozen other people. I held my response down to a "Yeah?"

He had a Chrysler roadster parked around the corner. We got into it and began bucking traffic and traffic signals towards Pacific Avenue.

I asked: "Who is Joseph?"

"Another cult. He's the head of it. He calls his place the Temple of the Holy Grail. It's the fashionable one just now. You know how they come and go in California. I don't like having Gabrielle there, if that's where she is—though—I don't know—they may be all right. He's one of Mr. Leggett's queer friends. Do you know that she's there?"

"Maybe. Is she a member of the cult?"

"She goes there, yes. I've been there with her."

"What sort of a layout is it?"

"Oh, it seems to be all right," he said somewhat reluctantly. "The right sort of people: Mrs. Payson Laurence, and the Ralph Colemans, and Mrs. Livingston Rodman, people like that. And the Haldorns—that's Joseph and his wife Aaronia—seem to be quite all right, but—but I don't like the idea of Gabrielle going there like this." He missed the end of a cable car with the Chrysler's right wheel. "I don't think it's good for her to come too much under their influence."

"You've been there; what is their brand of hocus-pocus?" I asked.

"It isn't hocus-pocus, really," he replied, wrinkling his forehead. "I don't know very much about their creed, or anything like that, but I've been to their services with Gabrielle, and they're quite as dignified, as beautiful even, as either Episcopalian or Catholic services. You mustn't think that this is the Holy Roller or House of David sort of thing. It isn't at all. Whatever it is, it is quite first-rate. The Haldorns are people of—of—well, more culture than I."

"Then what's the matter with them?"

He shook his head gloomily. "I honestly don't know that anything is. I don't like it. I don't like having Gabrielle go off like this without letting anybody know where she's gone. Do you think her parents knew where she had gone?"

"No."

"I don't think so either," he said.

From the street the Temple of the Holy Grail looked like what it had originally been, a six-story yellow brick apartment building. There was nothing about its exterior to show that it wasn't still that. I made Collinson drive past it to the corner where Mickey Linehan was leaning his lop-sided bulk against a stone wall. He came to the car as it stopped at the curb.

"The dark meat left ten minutes ago," he reported, "with Dick behind her. Nobody else that looks like anybody you listed has been out."

"Camp here in the car and watch the door," I told him. "We're going in," I said to Collinson. "Let me do most of the talking."

When we reached the Temple door I had to caution him: "Try not breathing so hard. Everything will probably be oke."

I rang the bell. The door was opened immediately by a broad-shouldered, meaty woman of some year close to fifty. She was a good three inches taller than my five feet six. Flesh hung in little bags on her face, but there was neither softness nor looseness in her eyes and mouth. Her long upper lip had been shaved. She was dressed in black, black clothes that covered her from chin and ear-lobes to within less than an inch of the floor.

"We want to see Miss Leggett," I said.

She pretended she hadn't understood me.

"We want to see Miss Leggett," I repeated, "Miss Gabrielle Leggett."

"I don't know." Her voice was bass. "But come in."

She took us not very cheerfully into a small, dimly lighted reception room to one side of the foyer, told us to wait there, and went away.

"Who's the village blacksmith?" I asked Collinson.

He said he didn't know her. He fidgeted around the room. I sat down. Drawn blinds let in too little light for me to make out much of the room, but the rug was soft and thick, and what I could see of the furniture leaned towards luxury rather than severity.

Except for Collinson's fidgeting, no sound came from anywhere in the building. I looked at the open door and saw that we were being examined. A small boy of twelve or thirteen stood there staring at us with big dark eyes that seemed to have lights of their own in the semi-darkness.

I said: "Hello, son."

Collinson jumped around at the sound of my voice.

The boy said nothing. He stared at me for at least another minute with the blank, unblinking, embarrassing stare that only children can manage completely, then turned his back on me and walked away, making no more noise going than he had made coming.

"Who's that?" I asked Collinson.

"It must be the Haldorns' son Manuel. I've never seen him before."

Collinson walked up and down. I sat and watched the door. Presently a woman, walking silently on the thick carpet, appeared there and came into the reception room. She was tall, graceful; and her dark eyes seemed to have lights of their own, like the boy's. That was all I could see clearly then.

I stood up.

She addressed Collinson: "How do you do? This is Mr. Collinson, isn't it?" Her voice was the most musical I had ever heard.

Collinson mumbled something or other and introduced me to the woman, calling her Mrs. Haldorn. She gave me a warm, firm hand and then crossed the room to raise a blind, letting in a fat rectangle of afternoon sun. While I blinked at her in the sudden brightness, she sat down and motioned us into chairs.

I saw her eyes first. They were enormous, almost black, warm, and heavily fringed with almost black lashes. They were the only live, human, real things in her face. There was warmth and there was beauty in her oval, olive-skinned face, but, except for the eyes, it was warmth and beauty that didn't seem to have anything to do with reality. It was as if her face were not a face, but a mask that she had worn until it had almost become a face. Even her mouth, which was a mouth to talk about, looked not so much like flesh as like a too perfect imitation of flesh, softer and redder and maybe warmer than genuine flesh, but not genuine flesh. Above this face, or mask, uncut black hair was tied close to her head, parted in the middle, and drawn across temples and upper ears to end in a knot on the nape of her neck. Her neck was long, strong, slender; her body tall, fully fleshed, supple; her clothes dark and silky, part of her body.

I said: "We want to see Miss Leggett, Mrs. Haldorn."

She asked curiously: "Why do you think she is here?"

"That doesn't make any difference, does it?" I replied quickly, before Collinson could say something wrong. "She is. We'd like to see her."

"I don't think you can," she said slowly. "She isn't well, and she came here to rest, particularly to get away from people for a while."

"Sorry," I said, "but it's a case of have to. We wouldn't have come like this if it hadn't been important."

"It is important?"

"Yeah."

She hesitated, said: "Well, I'll see," excused herself, and left us.

"I wouldn't mind moving in here myself," I told Collinson.

He didn't know what I was talking about. His face was flushed and excited.

"Gabrielle may not like our coming here like this," he said.

I said that would be too bad.

Aaronia Haldorn returned to us.

"I'm really very sorry," she said, standing in the doorway, smiling politely, "but Miss Leggett doesn't wish to see you."

"I'm sorry she doesn't," I said, "but we'll have to see her."

She drew herself up straight and her smile went away.

"I beg your pardon?" she said.

"We'll have to see her," I repeated, keeping my voice amiable. "It's important, as I told you."

"I am sorry." Even the iciness she got into her voice didn't keep it from being beautiful. "You cannot see her."

I said: "Miss Leggett's an important witness, as you probably know, in a robbery and murder job. Well, we've got to see her. If it suits you better, I'm willing to wait half an hour till we can get a policeman up here with whatever authority you make necessary. We're going to see her."

Collinson said something unintelligible, though it sounded apologetic.

Aaronia Haldorn made the slightest of bows.

"You may do as you see fit," she said coldly. "I do not approve of your disturbing Miss Leggett against her wishes, and so far as my permission is concerned, I do not give it. If you insist, I cannot prevent you."

"Thanks. Where is she?"

"Her room is on the fifth floor, just beyond the stairs, to the left."

She bent her head a little once more and went away.

Collinson put a hand on my arm, mumbling: "I don't know whether I—whether we ought to do this. Gabrielle's not going to like it. She won't—"

"Suit yourself," I growled, "but I'm going up. Maybe she won't like it, but neither do I like having people running away and hiding when I want to ask them about stolen diamonds."

He frowned, chewed his lips, and made uncomfortable faces, but he went along with me. We found an automatic elevator, rode to the fifth floor, and went down a purple-carpeted corridor to the door just beyond the stairs on the left-hand side.

I tapped the door with the back of my hand. There was no answer from inside. I tapped again, louder.

A voice sounded inside the room. It might have been anybody's voice, though probably a woman's. It was too faint for us to know what it said and too smothered for us to know who was saying it.

I poked Collinson with my elbow and ordered: "Call her."

He pulled at his collar with a forefinger and called hoarsely: "Gaby, it's Eric."

That didn't bring an answer.

I thumped the wood again, calling: "Open the door."

The voice inside said something that was nothing to me. I repeated my thumping and calling. Down the corridor a door opened and a sallow thin-haired old man's head stuck out and asked: "What's the matter?" I said: "None of your damned business," and pounded the door again.

The inside voice came strong enough now to let us know that it was complaining, though no words could be made out yet. I rattled the knob and found that the door was unlocked. Rattling the knob some more, I worked the door open an inch or so. Then the voice was clearer. I heard soft feet on the floor. I heard a choking sob. I pushed the door open.

Eric Collinson made a noise in his throat that was like somebody very far away yelling horribly.

Gabrielle Leggett stood beside the bed, swaying a little, holding the white foot-rail of the bed with one hand. Her face was white as lime. Her eyes were all brown, dull, focused on nothing, and her small forehead was wrinkled. She looked as if she knew there was something in front of her and was wondering what it was. She had on one yellow stocking, a brown velvet skirt that had been slept in, and a yellow chemise. Scattered around the room were a pair of brown slippers, the other stocking, a brown and gold blouse, a brown coat, and a brown and yellow hat.

Everything else in the room was white: white-papered walls and white-painted ceiling; white-enameled chairs, bed, table, fixtures—even to the telephone—and woodwork; white felt on the floor. None of the furniture was hospital furniture, but solid whiteness gave it that appearance. There were two windows, and two doors besides the one I had opened. The door on the left opened into a bathroom, the one on the right into a small dressing-room.

I pushed Collinson into the room, followed him, and closed the door. There was no key in it, and no place for a key, no lock of any fixable sort. Collinson stood gaping at the girl, his jaw sagging, his eyes as vacant as hers; but there was more horror in his face. She leaned against the foot of the bed and stared at nothing with dark, blank eyes in a ghastly, puzzled face.

I put an arm around her and sat her on the side of the bed, telling Collinson: "Gather up her clothes." I had to tell him twice before he came out of his trance.

He brought me her things and I began dressing her. He dug his fingers into my shoulder and protested in a voice that would have been appropriate if I had been robbing a poor-box:

"No! You can't—"

"What the hell?" I asked, pushing his hand away. "You can have the job if you want it."

He was sweating. He gulped and stuttered: "No, no! I couldn't—it—" He broke off and walked to the window.

"She told me you were an ass," I said to his back, and discovered I was putting the brown and gold blouse on her backwards. She might as well have been a wax figure, for all the help she gave me, but at least she didn't struggle when I wrestled her around, and she stayed where I shoved her.

By the time I had got her into coat and hat, Collinson had come away from the window and was spluttering questions at me. What was the matter with her? Oughtn't we to get a doctor? Was it safe to take her out? And when I stood up, he took her away from me, supporting her with his long, thick arms, babbling: "It's Eric, Gaby. Don't you know me? Speak to me. What is the matter, dear?"

"There's nothing the matter except that she's got a skinful of dope," I said. "Don't try to bring her out of it. Wait till we get her home. You take this arm and I'll take that. She can walk all right. If we run into anybody, just keep going and let me handle them. Let's go."

We didn't meet anybody. We went out to the elevator, down in it to the ground floor, across the foyer, and into the street without seeing a single person.

We went down to the corner where we had left Mickey in the Chrysler.

"That's all for you," I told him.

He said: "Right, so long," and went away.

Collinson and I wedged the girl between us in the roadster, and he put it in motion.

We rode three blocks. Then he asked: "Are you sure home's the best place for her?"

I said I was. He didn't say anything for five more blocks and then repeated his question, adding something about a hospital.

"Why not a newspaper office?" I sneered.

Three blocks of silence, and he started again: "I know a doctor who—"

"I've got work to do," I said; "and Miss Leggett home now, in the shape she's in now, will help me get it done. So she goes home."

He scowled, accusing me angrily: "You'd humiliate her, disgrace her, endanger her life, for the sake of—"

"Her life's in no more danger than yours or mine. She's simply got a little more of the junk in her than she can stand up under. And she took it. I didn't give it to her."

The girl we were talking about was alive and breathing between us—even sitting up with her eyes open—but knowing no more of what was going on than if she had been in Finland.

We should have turned to the right at the next corner. Collinson held the car straight and stepped it up to forty-

43

five miles an hour, staring ahead, his face hard and lumpy.

"Take the next turn," I commanded.

"No," he said, and didn't. The speedometer showed a 50, and people on the sidewalks began looking after us as we whizzed by.

"Well?" I asked, wriggling an arm lose from the girl's side.

"We're going down the peninsula," he said firmly. "She's not going home in her condition."

I grunted: "Yeah?" and flashed my free hand at the controls. He knocked it aside, holding the wheel with one hand, stretching the other out to block me if I tried again.

"Don't do that," he cautioned me, increasing our speed another half-dozen miles. "You know what will happen to all of us if you—"

I cursed him, bitterly, fairly thoroughly, and from the heart. His face jerked around to me, full of righteous indignation because, I suppose, my language wasn't the kind one should use in a lady's company.

And that brought it about.

A blue sedan came out of a cross-street a split second before we got there. Collinson's eyes and attention got back to his driving in time to twist the roadster away from the sedan, but not in time to make a neat job of it. We missed the sedan by a couple of inches, but as we passed behind it our rear wheels started sliding out of line. Collinson did what he could, giving the roadster its head, going with the skid, but the corner curb wouldn't co-operate. It stood stiff and hard where it was. We hit it sidewise and rolled over on the lamp-post behind it. The lamp-post snapped, crashed down on the sidewalk. The roadster, over on its side, spilled us out around the lamp-post. Gas from the broken post roared up at our feet.

Collinson, most of the skin scraped from one side of his face, crawled back on hands and knees to turn off the roadster's engine. I sat up, raising the girl, who was on my chest, with me. My right shoulder and arm were out of whack, dead. The girl was making whimpering noises in her chest, but I couldn't see any marks on her except a shallow scratch on one cheek. I had been her cushion, had taken the jolt for her. The soreness of my chest, belly, and back, the lameness of my shoulder and arm, told me how much I had saved her.

People helped us up. Collinson stood with his arms around the girl, begging her to say she wasn't dead, and so on. The smash had jarred her into semi-consciousness, but she still didn't know whether there had been an accident or what. I went over and helped Collinson hold her up—though neither needed help—saying earnestly to the gathering crowd: "We've got to get her home. Who can—?"

A pudgy man in plus fours offered his services. Collinson and I got in the back of his car with the girl, and I gave the pudgy man her address. He said something about a hospital, but I insisted that home was the place for her. Collinson was too upset to say anything. Twenty minutes later we took the girl out of the car in front of her house. I thanked the pudgy man profusely, giving him no opportunity to follow us indoors.

VI: THE MAN FROM DEVIL'S ISLAND

After some delay—I had to ring twice—the Leggetts' door was opened by Owen Fitzstephan. There was no sleepiness in his eyes: they were hot and bright, as they were when he found life interesting. Knowing the sort of things that interested him, I wondered what had happened.

"What have you been doing?" he asked, looking at our clothes, at Collinson's bloody face, at the girl's scratched cheek.

"Automobile accident," I said. "Nothing serious. Where's everybody?"

"Everybody," he said, with peculiar emphasis on the word, "is up in the laboratory;" and then to me: "Come here."

I followed him across the reception hall to the foot of the stairs, leaving Collinson and the girl standing just inside the street door. Fitzstephan put his mouth close to my ear and whispered:

"Leggett's committed suicide."

I was more annoyed than surprised. I asked: "Where is he?"

"In the laboratory. Mrs. Leggett and the police are up there. It happened only half an hour ago."

"We'll all go up," I said.

"Isn't it rather unnecessary," he asked, "taking Gabrielle up there?"

"Might be tough on her," I said irritably, "but it's necessary enough. Anyway, she's coked-up and better able to stand the shock than she will be later, when the stuff's dying out in her." I turned to Collinson. "Come on, we'll go up to the laboratory."

I went ahead, letting Fitzstephan help Collinson with the girl. There were six people in the laboratory: a uniformed copper—a big man with a red mustache—standing beside the door; Mrs. Leggett, sitting on a wooden chair in the far end of the room, her body bent forward, her hands holding a handkerchief to her face, sobbing quietly; O'Gar and Reddy, standing by one of the windows, close together, their heads rubbing over a sheaf of papers that the detective-sergeant held in his thick fists; a gray-faced, dandified man in dark clothes, standing beside the zinc table, twiddling eye-glasses on a black ribbon in his hand; and Edgar Leggett, seated on a chair at the table, his head and upper body resting on the table, his arms sprawled out.

O'Gar and Reddy looked up from their reading as I

came in. Passing the table on my way to join them at the window, I saw blood, a small black automatic pistol lying close to one of Leggett's hands, and seven unset diamonds grouped by his head.

O'Gar said, "Take a look," and handed me part of his sheaf of paper—four stiff white sheets covered with very small, precise, and regular handwriting in black ink. I was getting interested in what was written there when Fitz-stephan and Collinson came in with Gabrielle Leggett.

Collinson looked at the dead man at the table. Collin-son's face went white. He put his big body between the girl and her father.

"Come in," I said.

"This is no place for Miss Leggett now," he said hotly, turning to take her away.

"We ought to have everybody in here," I told O'Gar. He nodded his bullet head at the policeman. The policeman put a hand on Collinson's shoulder and said: "You'll have to come in, the both of you."

Fitzstephan placed a chair by one of the end windows for the girl. She sat down and looked around the room— at the dead man, at Mrs. Leggett, at all of us—with eyes that were dull but no longer completely blank. Collinson stood beside her, glaring at me. Mrs. Leggett hadn't looked up from her handkerchief.

I spoke to O'Gar, clearly enough for the others to hear: "Let's read the letter out loud."

He screwed up his eyes, hesitated, then thrust the rest of his sheaf at me, saying: "Fair enough. You read it."

I read:

"To the police:—

"My name is Maurice Pierre de Mayenne. I was born in Fécamp, department of Seine-Inférieure, France, on March 6, 1883, but was chiefly educated in England. In 1903 I went to Paris to study paint-ing, and there, four years later, I made the acquaint-ance of Alice and Lily Dain, orphan daughters of a British naval officer. I married Lily the following year, and in 1909 our daughter Gabrielle was born.

"Shortly after my marriage I had discovered that I had made a most horrible mistake, that it was Alice, and not my wife Lily, whom I really loved. I kept this discovery to myself until the child was past the most difficult baby years; that is, until she was nearly five, and then told my wife, asking that she divorce me so I could marry Alice. She refused.

"On June 6, 1913, I murdered Lily and fled with Alice and Gabrielle to London, where I was soon arrested and returned to Paris, to be tried, found guilty, and sentenced to life imprisonment on the Iles du Salut. Alice, who had had no part in the murder, no knowledge of it until after it was done, and who had accompanied us to London only because of her love for Gabrielle, was also tried, but justly acquitted. All this is a matter of record in Paris.

"In 1918 I escaped from the islands with a fellow convict named Jacques Labaud, on a flimsy raft. I do not know—we never knew—how long we were adrift on the ocean, nor, toward the last, how long we went without food and water. Then Labaud could stand no more, and died. He died of starvation and exposure. I did not kill him. No living creature could have been feeble enough for me to have killed it, no matter what my desire. But when Labaud was dead there was enough food for one, and I lived to be washed ashore in the Golfo Triste.

"Calling myself Walter Martin, I secured employment with a British copper mining company at Aroa, and within a few months had become private secretary to Philip Howart, the resident manager. Shortly after this promotion I was approached by a cockney named John Edge, who outlined to me a plan by which we could defraud the company of a hundred-odd pounds monthly. When I refused to take part in the fraud, Edge revealed his knowledge of my identity, and threatened exposure unless I assisted him. That Venezuela had no extradition treaty with France might save me from being returned to the islands, Edge said; but that was not my chief danger: Labaud's body had been cast ashore, undecomposed enough to show what had happened to him, and I, an escaped murderer, would be under the necessity of proving to a Venezuelan court that I had not killed Labaud in Venezuelan waters to keep from starving.

"I still refused to join Edge in his fraud, and prepared to go away. But while I was making my preparations he killed Howart and looted the company safe. He urged me to flee with him, arguing that I could not face the police investigation even if he did not expose me. That was true enough: I went with him. Two months later, in Mexico City, I learned why Edge had been so desirous of my company. He had a firm hold on me, through his knowledge of my identity, and a great—an unjustified—opinion of my ability; and he intended using me to commit crimes that were beyond his grasp. I was determined, no matter what happened, no matter what became necessary, never to return to the Iles du Salut; but neither did I intend becoming a professional criminal. I attempted to desert Edge in Mexico City; he found me; we fought; and I killed him. I killed him in self-defense: he struck me first.

"In 1920 I came to the United States, to San Francisco, changed my name once more—to Edgar Leggett—and began making a new place for myself in the world, developing experiments with color that I had attempted as a young artist in Paris. In 1923, believing that Edgar Leggett could never now be connected with Maurice de Mayenne, I sent for Alice and Gabrielle, who were then living in New York, and Alice and I were married. But the past was not dead, and there was no unbridgeable chasm between Leggett and Mayenne. Alice, not hearing from me after my escape, not knowing what had happened to me, employed a private detective to find me, a Louis Upton. Upton sent a man named Ruppert to South America, and Ruppert succeeded in tracing me step by step from my landing in the Golfo Triste up to, but no farther than, my departure from Mexico City after Edge's death. In doing this, Ruppert of course learned of the deaths of Labaud, Howart and Edge; three deaths of which I was guiltless, but of which—or at least of one or more of which—I most certainly, my record being what it is, would be convicted if tried.

"I do not know how Upton found me in San Francisco. Possibly he traced Alice and Gabrielle to me. Late last Saturday night he called upon me and demanded money as the price of silence. Having no money available at the time, I put him off until Tuesday, when I gave him the diamonds as part payment. But I was desperate. I knew what being at Upton's mercy would mean, having experienced the same thing with Edge. I determined to kill him. I decided to pretend the diamonds had been stolen, and to so inform you, the police. Upton, I was confident, would thereupon immediately communicate with me. I would make an appointment with him and shoot him down in cold blood, confident that I would have no difficulty in arranging a story that would make me seem justified in having killed this known burglar, in whose possession, doubtless, the stolen diamonds would be found.

"I think the plan would have been successful. However, Ruppert—pursuing Upton with a grudge of his own to settle—saved me from killing Upton by himself killing him. Ruppert, the man who had traced my course from Devil's Island to Mexico City, had also, either from Upton or by spying on Upton, learned that Mayenne was Leggett, and, with the police after him for Upton's murder, he came here, demanding that I shelter him, returning the diamonds, claiming money in their stead.

"I killed him. His body is in the cellar. Out front, a detective is watching my house. Other detectives are busy elsewhere inquiring into my affairs. I have not been able satisfactorily to explain certain of my actions, nor to avoid contradictions, and, now that I am actually suspect, there is little chance of the past's being kept secret. I have always known—have known it most surely when I would not admit it to myself—that this would one day happen. I am not going back to Devil's Island. My wife and daughter had neither knowledge of nor part in Ruppert's death.

"Maurice de Mayenne."

VII : THE CURSE

Nobody said anything for some minutes after I had finished reading. Mrs. Leggett had taken her handkerchief from her face to listen, sobbing softly now and then. Gabrielle was looking jerkily around the room, light fighting cloudiness in her eyes, her lips twitching as if she was trying to get words out but couldn't.

I went to the table, bent over the dead man, and ran my hand over his pockets. The inside coat pocket bulged. I reached under his arm, unbuttoned and pulled open his coat, taking a brown wallet from the pocket. The wallet was thick with paper money—fifteen thousand dollars when we counted it later.

Showing the others the wallet's contents, I asked:

"Did he leave any message besides the one I read?"

"None that's been found," O'Gar said. "Why?"

"Any that you know of, Mrs. Leggett?" I asked.

She shook her head.

"Why?" O'Gar asked again.

"He didn't commit suicide," I said. "He was murdered."

Gabrielle Leggett screamed shrilly and sprang out of her chair, pointing a sharp-nailed white finger at Mrs. Leggett.

"She killed him," the girl shrieked. "She said, 'Come back here,' and held the kitchen door open with one hand, and picked up the knife from the drain-board with the other, and when he went past her she pushed it in his back. I saw her do it. She killed him. I wasn't dressed, and when I heard them coming I hid in the pantry, and I saw her do it."

Mrs. Leggett got to her feet. She staggered, and would have fallen if Fitzstephan hadn't gone over to steady her. Amazement washed her swollen face empty of grief.

The gray-faced dandified man by the table—Doctor Riese, I learned later—said, in a cold, crisp voice:

"There is no stab wound. He was shot through the temple by a bullet from this pistol, held close, slanting up. Clearly suicide, I should say."

Collinson forced Gabrielle down to her chair again, trying to calm her. She was working her hands together and moaning.

I disagreed with the doctor's last statement, and said so while turning something else over in my mind.

"Murder. He had this money in his pocket. He was going away. He wrote that letter to the police to clear his wife and daughter, so they wouldn't be punished for complicity in his crimes. Did it," I asked O'Gar, "sound to you like the dying statement of a man who was leaving a wife and daughter he loved? No message, no word, to them—all to the police."

"Maybe you're right," the bullet-headed man said; "but supposing he was going away, he still didn't leave them any—"

"He would have told them—either on paper or talking—something before he went, if he had lived long enough. He was winding up his affairs, preparing to go away, and— Maybe he *was* going to commit suicide, though the money and the tone of the letter make me doubt it; but even in that case my guess is that he didn't, that he was killed before he had finished his preparations—maybe because he was taking too long a time. How was he found?"

"I heard," Mrs. Leggett sobbed; "I heard the shot, and ran up here, and he—he was like that. And I went down to the telephone, and the bell—the doorbell—rang, and it was Mr. Fitzstephan, and I told him. It couldn't—there was nobody else in the house to—to kill him."

"You killed him," I said to her. "He was going away. He wrote this statement, shouldering your crimes. You killed Ruppert down in the kitchen. That's what the girl was talking about. Your husband's letter sounded enough like a suicide letter to pass for one, you thought; so you murdered him—murdered him because you thought his confession and death would hush up the whole business, keep us from poking into it any further."

Her face didn't tell me anything. It was distorted, but in a way that might have meant almost anything. I filled my lungs and went on, not exactly bellowing, but getting plenty of noise out:

"There are half a dozen lies in your husband's statement—half a dozen that I can peg now. He didn't send for you and his daughter. You traced him here. Mrs. Begg said he was the most surprised man she had ever seen when you arrived from New York. He didn't give Upton the diamonds. His account of why he gave them to Upton and of what he intended doing afterwards is ridiculous: it's simply the best story he could think of on short notice to cover you up. Leggett would have given him money or he would have given him nothing; he wouldn't have been foolish enough to give him somebody else's diamonds and have all this stink raised.

"Upton traced you here and he came to you with his

53

demand—not to your husband. You had hired Upton to find Leggett; you were the one he knew; he and Ruppert had traced Leggett for you, not only to Mexico City, but all the way here. They'd have squeezed you before this if they hadn't been sent to Sing Sing for another trick. When they got out, Upton came here and made his play. You framed the burglary; you gave Upton the diamonds; and you didn't tell your husband anything about it. Your husband thought the burglary was on the level. Otherwise, would he—a man with his record—have risked reporting it to the police?

"Why didn't you tell him about Upton? Didn't you want him to know that you had had him traced step by step from Devil's Island to San Francisco? Why? His southern record was a good additional hold on him, if you needed one? You didn't want him to know you knew about Labaud and Howart and Edge?"

I didn't give her a chance to answer any of these questions, but sailed ahead, turning my voice loose:

"Maybe Ruppert, following Upton here, got in touch with you, and you had him kill Upton, a job he was willing to do on his own hook. Probably, because he did kill him and he did come to you afterwards, and you thought it necessary to put the knife into him down in the kitchen. You didn't know the girl, hiding in the pantry, saw you; but you did know that you were getting out of your depth. You knew that your chances of getting away with Ruppert's murder were slim. Your house was too much in the spotlight. So you played your only out. You went to your husband with the whole story—or as much of it as could be arranged to persuade him—and got him to shoulder it for you. And then you handed him this—here at the table.

"He shielded you. He had always shielded you. *You*," I thundered, my voice in fine form by now, "killed your sister Lily, his first wife, and let him take the fall for you. *You* went to London with him after that. Would you have gone with your sister's murderer if you had been innocent? *You* had him traced here, and *you* came here after

54

him, and *you* married him. *You* were the one who decided he had married the wrong sister, and *you* killed her."

"She did! She did!" cried Gabrielle Leggett, trying to get up from the chair in which Collinson was holding her. "She—"

Mrs. Leggett drew herself up straight, and smiled, showing strong yellowish teeth set edge to edge. She took two steps toward the center of the room. One hand was on her hip, the other hanging loosely at her side. The housewife—Fitzstephan's serene sane soul—was suddenly gone. This was a blonde woman whose body was rounded, not with the plumpness of contented, well-cared-for early middle age, but with the cushioned, soft-sheathed muscles of the hunting cats, whether in jungle or alley.

I picked up the pistol from the table and put it in my pocket.

"You wish to know who killed my sister?" Mrs. Leggett asked softly, speaking to me, her teeth clicking together between words, her mouth smiling, her eyes burning. "She, the dope fiend, Gabrielle—she killed her mother. She is the one he shielded."

The girl cried out something unintelligible.

"Nonsense," I said. "She was a baby."

"Oh, but it is not nonsense," the woman said. "She was nearly five, a child of five playing with a pistol that she had taken from a drawer while her mother slept. The pistol went off and Lily died. An accident, of course, but Maurice was too sensitive a soul to bear the thought of her growing up knowing that she had killed her mother. Besides, it was likely that Maurice would have been convicted in any event. It was known that he and I were intimate, that he wanted his freedom from Lily; and he was at the door of Lily's bedroom when the shot was fired. But that was a slight matter to him: his one desire was to save the child from memory of what she had done, so her life might not be blackened by the knowledge that she had, however accidentally, killed her mother."

What made this especially nasty was the niceness with

which the woman smiled as she talked, and the care—almost fastidious—with which she selected her words, mouthing them daintily. She went on:

"Gabrielle was always, even before she became addicted to drugs, a child of, one might say, limited mentality; and so, by the time the London police had found us, we had succeeded in quite emptying her mind of the last trace of memory, that is, of this particular memory. This is, I assure you, the entire truth. She killed her mother; and her father, to use your expression, took the fall for her."

"Fairly plausible," I conceded, "but it doesn't hang together right. There's a chance that you made Leggett believe that, but I doubt it. I think you're trying to hurt your step-daughter because she's told us of seeing you knife Ruppert downstairs."

She pulled her lips back from her teeth and took a quick step toward me, her eyes wide and white-ringed; then she checked herself, laughed sharply, and the glare went from her eyes—or maybe went back through them, to smolder behind them. She put her hands on her hips and smiled playfully, airily, at me and spoke playfully to me, while mad hatred glowed behind eyes, smile, and voice.

"Am I? Then I must tell you this, which I should not tell you unless it was true. I taught her to kill her mother. Do you understand? I taught her, trained her, drilled her, rehearsed her. Do you understand that? Lily and I were true sisters, inseparable, hating one another poisonously. Maurice, he wished to marry neither of us—why should he?—though he was intimate enough with both. You are to try to understand that literally. But we were poverty-ridden and he was not, and, because we were and he wasn't, Lily wished to marry him. And I, I wished to marry him because she did. We were true sisters, like that in all things. But Lily got him, first—trapped him—that is crude but exact—into matrimony.

"Gabrielle was born six or seven months later. What a happy little family we were. I lived with them—weren't

Lily and I inseparable?—and from the first Gabrielle had more love for me than for her mother. I saw to that: there was nothing her Aunt Alice wouldn't do for her dear niece; because her preferring me infuriated Lily, not that Lily herself loved the child so much, but that we were sisters; and whatever one wanted the other wanted, not to share, but exclusively.

"Gabrielle had hardly been born before I began planning what I should some day do; and when she was nearly five I did it. Maurice's pistol, a small one, was kept in a locked drawer high in a chiffonier. I unlocked the drawer, unloaded the pistol, and taught Gabrielle an amusing little game. I would lie on Lily's bed, pretending to sleep. The child would push a chair to the chiffonier, climb up on it, take the pistol from the drawer, creep over to the bed, put the muzzle of the pistol to my head, and press the trigger. When she did it well, making little or no noise, holding the pistol correctly in her tiny hands, I would reward her with candy, cautioning her against saying anything about the game to her mother or to anyone else, as we were going to surprise her mother with it.

"We did. We surprised her completely one afternoon when, having taken aspirin for a headache, Lily was sleeping in her bed. That time I unlocked the drawer but did not unload the pistol. Then I told the child she might play the game with her mother; and I went to visit friends on the floor below, so no one would think I had had any part in my dear sister's demise. I thought Maurice would be away all afternoon. I intended, when I heard the shot, to rush upstairs with my friends and find with them that the child playing with the pistol had killed her mother.

"I had little fear of the child's talking afterwards. Of, as I have said, limited mentality, loving and trusting me as she did, and in my hands both before and during any official inquiry that might be made, I knew I could very easily control her, make sure that she said nothing to reveal my part in the—ah—enterprise. But Maurice very nearly spoiled the whole thing. Coming home unexpectedly, he reached the bedroom door just as Gabrielle pressed the trigger. The tiniest fraction of a second earlier, and he would have been in time to save his wife's life.

"Well, that was unfortunate in that it led to his being convicted; but it certainly prevented his ever suspecting me; and his subsequent desire to wipe from the child's mind all remembrance of the deed relieved me of any further anxiety or effort. I did follow him to this country after his escape from Devil's Island, and I did follow him to San Francisco when Upton had found him for me; and I used Gabrielle's love for me and her hatred of him—I had carefully cultivated that with skilfully clumsy attempts to persuade her to forgive him for murdering her mother—and the necessity of keeping her in ignorance of the truth, and my record of faithfulness to him and her, to make him marry me, to make him think that marrying me would in some sense salvage our ruined lives. The day he married Lily I swore I would take him away from her. And I did. And I hope my dear sister in hell knows it."

The smile was gone. Mad hatred was no longer *behind* eyes and voice: it was *in* them, and in the set of her features, the pose of her body. This mad hatred—and she as part of it—seemed the only live thing in the room. The eight of us who looked at and listened to her didn't, for the moment, count: we were alive to her, but not to each other, nor to anything but her.

She turned from me to fling an arm out at the girl on the other side of the room; and now her voice was throaty, vibrant, with savage triumph in it; and her words were separated into groups by brief pauses, so that she seemed to be chanting them.

"You're her daughter," she cried; "and you're cursed with the same black soul and rotten blood that she and I and all the Dains have had; and you're cursed with your mother's blood on your hands in babyhood; and with the twisted mind and the need for drugs that are my gifts to you; and your life will be black as your mother's and mine were black; and the lives of those you touch will be black as Maurice's was black; and your—"

"Stop!" Eric Collinson gasped. "Make her stop."

Gabrielle Leggett, both hands to her ears, her face twisted with terror, screamed once—horribly—and fell forward out of her chair.

Pat Reddy was young at manhunting, but O'Gar and I should have known better than to stop watching Mrs. Leggett even for a half-second, no matter how urgently the girl's scream and fall pulled at our attention. But we did look at the girl—if for less than half a second—and that was long enough. When we looked at Mrs. Leggett again, she had a gun in her hand, and she had taken her first step towards the door.

Nobody was between her and the door: the uniformed copper had gone to help Collinson with Gabrielle Leggett. Nobody was behind her: her back was to the door and by turning she had brought Fitzstephan into her field of vision. She glared over the black gun, burning eyes darting from one to another of us, taking another step backward, snarling: "Don't you move."

Pat Reddy shifted his weight to the balls of his feet. I frowned at him, shaking my head. The hall and stairs were better places in which to catch her: in here somebody would die.

She backed over the sill, blew breath between her teeth with a hissing, spitting sound, and was gone down the hall.

Owen Fitzstephan was first through the door after her. The policeman got in my way, but I was second out. The woman had reached the head of the stairs, at the other end of the dim hall, with Fitzstephan, not far behind, rapidly overtaking her.

He caught her on the between-floors landing, just as I reached the top of the stairs. He pinned one of her arms to her body, but the other, with the gun, was free. He grabbed at it and missed. She twisted the muzzle in to his body as I—with my head bent to miss the edge of the floor—leaped down at them.

I landed on them just in time, crashing into them, smashing them into the corner of the wall, sending her bullet, meant for the sorrel-haired man, into a step.

We weren't standing up. I caught with both hands at the flash of her gun, missed, and had her by the waist. Close to my chin Fitzstephan's lean fingers closed on her gun-hand wrist.

She twisted her body against my right arm. My right arm was still lame from our spill out of the Chrysler. It wouldn't hold. Her thick body went up, turning over on me.

Gunfire roared in my ear, burnt my cheek.

The woman's body went limp.

When O'Gar and Reddy pulled us apart she lay still. The second bullet had gone through her throat.

I went up to the laboratory. Gabrielle Leggett, with the doctor and Collinson kneeling beside her, was lying on the floor.

I told the doctor: "Better take a look at Mrs. Leggett. She's on the stairs. Dead, I think, but you'd better take a look."

The doctor went out. Collinson, chafing the unconscious girl's hands, looked at me as if I were something there ought to be a law against, and said:

"I hope you're satisfied with the way your work got done."

"It got done," I said.

VIII : BUT AND IF

Fitzstephan and I ate one of Mrs. Schindler's good dinners that evening in her low-ceilinged basement, and drank her husband's good beer. The novelist in Fitzstephan was busy trying to find what he called Mrs. Leggett's psychological basis.

"The killing of her sister is plain enough, knowing her character as we now do," he said, "and so are the killing of her husband, her attempt to ruin her niece's life when she was exposed, and even her determination to kill herself on the stairs rather than be caught. But the quiet years in between—where do they fit in?"

"It's Leggett's murder that doesn't fit in," I argued. "The rest is all one piece. She wanted him. She killed her sister—or had her killed—in a way to tie him to her; but the law pulled them apart. There was nothing she could do about that, except wait and hope for the chance that always existed, that he would be freed some day. We don't know of anything else she wanted then. Why shouldn't she be quiet, holding Gabrielle as her hostage against the chance she hoped for, living comfortably enough, no doubt, on his money? When she heard of his escape, she came to America and set about finding him. When her detectives located him here she came to him. He was willing to marry her. She had what she wanted. Why should she be anything but quiet? She wasn't a trouble-maker for the fun of it—one of these people who act out of pure mischief. She was simply a woman who wanted what she wanted and was willing to go to any length to get it. Look how patiently, and for how many years, she hid her hatred from the girl. And her wants weren't even very extravagant. You won't find the key to her in any complicated derangements. She was simple as an animal, with an animal's simple ignorance of right and wrong, dislike for being thwarted, and spitefulness when trapped."

Fitzstephan drank beer and asked:

"You'd reduce the Dain curse, then, to a primitive strain in the blood?"

"To less than that, to words in an angry woman's mouth."

"It's fellows like you that take all the color out of life." He sighed behind cigarette smoke. "Doesn't Gabrielle's being made the tool of her mother's murder convince you of the necessity—at least the poetic necessity—of the curse?"

"Not even if she *was* the tool, and that's something I wouldn't bet on. Apparently Leggett didn't doubt it. He stuffed his letter with those ancient details to keep her covered up. But we've only got Mrs. Leggett's word that he actually saw the child kill her mother. On the other hand, Mrs. Leggett said, in front of Gabrielle, that Gabrielle had been brought up to believe her father the murderer—so we can believe that. And it isn't likely—though it's possible—that he would have gone that far except to save her from knowledge of her own guilt. But, from that point on, one guess at the truth is about as good as another. Mrs. Leggett wanted him and she got him. Then why in hell did she kill him?"

"You jump around so," Fitzstephan complained. "You answered that back in the laboratory. Why don't you stick to your answer? You said she killed him because the letter sounded enough like a pre-suicide statement to pass, and she thought it and his death would ensure her safety."

"That was good enough to say then," I admitted; "but not now, in cold blood, with more facts to fit in. She had worked and waited for years to get him. He must have had some value to her."

"But she didn't love him, or there is no reason to suppose she did. He hadn't that value to her. He was to her no more than a trophy of the hunt; and that's a value not affected by death—one has the head embalmed and nailed on the wall."

"Then why did she keep Upton away from him? Why did she kill Ruppert? Why should she have carried the load for him there? It was his danger. Why did she make it hers if he had no value to her? Why did she risk all that to keep him from learning that the past had come to life again?"

"I think I see what you're getting at," Fitzstephan said slowly. "You think—"

"Wait—here's another thing. I talked to Leggett and his wife together a couple of times. Neither of them addressed a word to the other either time, though the woman did a lot of acting to make me think she would have told me something about her daughter's disappearance if it had not been for him."

"Where did you find Gabrielle?"

"After seeing Ruppert murdered, she beat it to the Haldorns' with what money she had and her jewelry, turning the jewelry over to Minnie Hershey to raise money on. Minnie bought a couple of pieces for herself—her man had picked himself up a lot of dough in a crap game a night or two before: the police checked that—and sent the man out to peddle the rest. He was picked up in a hock-shop, just on general suspicion."

"Gabrielle was leaving home for good?" he asked.

"You can't blame her—thinking her father a murderer, and now catching her step-mother in the act. Who'd want to live in a home like that?"

"And you think Leggett and his wife were on bad terms? That may be: I hadn't seen much of them lately, and wasn't intimate enough with them to have been let in on a condition of that sort if it had existed. Do you think he had perhaps learned something—some of the truth about her?"

"Maybe, but not enough to keep him from taking the fall for her on Ruppert's murder; and what he had learned wasn't connected with this recent affair, because the first time I saw him he really believed in the burglary. But then—"

"Aw, shut up! You're never satisfied until you've got two buts and an if attached to everything. I don't see any reason for doubting Mrs. Leggett's story. She told us the whole thing quite gratuitously. Why should we suppose that she'd lie to implicate herself?"

"You mean in her sister's murder? She'd been acquitted of that, and I suppose the French system's like ours in that she couldn't be tried again for it, no matter what she confessed. She didn't give anything away, brother."

"Always belittling," he said. "You need more beer to expand your soul."

At the Leggett-Ruppert inquests I saw Gabrielle Leggett again, but was not sure that she even recognized me.

She was with Madison Andrews, who had been Leggett's attorney and was now his estate's executor. Eric Collinson was there, but, peculiarly, apparently not with Gabrielle. He gave me nods and nothing else.

The newspapers got hold of what Mrs. Leggett had said happened in Paris in 1913, and made a couple-day fuss over it. The recovery of Halstead and Beauchamp's diamonds let the Continental Detective Agency out: we wrote *Discontinued* at the bottom of the Leggett record. I went up in the mountains to snoop around for a gold-mine-owner who thought his employes were gypping him.

I expected to be in the mountains for at least a month: inside jobs of that sort take time. On the evening of my tenth day there I had a long-distance call from the Old Man, my boss.

"I'm sending Foley up to relieve you," he said. "Don't wait for him. Catch tonight's train back. The Leggett matter is active again."

Part Two: The Temple

IX : TAD'S BLIND MAN

Madison Andrews was a tall gaunt man of sixty with ragged white hair, eyebrows, and mustache that exaggerated the ruddiness of his bony hard-muscled face. He wore his clothes loose, chewed tobacco, and had twice in the past ten years been publicly named co-respondent in divorce suits.

"I dare say young Collinson has babbled all sorts of nonsense to you," he said. "He seems to think I'm in my second childhood, as good as told me so."

"I haven't seen him," I said. "I've only been back in town a couple of hours, long enough to go to the office and then come here."

"Well," he said, "he is her fiancé, but I am responsible for her, and I preferred following Doctor Riese's counsel. He is her physician. He said that letting her go to the Temple for a short stay would do more to restore her to mental health than anything else we could do. I couldn't disregard his advice. The Haldorns may be, probably are, charlatans, but Joseph Haldorn is certainly the only person to whom Gabrielle has willingly talked, and in whose company she has seemed at peace, since her parents' deaths. Doctor Riese said that to cross her in her desire to go to the Temple would be to send her mind deeper into its illness.

Could I snap my fingers at his opinion because young Collinson didn't like it?"

I said: "No."

"I have no illusions concerning the cult," he went on defending himself. "It is probably as full of quackery as any other. But we are not concerned with its religious aspect. We're interested in it as therapeutics, as a cure for Gabrielle's mind. Even if the character of its membership were not such that I could count with certainty on Gabrielle's safety, I should still have been tempted to let her go. Her recovery is, as I see it, the thing with which we should be most concerned, and nothing else should be allowed to interfere with that."

He was worried. I nodded and kept quiet, waiting to learn what was worrying him. I got it little by little as he went on talking around in circles.

On Doctor Riese's advice and over Collinson's protests he had let Gabrielle Leggett go to the Temple of the Holy Grail to stay awhile. She had wanted to go, no less prominently respectable a person than Mrs. Livingston Rodman was staying there at the time, the Haldorns had been Edgar Leggett's friends: Andrews let her go. That had been six days ago. She had taken the mulatto, Minnie Hershey, with her as maid. Doctor Riese had gone to see her each day. On four days he had found her improved. On the fifth day her condition had alarmed him. Her mind was more completely dazed than it had ever been, and she had the symptoms of one who had been subjected to some sort of shock. He couldn't get anything out of her. He couldn't get anything out of Minnie. He couldn't get anything out of the Haldorns. He had no way of learning what had happened, or if anything had happened.

Eric Collinson had held Riese up for daily reports on Gabrielle. Riese told him the truth about his last visit. Collinson hit the ceiling. He wanted the girl taken away from the Temple immediately: the Haldorns were preparing to murder her, according to his notion. He and Andrews had a swell row. Andrews thought that the girl had simply suffered a relapse from which she would most speedily recover if left where she wished to stay. Riese was inclined to agree with Andrews. Collinson didn't. He threatened to create a stink if they didn't yank her away *pronto*.

That worried Andrews. It wouldn't look so good for him, the hard-headed lawyer, letting his ward go to such a place, if anything happened to her. On the other hand, he said he really believed it was for her benefit to stay there. And he didn't want anything to happen to her. He finally reached a compromise with Collinson. Gabrielle should be allowed to remain in the Temple for a few more days at least, but somebody should be put in there to keep an eye on her, and to see that the Haldorns weren't playing any tricks on her.

Riese had suggested me: my luck in hitting on the manner of Leggett's death had impressed him. Collinson had objected that my brutality was largely responsible for Gabrielle's present condition, but he had finally given in. I already knew Gabrielle and her history, and I hadn't made such a total mess of that first job: my efficiency offset my brutality, or words to that effect. So Andrews had phoned the Old Man, offered him a high enough rate to justify pulling me off another job, and there I was.

"The Haldorns know you are coming," Andrews wound up. "It doesn't matter what they think about it. I simply told them that Doctor Riese and I had decided that, until Gabrielle's mind became more settled, it would be best to have a competent man on hand in case of emergency, as much perhaps to safeguard others as her. There is no need of my giving you instructions. It is simply a matter of taking every precaution."

"Does Miss Leggett know I'm coming?"

"No, and I don't think we need say anything to her about it. You'll make your watch over her as unobtrusive as possible, of course, and I doubt that she will, in her present state of mind, pay enough attention to your presence to resent it. If she does—well, we'll see."

Andrews gave me a note to Aaronia Haldorn.

An hour and a half later I was sitting opposite her in the Temple reception room while she read it. She put it aside and offered me long Russian cigarettes in a white jade box. I apologized for sticking to my Fatimas, and worked the lighter on the smoking stand she pushed out between us. When our cigarettes were burning, she said:

"We shall try to make you as comfortable as possible. We are neither barbarians nor fanatics. I explain this because so many people are surprised to find us neither. This is a temple, but none of us supposes that happiness, comfort, or any of the ordinary matters of civilized living, will desecrate it. You are not one of us. Perhaps—I hope—you will become one of us. However—do not squirm—you won't, I assure you, be annoyed. You may attend our services or not, as you choose, and you may come and go as you wish. You will show us, I am sure, the same consideration we show you, and I am equally sure that you will not interfere in any way with anything you may see—no matter how peculiar you may think it—so long as it does not promise to affect your—patient."

"Of course not," I promised.

She smiled, as if to thank me, rubbed her cigarette's end in the ash tray, and stood up, saying: "I'll show you your room."

Not a word had been said by either of us about my previous visit.

Carrying my hat and gladstone bag, I followed her to the elevator. We got out at the fifth floor.

"That is Miss Leggett's room," Aaronia Haldorn said, indicating the door that Collinson and I had taken turns knocking a couple of weeks before. "And this is yours." She opened the door that faced Gabrielle's across the corridor.

My room was a duplicate of hers, except that it was without a dressing-room. My door, like hers, had no lock.

"Where does her maid sleep?" I asked.

"In one of the servant's rooms on the top floor. Doctor Riese is with Miss Leggett now, I think. I'll tell him you have arrived."

I thanked her. She went out of my room, closing the door.

Fifteen minutes later Doctor Riese knocked and came in.

"I am glad you are here," he said, shaking hands. He had a crisp, precise way of turning out his words, sometimes emphasizing them by gesturing with the black-ribboned glasses in his hand. I never saw the glasses on his nose. "We shan't need your professional skill, I trust, but I am glad you are here."

"What's wrong?" I asked in what was meant for a tone that invited confidences.

He looked sharply at me, tapped his glasses on his left thumb-nail, and said:

"What is wrong is, so far as I know, altogether in my sphere. I know of nothing else wrong." He shook my hand again. "You'll find your part quite boring, I hope."

"But yours isn't?" I suggested.

He stopped turning away towards the door, frowned, tapped his glasses with his thumb-nail again, and said:

"No, it is not." He hesitated, as if deciding whether to say something more, decided not to, and moved to the door.

"I've a right to know what you honestly think about it," I said.

He looked sharply at me again. "I don't know what I honestly think about it." A pause. "I am not satisfied." He didn't look satisfied. "I'll be in again this evening."

He went out and shut the door. Half a minute later he opened the door, said, "Miss Leggett is extremely ill," shut the door again and went away.

I grumbled, "This is going to be a lot of fun," to myself, sat down at a window and smoked a cigarette.

A maid in black and white knocked on the door and asked me what I wanted for luncheon. She was a hearty pink and plump blonde somewhere in the middle twenties, with blue eyes that looked curiously at me and had jokes in them. I took a shot of Scotch from the bottle in my bag, ate the luncheon the maid presently returned with, and spent the afternoon in my room.

By keeping my ears open I managed to catch Minnie as she came out of her mistress's room at a little after four.

The mulatto's eyes jerked wide when she saw me standing in my doorway.

"Come in," I said. "Didn't Doctor Riese tell you I was here?"

"No, sir. Are—are you—? You're not wanting anything with Miss Gabrielle?"

"Just looking out for her, seeing that nothing happens to her. And if you'll keep me wised up, let me know what she says and does, and what others say and do, you'll be helping me, and helping her; because then I won't have to bother her."

The mulatto said, "Yes, yes," readily enough, but, as far as I could learn from her brown face, my coöperative idea wasn't getting across any too well.

"How is she this afternoon?" I asked.

"She's right cheerful this afternoon, sir. She like this place."

"How'd she spend the afternoon?"

"She—I don't know, sir. She just kind of spent it—quiet like."

Not much news there. I said:

"Doctor Riese thinks she'll be better off not knowing I'm here, so you needn't say anything to her about me."

"No, sir, I sure won't," she promised, but it sounded more polite than sincere.

In the early evening Aaronia Haldorn came in and invited me down to dinner. The dining-room was paneled and furnished in dark walnut. There were ten of us at the table.

Joseph Haldorn was tall, built like a statue, and wore a black silk robe. His hair was thick, long, white, and glossy. His thick beard, trimmed round, was white and glossy. Aaronia Haldorn introduced me to him, calling him, "Joseph," as if he had no last name. All the others addressed him in the same way. He gave me a white even-toothed smile and a warm strong hand. His face, healthily pink, was without line or wrinkle. It was a tranquil face, especially the clear brown eyes, somehow making you feel at peace with the world. The same soothing quality was in his baritone voice.

He said: "We are happy to have you here."

The words were merely polite, meaningless, yet, as he said them, I actually believed that for some reason he was happy. Now I understood Gabrielle Leggett's desire to come to this place. I said that I, too, was happy to be there, and while I was saying it I actually thought I was.

Besides Joseph and his wife and their son at the table there was Mrs. Rodman, a tall frail woman with transparent skin, faded eyes, and a voice that never rose above a murmur; a man named Fleming, who was young, dark, very thin, and wore a dark mustache and the detached air of one busy with his own thoughts; Major Jeffries, a well-tailored, carefully mannered man, stout and bald and sallow; his wife, a pleasant sort of person in spite of a kittenishness thirty years too young for her; a Miss Hillen, sharp of chin and voice, with an intensely eager manner; and Mrs. Pavlov, who was quite young, had a high-cheek-boned dark face, and avoided everybody's eyes.

The food, served by two Filipino boys, was good. There was not much conversation and none of it was religious. It wasn't so bad.

After dinner I returned to my room. I listened at Gabrielle Leggett's door for a few minutes, but heard nothing. In my room I fidgeted and smoked and waited for Doctor Riese to show up as he had promised. He didn't show up. I supposed that one of the emergencies that are regular parts of doctors' lives had kept him elsewhere, but his not coming made me irritable. Nobody went in or out of Gabrielle's room. I tiptoed over to listen at her door a couple of times. Once I heard nothing. Once I heard faint meaningless rustling sounds.

At a little after ten o'clock I heard some of the inmates going past my door, probably on their way to their rooms for the night.

At five minutes past eleven I heard Gabrielle's door open. I opened mine. Minnie Hershey was going down the corridor toward the rear of the building. I was tempted to call her, but didn't. My last attempt to get anything out of her had been a flop, and I wasn't feeling tactful enough now to stand much chance of having better luck.

By this time I had given up hopes of seeing Riese before the following day.

I switched off my lights, left my door open, and sat there in the dark, looking at the girl's door and cursing the world. I thought of Tad's blind man in a dark room hunting for a black hat that wasn't there, and knew how he felt.

At a little before midnight Minnie Hershey, in hat and coat as if she had just come in from the street, returned to Gabrielle's room. She didn't seem to see me. I stood up silently and tried to peep past her when she opened the door, but didn't have any luck.

Minnie remained there until nearly one o'clock, and when she came out she closed the door very softly, walking tiptoe. That was an unnecessary precaution on the thick carpet. Because it was unnecessary it made me nervous. I went to my door and called in a low voice:

"Minnie."

Maybe she didn't hear me. She went on tiptoeing down the corridor. That increased my jumpiness. I went after her quickly and stopped her by catching one of her wiry wrists.

Her Indian face was expressionless.

"How is she?" I asked.

"Miss Gabrielle's all right, sir. You just leave her alone," she mumbled.

"She's not all right. What's she doing now?"

"She's sleeping."

"Coked?"

She raised angry maroon eyes and let them drop again, saying nothing.

"She sent you out to get dope?" I demanded, tightening my grip on her wrist.

"She sent me out to get some—some medicine—yes, sir."

"And took some and went to sleep?"

"Y-yes, sir."

"We'll go back and take a look at her," I said.

The mulatto tried to jerk her wrist free. I held it. She said:

"You leave me alone, Mister, or else I'll yell."

"I'll leave you alone after we've had our look, maybe," I said, turning her around with my other hand on her shoulder. "So if you're going to yell you can get started right now."

She wasn't willing to go back to her mistress's room, but she didn't make me drag her. Gabrielle Leggett was lying on her side in bed, sleeping quietly, the bedclothes stirring gently with her breathing. Her small white face, at rest, with brown curls falling over it, looked like a sick child's.

I turned Minnie loose and went back to my room. Sitting there in the dark I understood why people bit their fingernails. I sat there for an hour or more, and then, God-damning myself for an old woman, I took off my shoes, picked the most comfortable chair, put my feet on another, hung a blanket over me, and went to sleep facing Gabrielle Leggett's door through my open doorway.

X : DEAD FLOWERS

I opened my eyes drowsily, decided that I had dozed off for only a moment, closed my eyes, drifted back into slumber, and then roused myself sluggishly again. Something wasn't right.

I forced my eyes open, then closed them, and opened them again. Whatever wasn't right had to do with that.

Blackness was there when they were open and when they were closed. That should have been reasonable enough: the night was dark, and my windows were out of the street lights' range. That should have been reasonable enough, but it wasn't: I remembered that I had left my door open, and the corridor lights had been on. Facing me was no pale rectangle of light framed by my doorway, with Gabrielle's door showing through.

I was too awake by now to jump up suddenly. I held my breath and listened, hearing nothing but the tick of my wrist-watch. Cautiously moving my hand, I looked at the luminous dial—3:17. I had been asleep longer than I had supposed, and the corridor light had been put out.

My head was numb, my body stiff and heavy, and there was a bad taste in my mouth. I got out from under the blanket, and out of my chairs, moving awkwardly, my muscles stubborn. I crept on stockinged feet to the door, and bumped into the door. It had been closed. When I opened it the corridor light was burning as before. The air that came in from the corridor seemed surprisingly fresh, sharp, pure.

I turned my face back into the room, sniffing. There was an odor of flowers, faint, stuffy, more the odor of a closed place in which flowers had died than of flowers themselves. Lilies of the valley, moonflowers, perhaps another one or two. I spent time trying to divide the odor into its parts, seriously trying to determine whether a trace of honeysuckle was actually present. Then I vaguely remembered having dreamed of a funeral. Trying to recall exactly what I had dreamed, I leaned against the doorframe and let sleep come into me again.

The jerking up of my neck muscles when my head sunk too low aroused me. I wrestled my eyes open, standing there on legs that weren't part of me, stupidly wondering why I didn't go to bed. While I drowsed over the idea that there might be some reason why I shouldn't sleep, if I could only think of it, I put a hand against the wall to steady myself. The hand touched the light button. I had sense enough to push it.

Light scorched my eyes. Squinting, I could see a world that was real to me, and could remember that I had work to do. I made for the bathroom, where cold water on head and face left me still stupid and muddled, but at least partly conscious.

I turned off my lights, crossed to Gabrielle's door, listened, and heard nothing. I opened the door, stepped inside, and closed the door. My flashlight showed me an empty bed with covers thrown down across the foot. I put a hand in the hollow her body had made in the bed—cold. There was nobody in bathroom or dressing-alcove. Under the edge of the bed lay a pair of green mules, and a green dressing-gown, or something of the sort, was hanging over the back of a chair.

I went to my room for my shoes, and then walked down the front stairs, intending to go through the house from bottom to top. I would go silently first, and then, if, as was likely enough, I ran across nothing, I could start kicking in doors, turning people out of bed, and raising hell till I turned up the girl. I wanted to find her as soon as possible, but she had too long a start for a few minutes to make much difference now; so if I didn't waste any time, neither did I run.

I was half-way between the second and first floors when I saw something move below—or, rather, saw the movement of something without actually seeing it. It moved from the direction of the street-door towards the interior of the house. I was looking towards the elevator at the time as I walked down the stairs. The banister shut off my view of the street-door. What I saw was a flash of movement across half a dozen of the spaces between the banister's uprights. By the time I had brought my eyes into focus there, there was nothing to see. I thought I had seen a face, but that's what anybody would have thought in my position, and all I had actually seen was the movement of something pale.

The lobby, and what I could see of the corridors, were vacant when I reached the ground-floor. I started towards the rear of the building, and stopped. I heard, for the first time since I had awakened, a noise that I hadn't made. A shoe-sole had scuffed on the stone steps the other side of the street-door.

I walked to the front door, got one hand on the bolt, the other hand on the latch, snapped them back together, and yanked the door open with my left hand, letting my right hang within a twist of my gun.

Eric Collinson stood on the top step.

"What the hell are you doing here?" I asked sourly.

It was a long story, and he was too excited to make it a clear one. As nearly as I could untangle it from his words, he had been in the habit of phoning Doctor Riese daily for reports on Gabrielle's progress. Today—or rather yesterday —and last night, he had failed to get the doctor on the wire. He had called up as late as two o'clock this morning. Doctor Riese was not at home, he had been told, and none of the household knew where he was or why he was not at home. Collinson had then, after the two-o'clock call, come to the neighborhood of the Temple, on the chance that he might see me and get some word of the girl. He hadn't intended, he said, coming to the door until he saw me looking out.

"Until you did what?" I asked.

"Saw you."

"When?"

"A minute ago, when you looked out."

"You didn't see me," I said. "What did you see?"

"Somebody looking out, peeping out. I thought it was you, and came up from the corner where I was sitting in the car. Is Gabrielle all right?"

"Sure," I said. There was no use telling him I was hunting for her, and have him blow up on me. "Don't talk so loud. Riese's people don't know where he is?"

"No—they seem worried. But that's all right if Gabrielle's all right." He put a hand on my upper arm. "Could— could I see her? Just for a second? I won't say anything. She needn't even know I've seen her. I don't mean now— but can't you arrange it?"

This bird was young, tall, strong, and perfectly willing

to have himself broken into pieces for Gabrielle Leggett. I knew something was wrong. I didn't know what. I didn't know what I would have to do to make it right, and how much help I would need. I couldn't afford to turn him away. On the other hand, I couldn't give him the low-down on the racket—that would have turned him into a wild man. I said:

"Come in. I'm on an inspection trip. You can go along if you keep quiet, and afterwards we'll see what we can do."

He came in, looking and acting as if I were St. Peter letting him into Heaven. I closed the door and led him through the lobby, down the main corridor. So far as we could see we had the joint to ourselves. And then we didn't.

Gabrielle Leggett came around a corner just ahead of us. She was barefooted. Her only clothing was a yellow silk nightgown that was splashed with dark stains. In both hands, held out in front of her as she walked, she carried a large dagger, almost a sword. It was red and wet. Her hands and bare arms were red and wet. There was a dab of blood on one of her cheeks. Her eyes were clear, bright, and calm. Her small forehead was smooth, her mouth and chin firmly set.

She walked up to me, her untroubled gaze holding my probably troubled one, and said evenly, just as if she had expected to find me there, had come there to find me:

"Take it. It is evidence. I killed him."

I said: "Huh?"

Still looking straight into my eyes, she said:

"You are a detective. Take me to where they will hang me."

It was easier to move my hand than my tongue. I took the bloody dagger from her. It was a broad, thick-bladed weapon, double-edged, with a bronze hilt like a cross.

Eric Collinson pushed past me, babbling words that nobody could have made out, going for the girl with shaking outstretched hands. She shrank over against the wall, away from him, fear in her face.

"Don't let him touch me," she begged.

"Gabrielle," he cried, reaching for her.

"No, no," she panted.

I walked into his arms, my body between him and her, facing him, pressing him back with a hand against his chest, growling at him: "Be still, you."

He took my shoulders in his big brown hands and began pushing me out of the way. I got ready to rap him on the chin with the heavy bronze dagger hilt. But we didn't have to go that far: looking over me at the girl he forgot his intentions of forcing me out of his path, and his hands went loose on my shoulders. I leaned on the hand that I had on his chest, moving him back until he was against the wall; and then stepped away from him, a little to one side, so I could see both him and her facing each other from opposite walls.

"Be still till we see what's happened," I told him, and turned to the girl, pointing the dagger at her. "What's happened?"

She was calm again.

"Come," she said. "I'll show you. Don't let Eric come, please."

"He won't bother you," I promised.

She nodded at that, gravely, and led us back down the corridor, around the corner, and up to a small iron door that stood ajar. She went through first. I followed her. Collinson was at my heels. Fresh air hit us when we went through the door. I looked up and saw dim stars in a dark sky. I looked down again. In the light that came through the open door behind us I saw that we were walking on a floor of white marble, or pentagonal tiles that imitated white marble. The place was dark except for the light from behind us. I took my flashlight out.

Walking unhurriedly on bare feet that must have found the tiled floor chilly, she led us straight to a square grayish shape that loomed up ahead. When she halted close to it and said, "There," I clicked on my light.

The light glittered and glistened on a wide altar of brilliant white, crystal, and silver.

On the lowest of the three altar steps Doctor Riese lay dead on his back.

His face was composed, as if he were sleeping. His arms were straight down at his sides. His clothes were not rumpled, though his coat and vest were unbuttoned. His shirt was all blood. There were four holes in his shirt-front, all alike, all the size and shape that the weapon the girl had given me would have made. No blood was coming from his wounds now, but when I put a hand on his forehead I found it not quite cold. There was blood on the altar steps, and on the floor below, where his noseglasses, unbroken, on the end of their black ribbon, lay.

I straightened up and swung the beam of my light into the girl's face. She blinked and squinted, but her face showed nothing except that physical discomfort.

"You killed him?" I asked.

Young Collinson came out of his trance to bawl: "No."

"Shut up," I told him, stepping closer to the girl, so he couldn't wedge himself between us. "Did you?" I asked her again.

"Are you surprised?" she inquired quietly. "You were there when my step-mother told of the cursed Dain blood in me, and of what it had done and would do to me and those who touched me. Is this," she asked, pointing at the dead man, "anything you should not have expected?"

"Don't be silly," I said while I tried to figure out her calmness. I had seen her coked to the ears before, but this wasn't that. I didn't know what this was. "Why did you kill him?"

Collinson grabbed my arm and yanked me around to face him. He was all on fire.

"We can't stand here talking," he cried. "We've got to get her out of here, away from this. We've got to hide the body, or put it some place where they'll think somebody else did it. You know how those things are done. I'll take her home. You fix it."

"Yeah?" I asked. "What'll I do? Frame it on one of the Filipino boys, so they'll hang him instead of her?"

81

"Yes, that's it. You know how to——"

"Like hell that's it," I said. "You've got nice ideas."

His face got redder. He stammered: "I didn't—didn't mean so they'll hang anybody, really. I wouldn't want you to do that. But couldn't it be fixed for him to get away? I—I'd make it worth his while. He could——"

"Turn it off," I growled. "You're wasting our time."

"But you've got to," he insisted. "You came here to see that nothing happened to Gabrielle and you've got to go through with it."

"Yeah? You're a smart boy."

"I know it's a lot to ask, but I'll pay——"

"Stop it." I took my arm out of his hands and turned to the girl again, asking: "Who else was here when it happened?"

"No one."

I played my light around, on the corpse and altar, all over the floor, on the walls, and saw nothing I hadn't seen before. The walls were white, smooth, and unbroken except for the door we had come through and another, exactly like it, on the other side. These four straight whitewashed walls, undecorated, rose six stories to the sky.

I put the dagger beside Riese's body, snapped off the light, and told Collinson: "We'll take Miss Leggett up to her room."

"For God's sake let's get her out of here—out of this house—now, while there's time!"

I said she'd look swell running through the streets barefooted and with nothing on but a bloodstained nightie.

I turned on the light again when I heard him making noises. He was jerking his arms out of his overcoat. He said: "I've got the car at the corner, and I can carry her to it," and started towards her with the coat held out.

She ran around to the other side of me, moaning: "Oh, don't let him touch me."

I put out an arm to stop him. It wasn't strong enough. The girl got behind me. Collinson pursued her and she came around in front. I felt like the center of a merry-go-round, and didn't like the feel of it. When Collinson came in front of me, I drove my shoulder into his side, sending him staggering over against the side of the altar. Following him, I planted myself in front of the big sap and blew off steam: "Stop it. If you want to play with us you've got to stop cutting up, and do what you're told, and let her alone. Yes or no?"

He straightened his legs under him and began: "But, man, you can't—"

"Let her alone," I said. "Let me alone. The next break you make I'm going to sock your jaw with the flat of a gun. If you want it now, say so. Will you behave?"

He muttered: "All right."

I turned around to see the girl, a gray shadow, running towards the open door, her bare feet making little noise on the tiles. My shoes made an ungodly racket as I went after her. Just inside the door I caught her with an arm around her waist. The next moment my arm was jerked away, and I was flung aside, smacking into the wall, slipping down on one knee. Collinson, looking eight feet tall in the darkness, stood close to me, storming down at me, but all I could pick out of his many words was a "damn you."

I was in a swell mood when I got up from my knee. Playing nursemaid to a crazy girl wasn't enough: I had to be chucked around by her boy friend. I put all the hypocrisy I had into my voice when I said casually, "You oughtn't to do that," to him and went over to where the girl was standing by the door.

"We'll go up to your room now," I told her.

"Not Eric," she protested.

"He won't bother you," I promised again, hoping there'd be more truth to it this time. "Go ahead."

She hesitated, then went through the doorway. Collinson, looking partly sheepish, partly savage, and altogether discontented, followed me through. I closed the door, asking the girl if she had the key. "No," she said, as if she hadn't known there was a key.

We rode up in the elevator, the girl keeping me always between her and her fiancé, if that's what he still was. He stared fixedly at nothing. I studied her face, still trying to dope her out, to decide whether she had been shocked back into sanity or farther away from it. Looking at her, the first guess seemed likely, but I had a hunch it wasn't. We saw nobody between the altar and her room. I switched on her lights and we went in. I closed the door and put my back against it. Collinson put his overcoat and hat on a chair and stood beside them, folding his arms, looking at Gabrielle. She sat on the edge of the bed and looked at my feet.

"Tell us the whole thing, quick," I commanded.

She looked up at my face and said: "I should like to go to sleep now."

That settled the question of her sanity, so far as I was concerned: she hadn't any. But now I had another thing to worry me. This room was not exactly as it had been before. Something had been changed in it since I had been there not many minutes ago. I shut my eyes, trying to shake up my memory for a picture of it then; I opened my eyes, looking at it now.

"Can't I?" she asked.

I let her question wait while I put my gaze around the room, checking it up item by item, as well as I could. The only change I could put my finger on was Collinson's coat and hat on the chair. There was no mystery to their presence; and the chair, I decided, was what had bothered me. It still did. I went to it and picked up his coat. There was nothing under it. That's what was wrong: a green dressing-gown, or something of the sort, had been there before, and was not there now. I didn't see it elsewhere in the room, and didn't have enough confidence in its being there to search for it. The green mules were under the bed.

I said to the girl:

"Not now. Go in the bathroom and wash the blood off, and then get dressed. Take your clothes in there with you. When you're dressed, give your nightgown to Collinson." I turned to him. "Put it in your pocket and keep it there. Don't go out of the room until I come back, and don't let anybody in. I won't be gone long. Got a gun?"

"No," he said, "but I—"

The girl got up from the bed, came over to stand close in front of me, and interrupted him.

"You can't leave me here with him," she said earnestly. "I won't have it. Isn't it enough that I've killed one man tonight? Don't make me kill another." She was earnest, but not excited, speaking as if her words were quite reasonable.

"I've got to go out for a while," I said. "And you can't stay alone. Do what I tell you."

"Do you know what you're doing?" she asked in a thin, tired voice. "You can't know, or you wouldn't do it." Her back was to Collinson. She lifted her face so that I saw rather than heard the nearly soundless words her lips formed: "Not Eric. Let him go."

She had me woozy: a little more of it and I would have been ready for the cell next to hers: I was actually tempted to let her have her way. I jerked a thumb at the bathroom and said: "You can stay in there till I come back, if you want, but he'll have to stay here."

She nodded hopelessly and went into the dressing-alcove. When she crossed from there to the bathroom, carrying clothes in her arms, a tear was shiny beneath each eye.

I gave my gun to Collinson. The hand in which he took it was tight and shaky. He was making a lot of noise with his breath. I said: "Now don't be a sap. Give me some help instead of trouble for once. Nobody in or out: if you have to shoot, shoot."

He tried to say something, couldn't, grabbed my nearest hand, and did his best to disable it. I took it away from him and went down to the scene of Doctor Riese's murder. I had some difficulty in getting there. The iron door through which we had passed a few minutes ago was now locked. The lock seemed simple enough. I went at it with the fancy attachments on my pocketknife, and presently had the door open.

I didn't find the green gown inside. I didn't find Riese's body on the altar steps. It was nowhere in sight. The dag-

ger was gone. Every trace of blood, except where the pool
on the white floor had left a faintly yellow stain, was gone.
Somebody had been tidying up.

XI : GOD

I went back to the lobby, to a recess where I had seen a
telephone. The phone was there, but dead. I put it down
and set out for Minnie Hershey's room on the sixth floor.
I hadn't been able to do much with the mulatto so far, but
she was apparently devoted to her mistress, and, with the
telephone useless, I needed a messenger.

I opened the mulatto's door—lockless as the others—
and went in, closing it behind me. Holding a hand over
the lens of my flashlight, I snapped it on. Enough light
leaked through my fingers to show me the brown girl in
her bed, sleeping. The windows were closed, the atmo-
sphere heavy, with a faint stuffiness that was familiar, the
odor of a place where flowers had died.

I looked at the girl in bed. She was on her back, breathing through open mouth, her face more like an Indian's
than ever with the heaviness of sleep on it. Looking at her,
I felt drowsy myself. It seemed a shame to turn her out.
Perhaps she was dreaming of—I shook my head, trying to
clear it of the muddle settling there. Lilies of the valley,
moonflowers—flowers that had died—was honeysuckle one
of the flowers? The question seemed to be important. The
flashlight was heavy in my hand, too heavy. Hell with it:
I let it drop. It hit my foot, puzzling me: who had touched
my foot? Gabrielle Leggett, asking to be saved from Eric

Collinson? That didn't make sense, or did it? I tried to shake my head again, tried desperately. It weighed a ton, and would barely move from side to side. I felt myself swaying; put out a foot to steady myself. The foot and leg were weak, limber, doughy. I had to take another step or fall, took it, forced my head up and my eyes open, hunting for a place to fall, and saw the window six inches from my face.

I swayed forward till the sill caught my thighs, holding me up. My hands were on the sill. I tried to find the handles on the bottom of the window, wasn't sure that I had found them, but put everything I had into an upward heave. The window didn't budge. My hands seemed nailed down. I think I sobbed then; and, holding the sill with my right hand, I beat the glass from the center of the pane with my open left.

Air that stung like ammonia came through the opening. I put my face to it, hanging to the sill with both hands, sucking air in through mouth, nose, eyes, ears, and pores, laughing, with water from my stinging eyes trickling down into my mouth. I hung there drinking air until I was reasonably sure of my legs under me again, and of my eyesight, until I knew myself able to think and move again, though neither speedily nor surely. I couldn't afford to wait longer. I put a handkerchief over my mouth and nose and turned away from the window.

Not more than three feet away, there in the black room, a pale bright thing like a body, but not like flesh, stood writhing before me.

It was tall, yet not so tall as it seemed, because it didn't stand on the floor, but hovered with its feet a foot or more above the floor. Its feet—it had feet, but I don't know what their shape was. They had no shape, just as the thing's legs and torso, arms and hands, head and face, had no shape, no fixed form. They writhed, swelling and contracting, stretching and shrinking, not greatly, but without pause. An arm drifted into the body, was swallowed by the body, came out again as if poured out. The nose stretched down over the gaping shapeless mouth, shrank back up into the face till it was flush with the pulpy cheeks, grew out again. Eyes spread until they were one gigantic eye that blotted out the whole upper face, diminished until there was no eye, and opened in their places again. The legs were now one leg like a twisting, living pedestal, and then three, and then two. No feature or member ever stopped twisting, quivering, writhing long enough for its average outline, its proper shape, to be seen. The thing was a thing like a man who floated above the floor, with a horrible grimacing greenish face and pale flesh that was not flesh, that was visible in the dark, and that was as fluid and as unresting and as transparent as tidal water.

I knew—then—that I was off-balance from breathing the dead-flower stuff, but I couldn't—though I tried to— tell myself that I did not see this thing. It was there. It was there within reach of my hand if I leaned forward, shivering, writhing, between me and the door. I didn't believe in the supernatural—but what of that? The thing was there. It was there and it was not, I knew, a trick of luminous paint, a man with a sheet over him. I gave it up. I stood there with my handkerchief jammed to my nose and mouth, not stirring, not breathing, possibly not even letting my blood run through me. I was there, and the thing was there, and I stayed where I was.

The thing spoke, though I could not say that I actually heard the words: it was as if I simply became, through my entire body, conscious of the words:

"Down, enemy of the Lord God; down on your knees."

I stirred then, to lick my lips with a tongue drier than they were.

"Down, accursed of the Lord God, before the blow falls."

An argument was something I understood. I moved my handkerchief sufficiently to say: "Go to hell." It had a silly sound, especially in the creaking voice I had used.

The thing's body twisted convulsively, swayed, and bent towards me.

I dropped my handkerchief and reached for the thing with both hands. I got hold of the thing, and I didn't. My hands were on it, *in* it to the wrists, into the center of it, and shut on it. And there was nothing in my hands but dampness without temperature, neither warm nor cold.

That same dampness came into my face when the thing's face floated into mine. I bit at its face—yes—and my teeth closed on nothing, though I could see and feel that my face was *in* its face. And in my hands, on my arms, against my body, the thing squirmed and writhed, shuddered and shivered, swirling wildly now, breaking apart, reuniting madly in the black air.

Through the thing's transparent flesh I could see my hands clenched in the center of its damp body. I opened them, struck up and down inside it with stiff crooked fingers, trying to gouge it open; and I could see it being torn apart, could see it flowing together after my clawing fingers had passed; but all I could feel was its dampness.

Now another feeling came to me, growing quickly once it had started—of an immense suffocating weight bearing me down. This thing that had no solidity had weight, weight that was pressing me down, smothering me. My knees were going soft. I spit its face out of my mouth, tore my right hand free from its body and struck up at its face, and felt nothing but its dampness brushing my fist.

I clawed at its insides again with my left hand, tearing at this substance that was so plainly seen, so faintly felt. And then on my left hand I saw something else—blood. Blood that was dark and thick and real covered my hand, dripped from it, running out between my fingers.

I laughed and got strength to straighten my back against the monstrous weight on me, wrenching at the thing's insides again, croaking: "I'll gut you plenty." More blood came through my fingers. I tried to laugh again, triumphantly, and couldn't, choking instead. The thing's weight on me was twice what it had been. I staggered back, sagging against the wall, flattening myself against it to keep from sliding down it.

Air from the broken window, cold, pure, bitter, came over my shoulder to sting my nostrils, to tell me—by its difference from the air I had been breathing—that not the

the thing's weight, but the poisonous flower-smelling stuff, had been bearing me down.

The thing's greenish pale dampness squirmed over my face and body. Coughing, I stumbled through the thing, to the door, got the door open, and sprawled out in the corridor that was now as dark as the room I had just left.

As I fell, somebody fell over me. But this was no indescribable thing. It was human. The knees that hit my back were human, sharp. The grunt that blew hot breath in my ear was human, surprised. The arm my fingers caught was human, thin. I thanked God for its thinness. The corridor air was doing me a lot of good, but I was in no shape to do battle with an athlete.

I put what strength I had into my grip on the thin arm, dragging it under me as I rolled over on as much of the rest of its owner as I could cover. My other hand, flung out across the man's thin body as I rolled, struck something that was hard and metallic on the floor. Bending my wrist, I got my fingers on it, and recognized its feel: it was the over-size dagger with which Riese had been killed. The man I was lolling on had, I guessed, stood beside the door of Minnie's room, waiting to carve me when I came out; and my fall had saved me, making him miss me with the blade, tripping him. Now he was kicking, jabbing, and butting up at me from his face-down position on the floor, with my hundred and ninety pounds anchoring him there.

Holding on to the dagger, I took my right hand from his arm and spread it over the back of his head, grinding his face into the carpet, taking it easy, waiting for more of the strength that was coming back into me with each breath. A minute or two more and I would be ready to pick him up and get words out of him.

But I wasn't allowed to wait that long. Something hard pounded my right shoulder, then my back, and then struck the carpet close to our heads. Somebody was swinging a club at me.

I rolled off the skinny man. The club-swinger's feet stopped my rolling. I looped my right arm above the feet, took another rap on the back, missed the legs with my circling arm, and felt skirts against my hand. Surprised, I pulled my hand back. Another chop of the club—on my side this time—reminded me that this was no place for gallantry. I made a fist of my hand and struck back at the skirt. It folded around my fist: a meaty shin stopped my fist. The shin's owner snarled above me and backed off before I could hit out again.

Scrambling up on hands and knees, I bumped my head into wood—a door. A hand on the knob helped me up. Somewhere inches away in the dark the club swished again. The knob turned in my hand. I went in with the door, into the room, and made as little noise as I could, practically none, shutting the door.

Behind me in the room a voice said, very softly, but also very earnestly:

"Go right out of here or I'll shoot you."

It was the plump blonde maid's voice, frightened. I turned, bending low in case she did shoot. Enough of the dull gray of approaching daylight came into this room to outline a shadow sitting up in bed, holding something small and dark in one outstretched hand.

"It's me," I whispered.

"Oh, you!" She didn't lower the thing in her hand.

"You in on the racket?" I asked, risking a slow step towards the bed.

"I do what I'm told and I keep my mouth shut, but I'm not going in for strong-arm work, not for the money they're paying me."

"Swell," I said, taking more and quicker steps towards the bed. "Could I get down through this window to the floor below if I tied a couple of sheets together?"

"I don't know— Ouch! Stop!"

I had her gun—a .32 automatic—in my right hand, her wrist in my left, and was twisting them. "Let go," I ordered, and she did. Releasing her hand, I stepped back, picking up the dagger I had dropped on the foot of the bed.

I tiptoed to the door and listened. I couldn't hear anything. I opened the door slowly, and couldn't hear anything, couldn't see anything in the dim grayness that went through the door. Minnie Hershey's door was open, as I had left it when I tumbled out. The thing I had fought wasn't there. I went into Minnie's room, switching on the lights. She was lying as she had lain before, sleeping heavily. I pocketed my gun, pulled down the covers, picked Minnie up, and carried her over to the maid's room.

"See if you can bring her to life," I told the maid, dumping the mulatto on the bed beside her.

"She'll come around all right in a little while: they always do."

I said, "Yeah?" and went out, down to the fifth floor, to Gabrielle Leggett's room.

Gabrielle's room was empty. Collinson's hat and overcoat were gone; so were the clothes she had taken into the bathroom; and so was the bloody nightgown.

I cursed the pair of them, trying to show no favoritism, but probably concentrating most on Collinson; snapped off the lights; and ran down the front stairs, feeling as violent as I must have looked, battered and torn and bruised, with a red dagger in one hand, a gun in the other. For four flights of down-going I heard nothing, but when I reached the second floor a noise like small thunder was audible below me. Dashing down the remaining flight, I identified it as somebody's knocking on the front door. I hoped the somebody wore a uniform. I went to the door, unlocked it, and pulled it open.

Eric Collinson was there, wild-eyed, white-faced, and frantic.

"Where's Gaby?" he gasped.

"God damn you," I said and hit him in the face with the gun.

He drooped, bending forward, stopped himself with hands on the vestibule's opposite walls, hung there a moment, and slowly pulled himself upright again. Blood leaked from a corner of his mouth.

"Where's Gaby?" he repeated doggedly.

"Where'd you leave her?"

"Here. I was taking her away. She asked me to. She

sent me out first to see if anybody was in the street. Then the door closed."

"You're a smart boy," I grumbled. "She tricked you, still trying to save you from that lousy curse. Why in hell couldn't you do what I told you? But come on; we'll have to find her."

She wasn't in any of the reception rooms off the lobby. We left the lights on in them and hurried down the main corridor.

A small figure in white pajamas sprang out of a doorway and fastened itself on me, tangling itself in my legs, all but upsetting me. Unintelligible words came out of it. I pulled it loose from me and saw that it was the boy Manuel. Tears wet his panic-stricken face and crying ruined all the words he was trying to speak.

"Take it easy, son." I said. "I can't understand a word you're saying."

I understood, "Don't let him kill her."

"Who kill who?" I asked. "And take your time."

He didn't take his time, but I managed to hear "father" and "mama."

"Your father's trying to kill your mother?" I asked, since that seemed the most likely combination.

His head went up and down.

"Where?" I asked.

He fluttered a hand at the iron door ahead. I started towards it, and stopped.

"Listen, son," I bargained. "I'd like to help your mother, but I've got to know where Miss Leggett is first. Do you know where she is?"

"In there with them," he cried. "Oh, hurry, do hurry!"

"Right. Come on, Collinson," and we raced for the iron door.

The door was closed, but not locked. I yanked it open. The altar was glaring white, crystal, and silver in an immense beam of blue-white light that slanted down from an edge of the roof.

At one end of the altar Gabrielle crouched, her face turned up into the beam of light. Her face was ghastly white and expressionless in the harsh light. Aaronia Haldorn lay on the altar step where Riese had lain. There was a dark bruise on her forehead. Her hands and feet were tied with broad white bands of cloth, her arms tied to her body. Most of her clothes had been torn off.

Joseph, white-robed, stood in front of the altar, and of his wife. He stood with both arms held high and widespread, his back and neck bent so that his bearded face was lifted to the sky. In his right hand he held an ordinary horn-handled carving knife, with a long curved blade. He was talking to the sky, but his back was to us, and we couldn't hear his words. As we came through the door, he lowered his arms and bent over his wife. We were still a good thirty feet from him. I bellowed:

"Joseph!"

He straightened again, turning, and when the knife came into view I saw that it was still clean, shiny.

"Who calls Joseph, a name that is no more?" he asked, and I'd be a liar if I didn't admit that, standing there—for I had halted ten feet from him, with Collinson beside me—looking at him, listening to his voice, I didn't begin to feel that perhaps, after all, nothing very terrible had been about to happen. "There is no Joseph," he went on, not waiting for an answer to his question. "You may now know, as the world shall soon know, that he who went among you as Joseph was not Joseph, but God Himself. Now that you know, go."

I should have said, "Bunk," and jumped him. To any other man, I would have. To this one I didn't. I said: "I'll have to take Miss Leggett and Mrs. Haldorn with me," and said it indecisively, almost apologetically.

He drew himself up taller, and his white-bearded face was stern.

"Go," he commanded; "go from me before your defiance leads to destruction."

Aaronia Haldorn spoke from where she lay tied on the step, spoke to me:

"Shoot. Shoot now—quick. Shoot."

I said to the man:

"I don't care what your right name is. You're going to the can. Now put your knife down."

"Blasphemer," he thundered, and took a step towards me. "Now you will die."

That should have been funny. It wasn't.

I yelled, "Stop," at him. He wouldn't stop. I was afraid. I fired. The bullet hit his cheek. I saw the hole it made. No muscle twitched in his face; not even his eyes blinked. He walked deliberately, not hurrying, towards me.

I worked the automatic's trigger, pumping six more bullets into his face and body. I saw them go in. And he came on steadily, showing in no way that he was conscious of them. His eyes and face were stern, but not angry. When he was close to me the knife in his hand went up high above his head. That's no way to fight with a knife; but he wasn't fighting: he was bringing retribution to me, and he paid as little attention to my attempts to stop him as a parent does to those of a small child he's punishing.

I was fighting. When the knife, shining over our heads, started down I went in under it, bending my right forearm against his knife-arm, driving the dagger in my left hand at his throat. I drove the heavy blade into his throat, in till the hilt's cross stopped it. Then I was through.

I didn't know I had closed my eyes until I found myself opening them. The first thing I saw was Eric Collinson kneeling beside Gabrielle Leggett, turning her face from the glaring light-beam, trying to rouse her. Next I saw Aaronia Haldorn, apparently unconscious on the altar step, with the boy Manuel crying on her and pulling with too nervous hands at her bonds. Then I saw that I was standing with my legs apart, and that Joseph was lying between my feet, dead, with the dagger through his neck.

"Thank God he wasn't really God," I mumbled to myself.

A brown body in white brushed past me, and Minnie Hershey was throwing herself down in front of Gabrielle Leggett, crying:

"Oh, Miss Gabrielle, I thought that devil had come alive and was after you again."

I went over to the mulatto and took her by the shoulder, lifting her up, asking her: "How could he? Didn't you kill him dead?"

"Yes, sir, but—"

"But you thought he might have come back in another shape?"

"Y-yes, sir. I thought he was—" She stopped and worked her lips together.

"Me?" I asked.

She nodded, not looking at me.

XII : THE UNHOLY GRAIL

Owen Fitzstephan and I ate another of Mrs. Schindler's good dinners that evening, though my eating was a matter of catching bites between words. His curiosity poked at me with questions, requests to have this or that point made clear, and orders to keep talking whenever I stopped for breath or food.

"You could have got me in on it," he had complained before our soup was in front of us. "I knew the Haldorns, you know, or, at least, had met them once or twice at Leggett's. You could have used that as an excuse for somehow letting me in on the affair, so that I'd now have first-hand knowledge of what happened, and why; instead of having to depend on what I can get out of you and what the newspapers imagine their readers would like to think had happened."

"I had," I said, "enough grief with the one guy I did let in on it—Eric Collinson."

"Whatever trouble you had with him was your own fault, for selecting the wrong assistant, when such a better one was available. But come, my boy, I'm listening. Let's have the story, and then I can tell you where you erred."

"Sure," I agreed, "you'll be able to do that. Well, the Haldorns were originally actors. Most of what I can tell you comes from her, so a lot of maybes will have to be hung on it in spots. Fink won't talk at all; and the other help—maids, Filipino boys, Chinese cook, and the like—don't seem to know anything that helps much. None of them seems to have been let in on the trick stuff.

"As actors, Aaronia Haldorn says, she and Joseph were just pretty good, not getting on as well as they wanted to. About a year ago she ran into an old acquaintance—a one-time trouper—who had chucked the stage for the pulpit, and had made a go of it, now riding in Packards instead of day-coaches. That gave her something to think about. Thinking in that direction meant, pretty soon, thinking about Aimee, Buchman, Jeddu what's-his-name, and the other headliners. And in the end her thinking came to, why not us? They—or she: Joseph was a lightweight—rigged up a cult that pretended to be the revival of an old Gaelic church, dating from King Arthur's time, or words to that effect."

"Yes," said Fitzstephan; "Arthur Machen's. But go on."

"They brought their cult to California because everybody does, and picked San Francisco because it held less competition than Los Angeles. With them they brought a little fellow named Tom Fink who had at one time or another been in charge of the mechanical end of most of the well-known stage magicians' and illusionists' acts; and Fink's wife, a big village-smith of a woman.

"They didn't want a mob of converts: they wanted them few but wealthy. The racket got away to a slow start—until they landed Mrs. Rodman. She fell plenty. They took her for one of her apartment buildings, and she also footed the remodeling bill. The stage mechanic Fink was in charge of the remodeling, and did a neat job. They didn't need the kitchens that were dotted, one to an apartment, through the building, and Fink knew how to use part of that scattered kitchen-space for concealed rooms and cabinets; and he knew how to adapt the gas and water pipes, and the electric wiring, to his hocus-pocus.

"I can't give you the mechanical details now; not till we've had time to take the joint apart. It's going to be interesting. I saw some of their work—mingled right in with it—a ghost made by an arrangement of lights thrown up on steam rising from a padded pipe that had been pushed into a dark room through a concealed opening in the wainscoting under a bed. The part of the steam that wasn't lighted was invisible in the darkness, showing only a man-shape that quivered and writhed, and that was damp and real to the touch, without any solidity. You can take my word for its being a weird stunt, especially when you've been filled up with the stuff they pumped into the room before they turned their spook loose on you. I don't know whether they used ether or chloroform or what: its odor was nicely disguised with some sort of flower perfume. This spook—I fought with it, on the level, and even thought I had it bleeding, not knowing I had cut my hand breaking a window to let air in. It was a beaut: it made a few minutes seem like a lot of hours to me.

"Till the very last, when Haldorn went wild, there wasn't anything crude about their work. They kept the services—the whole public end of the cult—as dignified and orderly and restrained as possible. The hocus-pocusing was all done in the privacy of the victim's bedroom. First the perfumed gas was pumped in. Then the illuminated steam spook was sicked on him, with a voice coming out of the same pipe—or maybe there was another arrangement for that—to give him his orders, or whatever was to be given. The gas kept him from being too sharp-eyed and suspicious, and also weakened his will, so he'd be more likely to do what he was told. It was slick enough; and I imagine they squeezed themselves out a lot of pennies that way.

"Happening in the victim's room, when he was alone, these visions had a lot of authority, and the Haldorns gave them more by the attitude they took towards them. Discussion of these visions was not absolutely prohibited, but was discouraged. They were supposed—these spook sessions—to be confidential between the victim and his God, to be too sacred to be bragged about. Mentioning them, even to Joseph, unless there was some special reason for having to mention them, was considered in bad taste, indelicate. See how nicely that would work out? The Haldorns seemed to be *not* trying to capitalize on these spook sessions, seemed not to know what took place in them, and therefore to have no interest in whether the victim carried out his spook-given instructions or not. Their stand was that that was simply and strictly a concern of the victim's and his God's."

"That's very good," Fitzstephan said, smiling delightedly, "a neat reversal of the usual cult's—the usual sect's, for that matter—insistence on confession, public testimony, or some other form of advertising the mysteries. Go on."

I tried to eat. He said:

"What of the members, the customers? How do they like their cult now? You've talked to some of them, haven't you?"

"Yeah," I said; "but what can you do with people like them? Half of them are still willing to string along with Aaronia Haldorn. I showed Mrs. Rodman one of the pipes that the spooks came out of. When she had gasped once and gulped twice she offered to take us to the cathedral and show us that the images there, including the one on the cross, were made out of even more solid and earthly materials than steam; and asked us if we would arrest the bishop on proof that no actual flesh and blood—whether divine or not—was in the monstrance. I thought O'Gar, who's a good Catholic, would blackjack her."

"The Colemans weren't there, were they? The Ralph Colemans?"

"No."

"Too bad," he said, grinning. "I must look Ralph up and question him. He'll be in hiding by now, of course, but he's worth hunting out. He always has the most consistently logical and creditable reasons for having done the most idiotic things. He is"—as if that explained it—"an advertising man." Fitzstephan frowned at the discovery that I was eating again, and said impatiently: "Talk, my boy, talk."

"You've met Haldorn," I said. "What did you think of him?"

"I saw him twice, I think. He was, undoubtedly, impressive."

"He was," I agreed. "He had what he needed. Ever talk to him?"

"No; that is, not except to exchange the polite equivalents of 'pleased to meet you.'"

"Well, he looked at you and spoke to you, and things happened inside you. I'm not the easiest guy in the world to dazzle, I hope; but he had me going. I came damned near to believing he was God toward the last. He was quite young—in his thirties: they'd had the coloring—the pigment—in his hair and beard killed to give him that Father Joseph front. His wife says she used to hypnotize him before he went into action, and that without being hypnotized he wasn't so effective on people. Later he got so that he could hypnotize himself without her help, and toward the last it became a permanent condition with him.

"She didn't know her husband had fallen for Gabrielle till after the girl had come to stay in the Temple. Until then she thought that Gabrielle was to him, as to her, just another customer—one whose recent troubles made her a very likely prospect. But Joseph had fallen for her, and wanted her. I don't know how far he had worked on her, nor even how he had worked on her, but I suppose he was sewing her up by using his hocus-pocus against her fear of the Dain curse. Anyway, Doctor Riese finally discovered that everything wasn't going well with her. Yesterday morning he told me he was coming back to see her that evening, and he did come back, but he didn't see her; and I didn't see him—not then.

"He went back to see Joseph before he came up to the girl's room, and managed to overhear Joseph giving instructions to the Finks. That should have been fine, but wasn't. Riese was foolish enough to let Joseph know he had over-heard him. Joseph locked Riese up—a prisoner.

"They had cut loose on Minnie from the very beginning. She was a mulatto, and therefore susceptible to that sort of game, and she was devoted to Gabrielle Leggett. They had chucked visions and voices at the poor girl until she was dizzy. Now they decided to make her kill Riese. They drugged him and put him on the altar. They ghosted her into thinking that he was Satan—this is serious: they did this—come up from hell to carry Gabrielle down and keep her from becoming a saint. Minnie was ripe for it—poor boogie—and when the spirit told her that she had been selected to save her mistress, that she'd find the anointed weapon on her table, she followed the instructions the spirit gave her. She got out of bed, picked up the dagger that had been put on her table, went down to the altar, and killed Riese.

"To play safe, they pumped some of the gas into my room, to keep me slumbering while Minnie was at work. But I had been nervous, jumpy, and was sleeping in a chair in the center of the room, instead of on the bed, close to the gas-pipe; so I came out of the dope before the night was far gone.

"By this time, Aaronia Haldorn had made a couple of discoveries: first, that her husband's interest in the girl wasn't altogether financial; and second, that he had gone off center, was a dangerous maniac. Going around hypno-tized all the time, what brains he had—not a whole lot to start with, she says—had become completely scrambled. His success in flimflamming his followers had gone to his head. He thought he could do anything, get away with anything. He had dreams, she says, of the entire world de-luded into belief in his divinity: he didn't see why that would be any—or much—more difficult than fooling the handful that he had fooled. She thinks he actually had in-sane notions of his own divinity. I don't go that far. I think he knew well enough that he wasn't divine, but thought he could kid the rest of the world. These details don't make much difference: the thing is that he was a nut who saw no limit to his power.

"Aaronia Haldorn had, she says, no knowledge of Riese's murder until after it was done. Joseph, using the vision-and-voice trick, sent Gabrielle down to see the corpse on the altar step. That would fit in, you see, with his original scheme to tie her to him by playing his divinity against her curse. Apparently, he intended joining her there, and putting on an act of some sort for her. But Collinson and I interrupted that. Joseph and Gabrielle heard us talking at the door, so Joseph held back, not joining her at the altar, and she came to meet us. Joseph's plan was successful this far: the girl actually believed the curse had been responsible for Riese's death. She told us she had killed him and ought to be hanged for it.

"As soon as I saw Riese's body I knew she hadn't killed him. He was lying in an orderly position. It was plain he had been doped before being killed. Then the door leading to the altar, which I imagined was kept locked, was open, and she didn't know anything about the key. There was a chance that she had been in on the killing, but none that she had done it alone as she confessed.

"The place was scientifically equipped for eavesdropping: both of the Haldorns heard her confession. Aaronia got busy manufacturing evidence to fit the confession. She went up to Gabrielle's room and got her dressing-gown; got the bloody dagger from where I had dropped it beside the body after taking it from the girl; wrapped the dagger in the dressing-gown, and stuck them in a corner where the police could find them easy enough. Meanwhile, Joseph is working in another direction. He doesn't—as his wife does—want Gabrielle carried off to jail or the booby-hatch. He wants her. He wants her belief in her guilt and responsibility to tie her to him, not take her away. He removes Riese's remains—tucking them in one of the concealed cabinets—and has the Finks clean up the mess. He's overheard Collinson trying to persuade me to hush up the doings, and so he knows he can count on the boy—the only other exactly sane witness—to keep quiet if I'm taken care of.

"Kill yourself into a hole, and the chances are a time comes when you have to kill yourself out. To this nut Joseph now, 'taking care of' me is simply a matter of another murder. He and the Finks—though I don't think we're going to prove their part—went to work on Minnie with the spooks again. She had killed Riese docilely enough: why not me? You see, they were handicapped by not being equipped for this wholesale murdering into which they had all of a sudden plunged. For instance, except for my gun and one of the maids'—which they didn't know anything about—there wasn't a firearm in the place; and the dagger was the only other weapon—until they got to dragging in carving sets and plumber's helpers. Then, too, I suppose, there were the sleeping customers to consider—Mrs. Rodman's probable dislike for being roused by the noise of her spiritual guides ganging up on a roughneck sleuth. Anyway, the idea was that Minnie could be induced to walk up to me and stick the dagger into me in a quiet way.

"They had found the dagger again, in the dressing-gown, where Aaronia had stuck it; and Joseph began suspecting that his wife was double-crossing him. When he caught her in the act of turning on the dead-flower stuff so strong in Minnie's room that it knocked her completely out—put her so soundly asleep that a dozen ghosts couldn't have stirred her into action—he was sure of her treachery; and, up to his neck now, decided to kill *her*."

"His wife?" Fitzstephan asked.

"Yeah, but what difference does that make? It might as well have been anybody else for all the sense it makes. I hope you're not trying to keep this nonsense straight in your mind. You know damned well all this didn't happen."

"Then what," he asked, looking puzzled, "did happen?"

"I don't know. I don't think anybody knows. I'm telling you what I saw plus the part of what Aaronia Haldorn told me which fits in with what I saw. To fit in with what I saw, most of it must have happened very nearly as I've told you. If you want to believe that it did, all right. I don't. I'd rather believe I saw things that weren't there."

"Not now," he pleaded. "Later, after you've finished the

story, you can attach your ifs and buts to it, distorting and twisting it, making it as cloudy and confusing and generally hopeless as you like. But first please finish it, so I'll see it at least once in its original state before you start improving it."

"You actually believe what I've told you so far?" I asked.

He nodded, grinning, and said that he not only believed it but liked it.

"What a childish mind you've got," I said. "Let me tell you the story about the wolf that went to the little girl's grandmother's house and——"

"I always liked that one, too; but finish this one now. Joseph had decided to kill his wife."

"All right. There's not much more. While Minnie was being worked on, I popped into her room, intending to rouse her and send her for help. Before I did any rousing, I was needing some myself: I had a couple of lungfuls of the gas. The Finks must have turned the ghost loose on me, because Joseph was probably on his way downstairs with his wife at that time. He had faith enough in his divinity-shield, or he was nutty enough, to take her down and tie her on the altar before he carved her. Or maybe he had a way of fitting that stunt into his scheme, or maybe he simply had a liking for bloody theatricals. Anyway, he probably took her down there while I was up in Minnie's room going around and around with the ghost.

"The ghost had me sweating ink, and when I finally left him and tottered out into the corridor, the Finks jumped me. I say they did, and know it; but it was too dark for me to see them. I beat them off, got a gun, and went downstairs. Collinson and Gabrielle were gone from where I had left them. I found Collinson: Gabrielle had put him outside and shut the door on him. The Haldorns' son—a kid of thirteen or so—came to us with the news that Papa was about to kill Mama, and that Gabrielle was with them. I killed Haldorn, but I almost didn't. I put seven bullets in him. Hard-coated .32's go in clean, without much of a thump, true enough; but I put seven of them in him—in his face and body—standing close and firing pointblank— and he didn't even know it. That's how completely he had himself hypnotized. I finally got him down by driving the dagger through his neck."

I stopped. Fitzstephan asked: "Well?"

"Well what?"

"What happened after that?"

"Nothing," I said. "That's the kind of a story it is. I warned you there was no sense to it."

"But what was Gabrielle doing there?"

"Crouching beside the altar, looking up at the pretty spotlight."

"But why was she there? What was her reason for being there? Had she been called there again? Or was she there of her own free will? How did she come to be there? What was she there for?"

"I don't know. She didn't know. I asked her. She didn't know she was there."

"But surely you could learn something from the others?"

"Yeah," I said; "what I've told you, chiefly from Aaronia Haldorn. She and her husband ran a cult, and he went crazy and began murdering people, and how could she help it? Fink won't talk. He's a mechanic, yes; and he put in his trick-machinery for the Haldorns and operated it; but he doesn't know what happened last night. He heard a lot of noises, but it was none of his business to go poking his nose out to see what it was: the first he knew anything was wrong was when some police came and started giving him hell. Mrs. Fink's gone. The other employes probably don't really know anything, though it's a gut they could make some good guesses. Manuel, the little boy, is too frightened to talk—and will be sure to know nothing when he gets over his fright. What we're up against is this: if Joseph went crazy and committed some murders on his own hook, the others, even though they unknowingly helped him, are in the clear. The worst any of them can draw is a light sentence for taking part in the cult swindle.

But if any of them admits knowing anything, then he lets himself in for trouble as an accomplice in the murder. Nobody's likely to do that."

"I see," Fitzstephan said slowly. "Joseph is dead, so Joseph did everything. How will you get around that?"

"I won't," I said; "though the police will at least try to. My end's done, so Madison Andrews told me a couple of hours ago."

"But if, as you say, you aren't satisfied that you've learned the whole truth of the affair, I should think you—"

"It's not me," I said. "There's a lot I'd like to do yet, but I was hired, this time, by Andrews, to guard her while she was in the Temple. She isn't there now, and Andrews doesn't think there's anything further to be learned about what happened there. And, as far as guarding her is necessary, her husband ought to be able to do that."

"Her what?"

"Husband."

Fitzstephan thumped his stein down on the table so that beer sloshed over the sides.

"Now there you are," he said accusingly. "You didn't tell me anything about that. God only knows how much else there is that you've not told me."

"Collinson took advantage of the confusion to carry her off to Reno, where they won't have to wait the Californian three days for their license. I didn't know they'd gone till Andrews jumped on my neck three or four hours later. He was kind of unpleasant about it, which is one of the ways we came to stop being client and operative."

"I didn't know he was opposed to Collinson as a husband for her."

"I don't know that he is, but he didn't think this the time, nor that the way, for their wedding."

"I can understand that," he said as we got up from the table. "Andrews likes to have his way in most things."

Part Three: Quesada

XIII : THE CLIFF ROAD

Eric Collinson wired me from Quesada:

COME IMMEDIATELY STOP NEED YOU STOP TROUBLE
DANGER STOP MEET ME AT SUNSET HOTEL STOP DO
NOT COMMUNICATE STOP GABRIELLE MUST NOT
KNOW STOP HURRY

ERIC CARTER

The telegram came to the agency on Friday morning.
I wasn't in San Francisco that morning. I was up in
Martinez dickering with a divorced wife of Phil Leach,
alias a lot of names. We wanted him for spreading reams
of orphan paper through the Northwest, and we wanted
him badly. This ex-wife—a sweet-looking little blonde
telephone operator—had a fairly recent photograph of Phil,
and was willing to sell it.

"He never thought enough of me to risk passing any
bum checks so I could have things," she complained. "I
had to bring in my own share of the nut. So why shouldn't
I make something out of him now, when I guess some
tramp's getting plenty? Now how much will you give for
it?"

She had an exaggerated idea of how much the photograph was worth to us, of course, but I finally made the

deal with her. But it was after six when I returned to the city, too late for a train that would put me in Quesada that night. I packed a bag, got my car from the garage, and drove down.

Quesada was a one-hotel town pasted on the rocky side of a young mountain that sloped into the Pacific Ocean some eighty miles from San Francisco. Quesada's beach was too abrupt and hard and jagged for bathing, so Quesada had never got much summer-resort money. For a while it had been a hustling rum-running port, but that racket was dead now: bootleggers had learned there was more profit and less worry in handling domestic hooch than imported. Quesada had gone back to sleep.

I got there at eleven-something that night, garaged my car, and crossed the street to the Sunset Hotel. It was a low, sprawled-out, yellow building. The night clerk was alone in the lobby, a small effeminate man well past sixty who went to a lot of trouble to show me that his fingernails were rosy and shiny.

When he had read my name on the register he gave me a sealed envelope—hotel stationery—addressed to me in Eric Collinson's handwriting. I tore it open and read:

> *Do not leave the hotel*
> *until I have seen you.*
> *E. C.*

"How long has this been here?" I asked.

"Since about eight o'clock. Mr. Carter waited for you for more than an hour, until after the last stage came in from the railroad."

"He isn't staying here?"

"Oh, dear, no. He and his bride have got the Tooker place, down in the cove."

Collinson wasn't the sort of person to whose instructions I'd pay a whole lot of attention. I asked:

"How do you get there?"

"You'd never be able to find it at night," the clerk assured me, "unless you went all the way around by the

East road, and not then, I'm sure, unless you knew the country."

"Yeah? How do you get there in the daytime?"

"You go down this street to the end, take the fork of the road on the ocean side, and follow that up along the cliff. It isn't really a road, more of a path. It's about three miles to the house, a brown house, shingled all over, on a little hill. It's easily enough found in the daytime if you remember to keep to the right, to the ocean side, all the way down. But you'd never, never in the world, be able to find—"

"Thanks," I said, not wanting to hear the story all over again.

He led me up to a room, promised to call me at five, and I was asleep by midnight.

The morning was dull, ugly, foggy, and cold when I climbed out of bed to say, "All right, thanks," into the phone. It hadn't improved much by the time I had got dressed and gone downstairs. The clerk said there was not a chance in the world of getting anything to eat in Quesada before seven o'clock.

I went out of the hotel, down the street until it became a dirt road, kept to the dirt road until it forked, and turned into the branch that bent toward the ocean. This branch was never really a road from its beginning, and soon was nothing but a rocky path climbing along the side of a rocky ledge that kept pushing closer to the water's edge. The side of the ledge became steeper and steeper, until the path was simply an irregular shelf on the face of a cliff—a shelf eight or ten feet wide in places, no more than four or five in others. Above and behind the path, the cliff rose sixty or seventy feet; below and in front, it slanted down a hundred or more to ravel out in the ocean. A breeze from the general direction of China was pushing fog over the top of the cliff, making noisy lather of sea water at its bottom.

Rounding a corner where the cliff was steepest—was, in fact, for a hundred yards or so, straight up and down—I stopped to look at a small ragged hole in the path's outer rim. The hole was perhaps six inches across, with fresh loose earth piled in a little semicircular mound on one side, scattered on the other. It wasn't exciting to look at, but it said plainly to even such a city man as I was: here a bush was uprooted not so long ago.

There was no uprooted bush in sight. I chucked my cigarette away and got down on hands and knees, putting my head out over the path's rim, looking down. I saw the bush twenty feet below. It was perched on the top of a stunted tree that grew almost parallel to the cliff, fresh brown earth sticking to the bush's roots. The next thing that caught my eye was also brown—a soft hat lying upside down between two pointed gray rocks, half-way down to the water. I looked at the bottom of the cliff and saw the feet and legs.

They were a man's feet and legs, in black shoes and dark trousers. The feet lay on the top of a water-smoothed boulder, lay on their sides, six inches apart, both pointing to the left. From the feet, dark-trousered legs slanted down into the water, disappearing beneath the surface a few inches above the knees. That was all I could see from the cliff road.

I went down the cliff, though not at that point. It was a lot too steep there to be tackled by a middle-aged fat man. A couple of hundred yards back, the path had crossed a crooked ravine that creased the cliff diagonally from top to bottom. I returned to the ravine and went down it, stumbling, sliding, sweating and swearing, but reaching the bottom all in one piece, with nothing more serious the matter with me than torn fingers, dirty clothes, and ruined shoes.

The fringe of rock that lay between cliff and ocean wasn't meant to be walked on, but I managed to travel over it most of the way, having to wade only once or twice, and then not up to my knees. But when I came to the spot where the feet and legs were I had to go waist-deep into the Pacific to lift the body, which rested on its back on the worn slanting side of a mostly submerged boulder, covered from thighs up by frothing water. I got my hands under the armpits, found solid ground for my feet, and lifted.

It was Eric Collinson's body. Bones showed through flesh and clothing on his shattered back. The back of his head—that half of it—was crushed. I dragged him out of the water and put him down on dry rocks. His dripping pockets contained a hundred and fifty-four dollars and eighty-two cents, a watch, a knife, a gold pen and pencil, papers, a couple of letters, and a memoranda book. I spread out the papers, letters, and book; and read them; and learned nothing except that what was written in them hadn't anything to do with his death. I couldn't find anything else—on him or near him—to tell me more about his death than the uprooted bush, the hat caught between rocks, and the position of his body had told me.

I left him there and went back to the ravine, panting and heaving myself up it to the cliff path, returning to where the bush had grown. I didn't find anything there in the way of significant marks, footprints, or the like. The path was chiefly hard rock. I went on along it. Presently the cliff began to bend away from the ocean, lowering the path along its side. After another half-mile there was no cliff at all, merely a bush-grown ridge at whose foot the path ran. There was no sun yet. My pants stuck disagreeably to my chilly legs. Water squunched in my torn shoes. I hadn't had any breakfast. My cigarettes had got wet. My left knee ached from a twist it had got sliding down the ravine. I cursed the detective business and slopped on along the path.

The path took me away from the sea for a while, across the neck of a wooded point that pushed the ocean back, down into a small valley, up the side of a low hill; and then I saw the house the night clerk had described.

It was a rather large two-story building, roof and walls brown-shingled, set on a hump in the ground close to where the ocean came in to take a quarter-mile u-shaped bite out of the coast. The house faced the water. I was behind it. There was nobody in sight. The ground-floor windows were closed, with drawn blinds. The second-story windows were open. Off to one side were some smaller farm buildings.

I went around to the front of the house. Wicker chairs and a table were on the screened front porch. The screened porch-door was hooked on the inside. I rattled it noisily. I rattled it off and on for at least five minutes, and got no response. I went around to the rear again, and knocked on the back door. My knocking knuckles pushed the door open half a foot. Inside was a dark kitchen and silence. I opened the door wider, knocking on it again, loudly. More silence.

I called: "Mrs. Collinson."

When no answer came I went through the kitchen and a darker dining room, found a flight of stairs, climbed them, and began poking my head into rooms.

There was nobody in the house.

In one bedroom, a .38 automatic pistol lay in the center of the floor. There was an empty shell close to it, another under a chair across the room, and a faint odor of burnt gunpowder in the air. In one corner of the ceiling was a hole that a .38 bullet could have made, and, under it on the floor, a few crumbs of plaster. The bed-clothes were smooth and undisturbed. Clothes in the closet, things on and in table and bureau, told me this was Eric Collinson's bedroom.

Next to it, according to the same sort of evidence, was Gabrielle's bedroom. Her bed had not been slept in, or had been made since being slept in. On the floor of her closet I found a black satin dress, a once-white handkerchief, and a pair of black suede slippers, all wet and muddy—the handkerchief also wet with blood. In her bathroom—in the tub—were a bath-towel and a face-towel, both stained with mud and blood, and still damp. On her dressing-table was a small piece of thick white paper that had been folded. White powder clung to one crease. I touched it with the end of my tongue—morphine.

I went back to Quesada, changed my shoes and socks, got breakfast and a supply of dry cigarettes, and asked the clerk—a dapper boy, this one—who was responsible for law and order there.

"The marshal's Dick Cotton," he told me; "but he went up to the city last night. Ben Rolly's deputy sheriff. You can likely find him over at his old man's office."

"Where's that?"

"Next door to the garage."

I found it, a one-story red brick building with wide glass windows labeled *J. King Rolly, Real Estate, Mortgages, Loans, Stocks and Bonds, Insurance, Notes, Employment Agency, Notary Public, Moving and Storage,* and a lot more that I've forgotten.

Two men were inside, sitting with their feet on a battered desk behind a battered counter. One was a man of fifty-and, with hair, eyes, and skin of indefinite, washed-out tan shades—an amiable, aimless-looking man in shabby clothes. The other was twenty years younger and in twenty years would look just like him.

"I'm hunting," I said, "for the deputy sheriff."

"Me," the younger man said, easing his feet from desk to floor. He didn't get up. Instead, he put a foot out, hooked a chair by its rounds, pulled it from the wall, and returned his feet to the desk-top. "Set down. This is Pa," wiggling a thumb at the other man. "You don't have to mind him."

"Know Eric Carter?" I asked.

"The fellow honeymooning down to the Tooker place? I didn't know his front name was Eric."

"Eric Carter," the elder Rolly said; "that's the way I made out the rent receipt for him."

"He's dead," I told them. "He fell off the cliff road last night or this morning. It could have been an accident."

The father looked at the son with round tan eyes. The son looked at me with questioning tan eyes and said: "Tch, tch, tch."

I gave him a card. He read it carefully, turning it over to see that there was nothing on its back, and passed it to his father.

"Go down and take a look at him?" I suggested.

"I guess I ought to," the deputy sheriff agreed, getting

up from his chair. He was a larger man than I had supposed—as big as the dead Collinson boy—and, in spite of his slouchiness, he had a nicely muscled body.

I followed him out to a dusty car in front of the office. Rolly senior didn't go with us.

"Somebody told you about it?" the deputy sheriff asked when we were riding.

"I stumbled on him. Know who the Carters are?"

"Somebody special?"

"You heard about the Riese murder in the San Francisco temple?"

"Uh-huh, I read the papers."

"Mrs. Carter was the Gabrielle Leggett mixed up in that, and Carter was the Eric Collinson."

"Tch, tch, tch," he said.

"And her father and step-mother were killed a couple of weeks before that."

"Tch, tch, tch," he said. "What's the matter with them?"

"A family curse."

"Sure enough?"

I didn't know how seriously he meant that question, though he seemed serious enough. I hadn't got him sized up yet. However, clown or not, he was the deputy sheriff stationed at Quesada, and this was his party. He was entitled to the facts. I gave them to him as we bounced over the lumpy road, gave him all I had, from Paris in 1913 to the cliff road a couple of hours ago.

"When they came back from being married in Reno, Collinson dropped in to see me. They had to stick around for the Haldorn bunch's trial, and he wanted a quiet place to take the girl: she was still in a daze. You know Owen Fitzstephan?"

"The writer fellow that was down here a while last year? Uh-huh."

"Well, he suggested this place."

"I know. The old man mentioned it. But what'd they take them aliases for?"

"To dodge publicity, and, partly, to try to dodge something like this."

He frowned vaguely and asked:

"You mean they expected something like this?"

"Well, it's easy to say, 'I told you so,' after things happen, but I've never thought we had the answer to either of the two mix-ups she's been in. And not having the answer —how could you tell what to expect? I didn't think so much of their going off into seclusion like this while whatever was hanging over her—if anything was—was still hanging over her, but Collinson was all for it. I made him promise to wire me if he saw anything funny. Well, he did."

Rolly nodded three or four times, then asked:

"What makes you think he didn't fall off the cliff?"

"He sent for me. Something was wrong. Outside of that, too many things have happened around his wife for me to believe in accidents."

"There's the curse, though," he said.

"Yeah," I agreed, studying his indefinite face, still trying to figure him out. "But the trouble with it is it's worked out too well, too regularly. It's the first one I ever ran across that did."

He frowned over my opinion for a couple of minutes, and then stopped the car. "We'll have to get out here: the road ain't so good the rest of the way." None of it had been. "Still and all, you do hear of them working out. There's things that happen that makes a fellow think there's things in the world—in life—that he don't know much about." He frowned again as we set off afoot, and found a word he liked. "It's inscrutable," he wound up.

I let that go at that.

He went ahead up the cliff path, stopping of his own accord where the bush had been torn up, a detail I hadn't mentioned. I didn't say anything while he stared down at Collinson's body, looked searchingly up and down the face of the cliff, and then went up and down the path, bent far over, his tan eyes intent on the ground.

He wandered around for ten minutes or more, then straightened up and said: "There's nothing here that I can find. Let's go down."

I started back toward the ravine, but he said there was a better way ahead. There was. We went down it to the dead man.

Rolly looked from the corpse to the edge of the path high above us, and complained: "I don't hardly see how he could have landed just thataway."

"He didn't. I pulled him out of the water," I said, showing the deputy exactly where I had found the body.

"That would be more like it," he decided.

I sat on a rock and smoked a cigarette while he went around examining, touching, moving rocks, pebbles, and sand. He didn't seem to have any luck.

XIV : THE CRUMPLED
CHRYSLER

We climbed to the path again and went on to the Collinsons' house. I showed Rolly the stained towels, handkerchief, dress, and slippers; the paper that had held morphine; the gun on Collinson's floor, the hole in the ceiling, and the empty shells on the floor.

"That shell under the chair is where it was," I said; "but the other—the one in the corner—was here, close to the gun, when I saw it before."

"You mean it's been moved since you were here?"

"Yeah."

"But what good would that do anybody?" he objected.

"None that I know of, but it's been moved."

He had lost interest. He was looking at the ceiling. He said:

"Two shots and one hole. I wonder. Maybe the other went out the window."

He went back to Gabrielle Collinson's bedroom and examined the black velvet gown. There were some torn places in it—down near the bottom—but no bullet-holes. He put the dress down and picked up the morphine paper from the dressing-table.

"What do you suppose this is doing here?" he asked.

"She uses it. It's one of the things her step-mother taught her."

"Tch, tch, tch. Kind of looks like she might have done it."

"Yeah?"

"You know it does. She's a dope fiend, ain't she? They had had trouble, and he sent for you, and—" He broke off, pursed his lips, then asked: "What time do you reckon he was killed?"

"I don't know. Maybe last night, on his way home from waiting for me."

"You were in the hotel all night?"

"From eleven-something till five this morning. Of course I could have sneaked out for long enough to pull a murder between those hours."

"I didn't mean nothing like that," he said. "I was just wondering. What kind of looking woman is this Mrs. Collinson-Carter? I never saw her."

"She's about twenty; five feet four or five; looks thinner than she really is; light brown hair, short and curly; big eyes that are sometimes brown and sometimes green; white skin; hardly any forehead; small mouth and teeth; pointed chin; no lobes on her ears, and they're pointed on top; been sick for a couple of months and looks it."

"Oughtn't be hard to pick her up," he said, and began poking into drawers, closets, trunks, and so on. I had poked into them on my first visit, and hadn't found anything interesting either.

"Don't look like she did any packing or took much of anything with her," he decided when he came back to where I was sitting by the dressing-table. He pointed a thick finger at the monogrammed silver toilet-set on the table. "What's the G. D. L. for?"

"Her name was Gabrielle Something Leggett before she was married."

"Oh, yes. She went away in the car, I reckon. Huh?"

"Did they have one down here?" I asked.

"He used to come to town in a Chrysler roadster when he didn't walk. She could only have took it out by the East road. We'll go out thataway and see."

Outside, I waited while he made circles around the house, finding nothing. In front of a shed where a car obviously had been kept he pointed at some tracks, and said, "Drove out this morning." I took his word for it.

We walked along a dirt road to a gravel one, and along that perhaps a mile to a gray house that stood in a group of red farm buildings. A small-boned, high-shouldered man who limped slightly was oiling a pump behind the house. Rolly called him Debro.

"Sure, Ben," he replied to Rolly's question. "She went by here about seven this morning, going like a bat out of hell. There wasn't anybody else in the car."

"How was she dressed?" I asked.

"She didn't have on any hat and a tan coat."

I asked him what he knew about the Carters: he was their nearest neighbor. He didn't know anything about them. He had talked to Carter two or three times, and thought him an agreeable enough young fellow. Once he had taken the missus over to call on Mrs. Carter, but Carter told them she was lying down, not feeling well. None of the Debros had ever seen her except at a distance, walking or riding with her husband.

"I don't guess there's anybody around here that's talked to her," he wound up, "except of course Mary Nunez."

"Mary working for them?" the deputy asked.

"Yes. What's the matter, Ben? Something the matter over there?"

"He fell off the cliff last night, and she's gone away without saying anything to anybody."

Debro whistled.

Rolly went into the house to use Debro's phone, reporting to the sheriff. I stayed outside with Debro, trying to get more—if only his opinions—out of him. All I got were expressions of amazement.

"We'll go over and see Mary," the deputy said when he came from the phone; and then, when we had left Debro, had crossed the road, and were walking through a field towards a cluster of trees: "Funny she wasn't there."

"Who is she?"

"A Mex. Lives down in the hollow with the rest of them. Her man, Pedro Nunez, is doing a life-stretch in Folsom for killing a bootlegger named Dunne in a high-jacking two-three years back."

"Local killing?"

"Uh-huh. It happened down in the cove in front of the Tooker place."

We went through the trees and down a slope to where half a dozen shacks—shaped, sized, and red-leaded to resemble box-cars—lined the side of a stream, with vegetable gardens spread out behind them. In front of one of the shacks a shapeless Mexican woman in a pink-checkered dress sat on an empty canned-soup box smoking a corncob pipe and nursing a brown baby. Ragged and dirty children played between the buildings, with ragged and dirty mongrels helping them make noise. In one of the gardens a brown man in overalls that had once been blue was barely moving a hoe.

The children stopped playing to watch Rolly and me cross the stream on conveniently placed stones. The dogs came yapping to meet us, snarling and snapping around us until one of the boys chased them. We stopped in front of the woman with the baby. The deputy grinned down at the baby and said:

"Well, well, ain't he getting to be a husky son-of-a-gun!"

The woman took the pipe from her mouth long enough to complain stolidly:

"Colic all the time."

"Tch, tch, tch. Where's Mary Nunez?"

The pipe-stem pointed at the next shack.

"I thought she was working for them people at the Tooker place," he said.

"Sometimes," the woman replied indifferently.

We went to the next shack. An old woman in a gray wrapper had come to the door, watching us while stirring something in a yellow bowl.

"Where's Mary?" the deputy asked.

She spoke over her shoulder into the shack's interior, and moved aside to let another woman take her place in the doorway. This other woman was short and solidly built, somewhere in her early thirties, with intelligent dark eyes in a wide, flat face. She held a dark blanket together at her throat. The blanket hung to the floor all around her.

"Howdy, Mary," Rolly greeted her. "Why ain't you over to the Carters'?"

"I'm sick, Mr. Rolly." She spoke without accent. "Chills —so I just stayed home today."

"Tch, tch, tch. That's too bad. Have you had the doc?"

She said she hadn't. Rolly said she ought to. She said she didn't need him: she had chills often. Rolly said that might be so, but that was all the more reason for having him: it was best to play safe and have things like that looked after. She said yes but doctors took so much money, and it was bad enough being sick without having to pay for it. He said in the long run it was likely to cost folks more not having a doctor than having him. I had begun to think they were going to keep it up all day when Rolly finally brought the talk around to the Carters again, asking the woman about her work there.

She told us she had been hired two weeks ago, when they took the house. She went there each morning at nine —they never got up before ten—cooked their meals, did the housework, and left after washing the dinner dishes in the evening—usually somewhere around seven-thirty. She seemed surprised at the news that Collinson—Carter to her —had been killed and his wife had gone away. She told us that Collinson had gone out by himself, for a walk, he said, right after dinner the previous night. That was at about half-past six, dinner having been, for no special reason, a little early. When she left for home, at a few minutes past seven, Mrs. Carter had been reading a book in the front second-story room.

Mary Nunez couldn't, or wouldn't, tell us anything on which I could base a reasonable guess at Collinson's reason for sending for me. She knew, she insisted, nothing about them except that Mrs. Carter didn't seem happy—wasn't happy. She—Mary Nunez—had figured it all out to her own satisfaction: Mrs. Carter loved someone else, but her parents had made her marry Carter; and so, of course, Carter had been killed by the other man, with whom Mrs. Carter had now run away. I couldn't get her to say that she had any grounds for this belief other than her woman's intuition, so I asked her about the Carters' visitors.

She said she had never seen any.

Rolly asked her if the Carters ever quarreled. She started to say, "No," and then, rapidly, said they did, often, and were never on good terms. Mrs. Carter didn't like to have her husband near her, and several times had told him, in Mary's hearing, that if he didn't go away from her and stay away she would kill him. I tried to pin Mary down to details, asking what had led up to these threats, how they had been worded, but she wouldn't be pinned down. All she remembered positively, she told us, was that Mrs. Carter had threatened to kill Mr. Carter if he didn't go away from her.

"That pretty well settles that," Rolly said contentedly when we had crossed the stream again and were climbing the slope toward Debro's.

"What settles what?"

"That his wife killed him."

"Think she did?"

"So do you."

I said: "No."

Rolly stopped walking and looked at me with vague worried eyes.

"Now how can you say that?" he remonstrated. "Ain't she a dope fiend? And cracked in the bargain, according to your own way of telling it? Didn't she run away? Wasn't them things she left behind torn and dirty and bloody? Didn't she threaten to kill him so much that he got scared and sent for you?"

"Mary didn't hear threats," I said. "They were warnings —about the curse. Gabrielle Collinson really believed in it, and thought enough of him to try to save him from it. I've been through that before with her. That's why she wouldn't have married him if he hadn't carried her off while she was too rattled to know what she was doing. And she was afraid on that account afterwards."

"But who's going to believe—?"

"I'm not asking anybody to believe anything," I growled, walking on again. "I'm telling you what I believe. And while I'm at it I'll tell you I believe Mary Nunez is lying when she says she didn't go to the house this morning. Maybe she didn't have anything to do with Collinson's death. Maybe she simply went there, found the Collinsons gone, saw the bloody things and the gun—kicking that shell across the floor without knowing it—and then beat it back to her shack, fixing up that chills story to keep herself out of it; having had enough of that sort of trouble when her husband was sent over. Maybe not. Anyway, that would be how nine out of ten women of her sort in her place would have played it; and I want more proof before I believe her chills just happened to hit her this morning."

"Well," the deputy sheriff asked; "if she didn't have nothing to do with it, what difference does all that make anyway?"

The answers I thought up to that were profane and insulting. I kept them to myself.

At Debro's again, we borrowed a loose-jointed touring car of at least three different makes, and drove down the East road, trying to trace the girl in the Chrysler. Our first stop was at the house of a man named Claude Baker. He was a lanky sallow person with an angular face three or four days behind the razor. His wife was probably younger than he, but looked older—a tired and faded thin woman who might have been pretty at one time. The oldest of their six children was a bowlegged, freckled girl of ten; the youngest was a fat and noisy infant in its first year. Some of the in-betweens were boys and some girls, but they all had colds in their heads. The whole Baker family came out on the porch to receive us. They hadn't seen her, they said: they were never up as early as seven o'clock. They knew the Carters by sight, but knew nothing about them. They asked more questions than Rolly and I did.

Shortly beyond the Baker house the road changed from gravel to asphalt. What we could see of the Chrysler's tracks seemed to show that it had been the last car over the road. Two miles from Baker's we stopped in front of a small bright green house surrounded by rose bushes. Rolly bawled:

"Harve! Hey, Harve!"

A big-boned man of thirty-five or so came to the door, said, "Hullo, Ben," and walked between the rose bushes to our car. His features, like his voice, were heavy, and he moved and spoke deliberately. His last name was Whidden. Rolly asked him if he had seen the Chrysler.

"Yes, Ben, I saw them," he said. "They went past around a quarter after seven this morning, hitting it up."

"They?" I asked, while Rolly asked: "Them?"

"There was a man and a woman—or a girl—in it. I didn't get a good look at them—just saw them whizz past. She was driving, a kind of small woman she looked like from here, with brown hair."

"What did the man look like?"

"Oh, he was maybe forty, and didn't look like he was very big either. A pinkish face, he had, and gray coat and hat."

"Ever see Mrs. Carter?" I asked.

"The bride living down the cove? No. I seen him, but not her. Was that her?"

I said we thought it was.

"The man wasn't him," he said. "He was somebody I never seen before."

"Know him again if you saw him?"

"I reckon I would—if I saw him going past like that."

Four miles beyond Whidden's we found the Chrysler. It was a foot or two off the road, on the left-hand side, standing on all fours with its radiator jammed into a eucalyptus tree. All its glass was shattered, and the front third of its metal was pretty well crumpled. It was empty. There was no blood in it. The deputy sheriff and I seemed to be the only people in the vicinity.

We ran around in circles, straining our eyes at the ground, and when we got through we knew what we had known at the beginning—the Chrysler had run into a eucalyptus tree. There were tire-marks on the road, and marks that could have been footprints on the ground by the car; but it was possible to find the same sort of marks in a hundred places along that, or any other, road. We got into our borrowed car again and drove on, asking questions wherever we found someone to question; and all the answers were: No, we didn't see her or them.

"What about this fellow Baker?" I asked Rolly as we turned around to go back. "Debro saw her alone. There was a man with her when she passed Whidden's. The Bakers saw nothing, and it was in their territory that the man must have joined her."

"Well," he said, argumentatively; "it could of happened that way, couldn't it?"

"Yeah, but it might be a good idea to do some more talking to them."

"If you want to," he consented without enthusiasm. "But don't go dragging me into any arguments with them. He's my wife's brother."

That made a difference. I asked:

"What sort of man is he?"

"Claude's kind of shiftless, all right. Like the old man says, he don't manage to raise nothing much but kids on that farm of his, but I never heard tell that he did anybody any harm."

"If you say he's all right, that's enough for me," I lied. "We won't bother him."

XV : I'VE KILLED HIM

Sheriff Feeney, fat, florid, and with a lot of brown mustache, and district attorney Vernon, sharp-featured, aggressive, and hungry for fame, came over from the county seat. They listened to our stories, looked the ground over, and agreed with Rolly that Gabrielle Collinson had killed her husband. When Marshal Dick Cotton—a pompous, unintelligent man in his forties—returned from San Francisco, he added his vote to the others. The coroner and his jury came to the same opinion, though officially they limited themselves to the usual "person or persons unknown," with recommendations involving the girl.

The time of Collinson's death was placed between eight and nine o'clock Friday night. No marks not apparently caused by his fall had been found on him. The pistol found in his room had been identified as his. No fingerprints were on it. I had an idea that some of the county officials half suspected me of having seen to that, though nobody said anything of that sort. Mary Nunez stuck to her story of being kept home by chills. She had a flock of Mexican witnesses to back it up. I couldn't find any to knock holes in it. We found no further trace of the man Whidden had seen. I tried the Bakers again, by myself, with no luck. The marshal's wife, a frail youngish woman with a weak pretty face and nice shy manners, who worked in the telegraph office, said Collinson had sent off his wire to me early Friday morning. He was pale and shaky, she said, with dark-rimmed, bloodshot eyes. She had supposed he was drunk, though she hadn't smelled alcohol on his breath.

Collinson's father and brother came down from San Francisco. Hubert Collinson, the father, was a big calm man who looked capable of taking as many more millions out of Pacific Coast lumber as he wanted. Laurence Collinson was a year or two older than his dead brother, and much like him in appearance. Both Collinsons were careful to say nothing that could be interpreted as suggesting they thought Gabrielle had been responsible for Eric's death, but there was little doubt that they did think so.

Hubert Collinson said quietly to me, "Go ahead; get to the bottom of it;" and thus became the fourth client for whom the agency had been concerned with Gabrielle's affairs.

Madison Andrews came down from San Francisco. He and I talked in my hotel room. He sat on a chair by the window, cut a cube of tobacco from a yellowish plug, put it in his mouth, and decided that Collinson had committed suicide.

I sat on the side of the bed, set fire to a Fatima, and contradicted him:

"He wouldn't have torn up the bush if he'd gone over willingly."

"Then it was an accident. That was a dangerous road to be walked in the dark."

"I've stopped believing in accidents," I said. "And he had sent me an SOS. And there was the gun that had been fired in his room."

He leaned forward in his chair. His eyes were hard and watchful. He was a lawyer cross-examining a witness.

"You think Gabrielle was responsible?"

I wouldn't go that far. I said:

"He was murdered. He was murdered by— I told you two weeks ago that we weren't through with that damned curse, and that the only way to get through with it was to have the Temple business sifted to the bottom."

"Yes, I remember," he said without quite sneering. "You advanced the theory that there was some connecting link between her parents' deaths and the trouble she had at the Haldorns'; but, as I recall it, you had no idea what the link might be. Don't you think that deficiency has a tendency to make your theory a little—say—vaporous?"

"Does it? Her father, step-mother, physician, and husband have been killed, one after the other, in less than two months; and her maid jailed for murder. All the people closest to her. Doesn't that look like a program? And"—I grinned at him—"are you sure it's not going further? And if it does, aren't you the next closest person to her?"

"Preposterous!" He was very much annoyed now. "We know about her parents' deaths, and about Riese's, and that there was no link between them. We know that those responsible for Riese's murder are now either dead or in prison. There's no getting around that. It's simply preposterous to say there are links between one and another of these crimes when we know there's none."

"We don't know anything of the kind," I insisted. "All we know is that we haven't found the links. Who profits—or could hope to profit—by what has happened?"

"Not a single person so far as I know."

"Suppose she died? Who'd get the estate?"

"I don't know. There are distant relations in England or France, I dare say."

"That doesn't get us very far," I growled. "Anyway, nobody's tried to kill her. It's her friends who get the knock-off."

The lawyer reminded me sourly that we couldn't say that nobody had tried to kill her—or had succeeded—until we found her. I couldn't argue with him about that. Her trail still ended where the eucalyptus tree had stopped the Chrysler.

I gave him a piece of advice before he left:

"Whatever you believe, there's no sense in your taking unnecessary chances: remember that there might be a program, and you might be next on it. It won't hurt to be careful."

He didn't thank me. He suggested, unpleasantly, that doubtless I thought he should hire private detectives to guard him.

Madison Andrews had offered a thousand-dollar reward for information leading to discovery of the girl's whereabouts. Hubert Collinson had offered another thousand, with an additional twenty-five hundred for the arrest and conviction of his son's murderer. Half the population of the county had turned bloodhound. Anywhere you went you found men walking, or even crawling, around, searching fields, paths, hills, and valleys for clues, and in the woods you were likely to find more amateur gumshoes than trees.

Her photographs had been distributed and published widely. The newspapers, from San Diego to Vancouver, gave us a tremendous play, whooping it up in all the colored ink they had. All the San Francisco and Los Angeles Continental operatives who could be pulled off other jobs were checking Quesada's exits, hunting, questioning, finding nothing. Radio broadcasters helped. The police everywhere, all the agency's branches, were stirred up.

And by Monday all this hubbub had brought us exactly nothing.

Monday afternoon I went back to San Francisco and told all my troubles to the Old Man. He listened politely, as if to some moderately interesting story that didn't concern him personally, smiled his meaningless smile, and, instead of any assistance, gave me his pleasantly expressed opinion that I'd eventually succeed in working it all out to a satisfactory conclusion.

Then he told me that Fitzstephan had phoned, trying to get in touch with me. "It may be important. He would have gone down to Quesada to find you if I hadn't told him I expected you."

I called Fitzstephan's number.

"Come up," he said. "I've got something. I don't know whether it's a fresh puzzle, or the key to a puzzle; but it's something."

I rode up Nob Hill on a cable car and was in his apartment within fifteen minutes.

"All right, spring it," I said as we sat down in his paper-, magazine-, and book-littered living room.

"Any trace of Gabrielle yet?" he asked.

"No. But spring the puzzle. Don't be literary with me, building up to climaxes and the like. I'm too crude for that —it'd only give me a bellyache. Just spread it out for me."

"You'll always be what you are," he said, trying to seem disappointed and disgusted, but not succeeding because he was—inwardly—too excited over something. "Somebody— a man—called me up early Saturday morning—half-past one—on the phone. He asked: 'Is this Fitzstephan?' I said: 'Yes;' and then the voice said: 'Well, I've killed him.' He said it just like that. I'm sure of those exact words, though they weren't very clear. There was a lot of noise on the line, and the voice seemed distant.

"I didn't know who it was—what he was talking about. I asked: 'Killed who? Who is this?' I couldn't understand any of his answer except the word 'money.' He said something about money, repeating it several times, but I could understand only that one word. There were some people here—the Marquards, Laura Joines with some man she'd brought, Ted and Sue Van Slack—and we had been in the middle of a literary free-for-all. I had a wisecrack on my tongue—something about Cabell being a romanticist in the same sense that the wooden horse was Trojan—and didn't want to be robbed of my opportunity to deliver it by this drunken joker, or whoever he was, on the phone. I couldn't make heads or tails of what he was saying, so I hung up and went back to my guests.

"It never occurred to me that the phone conversation could have had any meaning until yesterday morning, when I read about Collinson's death. I was at the Colemans', up in Ross. I went up there Saturday morning, for the week-end, having finally run Ralph to earth." He grinned. "And I made him glad enough to see me leave this morning." He became serious again. "Even after hearing of Collinson's death, I wasn't convinced that my phone call was of any importance, had any meaning. It was such a silly sort of thing. But of course I meant to tell you about it. But look—this was in my mail when I got home this morning."

He took an envelope from his pocket and tossed it over

to me. It was a cheap and shiny white envelope of the kind you can buy anywhere. Its corners were dark and curled, as if it had been carried in a pocket for some time. Fitzstephan's name and address had been printed on it, with a hard pencil, by someone who was a rotten printer, or who wanted to be thought so. It was postmarked San Francisco, nine o'clock Saturday morning. Inside was a soiled and crookedly torn piece of brown wrapping paper, with one sentence—as poorly printed with pencil as the address —on it:

ANY BODY THAT WANTS MRS. CARTER
CAN HAVE SAME BY PAYING $10000—

There was no date, no salutation, no signature.

"She was seen driving away alone as late as seven Saturday morning," I said. "This was mailed here, eighty miles away, in time to be postmarked at nine—taken from the box in the first morning collection, say. That's one to get wrinkles over. But even that's not as funny as its coming to you instead of to Andrews, who's in charge of her affairs, or her father-in-law, who's got the most money."

"It is funny and it isn't," Fitzstephan replied. His lean face was eager. "There may be a point of light there. You know I recommended Quesada to Collinson, having spent a couple of months there last spring finishing *The Wall of Ashdod,* and gave him a card to a real estate dealer named Rolly—the deputy sheriff's father—there, introducing him as Eric Carter. A native of Quesada might not know she was Gabrielle Collinson, née Leggett. In that case he wouldn't know how to reach her people except through me, who had sent her and her husband there. So the letter is sent to me, but starts off *Anybody that,* to be passed on to the interested persons."

"A native might have done that," I said slowly; "or a kidnapper who wanted us to think he was a native, didn't want us to think he knew the Collinsons."

"Exactly. And as far as I know none of the natives knew my address here."

"How about Rolly?"

"Not unless Collinson gave it to him. I simply scribbled the introduction on the back of a card."

"Said anything to anybody else about the phone call and this letter?" I asked.

"I mentioned the call to the people who were here Friday night—when I thought it was a joke or a mistake. I haven't shown this to anybody else. In fact," he said, "I was a little doubtful about showing it at all—and still am. Is it going to make trouble for me?"

"Yeah, it will. But you oughtn't mind that. I thought you liked first-hand views of trouble. Better give me the names and addresses of your guests. If they and Coleman account for your whereabouts Friday night and over the week-end, nothing serious will happen to you; though you'll have to go down to Quesada and let the county officials third-degree you."

"Shall we go now?"

"I'm going back tonight. Meet me at the Sunset Hotel there in the morning. That'll give me time to work on the officials—so they won't throw you in the dungeon on sight."

I went back to the agency and put in a Quesada call. I couldn't get hold of Vernon or the sheriff, but Cotton was reachable. I gave him the information I had got from Fitzstephan, promising to produce the novelist for questioning the next morning.

The marshal said the search for the girl was still going on without results. Reports had come in that she had been seen—practically simultaneously—in Los Angeles, Eureka, Carson City, Denver, Portland, Tijuana, Ogden, San Jose, Vancouver, Porterville, and Hawaii. All except the most ridiculous reports were being run out.

The telephone company could tell me that Owen Fitzstephan's Saturday morning phone-call had not been a long distance call, and that nobody in Quesada had called a San Francisco number either Friday night or Saturday morning.

Before I left the agency I visited the Old Man again, asking him if he would try to persuade the district attorney to turn Aaronia Haldorn and Tom Fink loose on bail.

"They're not doing us any good in jail," I explained, "and, loose, they might lead us somewhere if we shadowed them. He oughtn't to mind: he knows he hasn't a chance in the world of hanging murder-raps on them as things now stack up."

The Old Man promised to do his best, and to put an operative behind each of our suspects if they were sprung.

I went over to Madison Andrews' office. When I had told him about Fitzstephan's messages, and had given him our explanation of them, the lawyer nodded his bony white-thatched head and said:

"And whether that's the true explanation or not, the county authorities will now have to give up their absurd theory that Gabrielle killed her husband."

I shook my head sidewise.

"What?" he asked explosively.

"They're going to think the messages were cooked up to clear her," I predicted.

"Is that what you think?" His jaws got lumpy in front of his ears, and his tangled eyebrows came down over his eyes.

"I hope they weren't," I said; "because if it's a trick it's a damned childish one."

"How could it be?" he demanded loudly. "Don't talk nonsense. None of us knew anything then. The body hadn't been found when——"

"Yeah," I agreed; "and that's why, if it turns out to have been a stunt, it'll hang Gabrielle."

"I don't understand you," he said disagreeably. "One minute you're talking about somebody persecuting the girl, and the next minute you're talking as if you thought she was the murderer. Just what do you think?"

"Both can be true," I replied, no less disagreeably. "And what difference does it make what I think? It'll be up to the jury when she's found. The question now is: what are you going to do about the ten-thousand-dollar demand —if it's on the level?"

"What I'm going to do is increase the reward for her

recovery, with an additional reward for the arrest of her abductor."

"That's the wrong play," I said. "Enough reward money has been posted. The only way to handle a kidnapping is to come across. I don't like it any more than you do, but it's the only way. Uncertainty, nervousness, fear, disappointment, can turn even a mild kidnapper into a maniac. Buy the girl free, and then do your fighting. Pay what's asked when it's asked."

He tugged at his ragged mustache, his jaw set obstinately, his eyes worried. But the jaw won out.

"I'm damned if I'll knuckle down," he said.

"That's your business." I got up and reached for my hat. "Mine's finding Collinson's murderer, and having her killed is more likely to help me than not."

He didn't say anything.

I went down to Hubert Collinson's office. He wasn't in, but I told Laurence Collinson my story, winding up:

"Will you urge your father to put up the money? And to have it ready to pass over as soon as the kidnapper's instructions come?"

"It won't be necessary to urge him," he said immediately. "Of course we shall pay whatever is required to ensure her safety."

XVI : THE NIGHT HUNT

I caught the 5:25 train south. It put me in Poston, a dusty town twice Quesada's size, at 7:30; and a rattle-trap stage, in which I was the only passenger, got me to my destination half an hour later. Rain was beginning to fall as I was leaving the stage across the street from the hotel.

Jack Santos, a San Francisco reporter, came out of the telegraph office and said: "Hello. Anything new?"

"Maybe, but I'll have to give it to Vernon first."

"He's in his room in the hotel, or was ten minutes ago. You mean the ransom letter that somebody got?"

"Yeah. He's already given it out?"

"Cotton started to, but Vernon headed him off, told us to let it alone."

"Why?"

"No reason at all except that it was Cotton giving it to us." Santos pulled the corners of his thin lips down. "It's been turned into a contest between Vernon, Feeney, and Cotton to see which can get his name and picture printed most."

"They been doing anything except that?"

"How can they?" he asked disgustedly. "They spend ten hours a day trying to make the front page, ten more trying to keep the others from making it, and they've got to sleep some time."

In the hotel I gave "nothing new" to some more reporters, registered again, left my bag in my room, and went down the hall to 204. Vernon opened the door when I had knocked. He was alone, and apparently had been reading the newspapers that made a pink, green, and white pile on the bed. The room was blue-gray with cigar smoke.

This district attorney was a thirty-year-old dark-eyed man who carried his chin up and out so that it was more prominent than nature had intended, bared all his teeth when he talked, and was very conscious of being a gogetter. He shook my hand briskly and said:

"I'm glad you're back. Come in. Sit down. Are there any new developments?"

"Cotton pass you the dope I gave him?"

"Yes." Vernon posed in front of me, hands in pockets, feet far apart. "What importance do you attach to it?"

"I advised Andrews to get the money ready. He won't. The Collinsons will."

"They will," he said, as if confirming a guess I had made. "And?" He held his lips back so that his teeth remained exposed.

"Here's the letter." I gave it to him. "Fitzstephan will be down in the morning."

He nodded emphatically, carried the letter closer to the light, and examined it and its envelope minutely. When he had finished he tossed it contemptuously to the table.

"Obviously a fraud," he said. "Now what, exactly, is this Fitzstephan's—is that the name?—story?"

I told him, word for word. When that was done, he clicked his teeth together, turned to the telephone, and told someone to tell Feeney that he—Mr. Vernon, district attorney—wished to see him immediately. Ten minutes later the sheriff came in wiping rain off his big brown mustache.

Vernon jerked a thumb at me and ordered: "Tell him."

I repeated what Fitzstephan had told me. The sheriff listened with an attentiveness that turned his florid face purple and had him panting. As the last word left my mouth, the district attorney snapped his fingers and said:

"Very well. He claims there were people in his apartment when the phone call came. Make a note of their names. He claims to have been in Ross over the week-end, with the—who were they? Ralph Coleman? Very well. Sheriff, see that those things are checked up. We'll learn how much truth there is to it."

I gave the sheriff the names and addresses Fitzstephan had given me. Feeney wrote them on the back of a laundry list and puffed out to get the county's crime-detecting machinery going on them.

Vernon hadn't anything to tell me. I left him to his newspapers and went downstairs. The effeminate night clerk beckoned me over to the desk and said:

"Mr. Santos asked me to tell you that services are being held in his room tonight."

I thanked the clerk and went up to Santos' room. He,

three other newshounds, and a photographer were there. The game was stud. I was sixteen dollars ahead at twelve-thirty, when I was called to the phone to listen to the district attorney's aggressive voice:

"Will you come to my room immediately?"

"Yeah." I gathered up my hat and coat, telling Santos: "Cash me in. Important call. I always have one when I get a little ahead of the game."

"Vernon?" he asked as he counted my chips.

"Yeah."

"It can't be much," he sneered, "or he'd 've sent for Red too," nodding at the photographer, "so tomorrow's readers could see him holding it in his hand."

Cotton, Feeney, and Rolly were with the district attorney. Cotton—a medium-sized man with a round dull face dimpled in the chin—was dressed in black rubber boots, slicker, and hat that were wet and muddy. He stood in the middle of the room, his round eyes looking quite proud of their owner. Feeney, straddling a chair, was playing with his mustache; and his florid face was sulky. Rolly, standing beside him, rolling a cigarette, looked vaguely amiable as usual.

Vernon closed the door behind me and said irritably:

"Cotton thinks he's discovered something. He thinks—"

Cotton came forward, chest first, interrupting:

"I don't think nothing. I know durned well—"

Vernon snapped his fingers between the marshal and me, saying, just as snappishly:

"Never mind that. We'll go out there and see."

I stopped at my room for raincoat, gun, and flashlight. We went downstairs and climbed into a muddy car. Cotton drove. Vernon sat beside him. The rest of us sat in back. Rain beat on top and curtains, trickling in through cracks.

"A hell of a night to be chasing pipe dreams," the sheriff grumbled, trying to dodge a leak.

"Dick'd do a sight better minding his own business," Rolly agreed. "What's he got to do with what don't happen in Quesada?"

"If he'd take more care of what does happen there, he wouldn't have to worry about what's down the shore," Feeney said, and he and his deputy sniggered together.

Whatever point there was to this conversation was over my head. I asked:

"What's he up to?"

"Nothing," the sheriff told me. "You'll see that it's nothing, and, by God! I'm going to give him a piece of my mind. I don't know what's the matter with Vernon, paying any attention to him at all."

That didn't mean anything to me. I peeped out between curtains. Rain and darkness shut out the scenery, but I had an idea that we were headed for some point on the East road. It was a rotten ride—wet, noisy, and bumpy. It ended in as dark, wet, and muddy a spot as any we had gone through.

Cotton switched off the lights and got out, the rest of us following, slipping and slopping in wet clay up to our ankles.

"This is too damned much," the sheriff complained.

Vernon started to say something, but the marshal was walking away, down the road. We plodded after him, keeping together more by the sound of our feet squashing in the mud than by sight. It was black.

Presently we left the road, struggled over a high wire fence, and went on with less mud under our feet, but slippery grass. We climbed a hill. Wind blew rain down it into our faces. The sheriff was panting. I was sweating. We reached the top of the hill and went down its other side, with the rustle of sea-water on rocks ahead of us. Boulders began crowding grass out of our path as the descent got steeper. Once Cotton slipped to his knees, tripping Vernon, who saved himself by grabbing me. The sheriff's panting sounded like groaning now. We turned to the left, going along in single file, the surf close beside us. We turned to the left again, climbed a slope, and halted under a low shed without walls—a wooden roof propped on a dozen posts. Ahead of us a larger building made a black blot against the almost black sky.

Cotton whispered: "Wait till I see if his car's here."

He went away. The sheriff blew out his breath and grunted: "Damn such a expedition!" Rolly sighed.

The marshal returned jubilant.

"It ain't there, so he ain't here," he said. "Come on, it'll get us out of the wet anyways."

We followed him up a muddy path between bushes to the black house, up on its back porch. We stood there while he got a window open, climbed through, and unlocked the door. Our flashlights, used for the first time now, showed us a small neat kitchen. We went in, muddying the floor.

Cotton was the only member of the party who showed any enthusiasm. His face, from hat-brim to dimpled chin, was the face of a master of ceremonies who is about to spring what he is sure will be a delightful surprise. Vernon regarded him skeptically, Feeney disgustedly, Rolly indifferently, and I—who didn't know what we were there for —no doubt curiously.

It developed that we were there to search the house. We did it, or at least Cotton did it while the rest of us pretended to help him. It was a small house. There was only one room on the ground-floor besides the kitchen, and only one—an unfinished bedroom—above. A grocer's bill and a tax-receipt in a table-drawer told me whose house it was—Harvey Whidden's. He was the big-boned deliberate man who had seen the stranger in the Chrysler with Gabrielle Collinson.

We finished the ground-floor with a blank score, and went upstairs. There, after ten minutes of poking around, we found something. Rolly pulled it out from between bed-slats and mattress. It was a small flat bundle wrapped in a white linen towel.

Cotton dropped the mattress, which he had been holding up for the deputy to look under, and joined us as we crowded around Rolly's package. Vernon took it from the deputy sheriff and unrolled it on the bed. Inside the towel were a package of hair-pins, a lace-edged white handkerchief, a silver hair-brush and comb engraved G. D. L., and a pair of black kid gloves, small and feminine.

I was more surprised than anyone else could have been.

"G. D. L.," I said, to be saying something, "could be Gabrielle Something Leggett—Mrs. Collinson's name before she was married."

Cotton said triumphantly: "You're durned right it could."

A heavy voice said from the doorway:

"Have you got a search-warrant? What the hell are you doing here if you haven't? It's burglary, and you know it."

Harvey Whidden was there. His big body, in a yellow slicker, filled the doorway. His heavy-featured face was dark and angry.

Vernon began: "Whidden, I—"

The marshal screamed, "It's him!" and pulled a gun from under his coat.

I pushed his arm as he fired at the man in the doorway. The bullet hit the wall.

Whidden's face was now more astonished than angry. He jumped back through the doorway and ran downstairs. Cotton, upset by my push, straightened himself up, cursed me, and ran out after Whidden. Vernon, Feeney, and Rolly stood staring after them.

I said: "This is good clean sport, but it makes no sense to me. What's it all about?"

Nobody told me. I said: "This comb and brush were on Mrs. Collinson's table when we searched the house, Rolly."

The deputy sheriff nodded uncertainly, still staring at the door. No noise came through it now. I asked:

"Would there be any special reason for Cotton framing Whidden?"

The sheriff said: "They ain't good friends." (I had noticed that.) "What do you think, Vern?"

The district attorney took his gaze from the door, rolled the things in their towel again, and stuffed the bundle in his pocket. "Come on," he snapped, and strode downstairs.

The front door was open. We saw nothing, heard nothing, of Cotton and Whidden. A Ford—Whidden's—stood at the front gate soaking up rain. We got into it. Vernon took the wheel, and drove to the house in the cove. We hammered at its door until it was opened by an old man in gray underwear, put there as caretaker by the sheriff.

The old man told us that Cotton had been there at eight o'clock that night, just, he said, to look around again. He, the caretaker, didn't know no reason why the marshal had to be watched, so he hadn't bothered him, letting him do what he wanted, and, so far as he knew, the marshal hadn't taken any of the Collinsons' property, though of course he might of.

Vernon and Feeney gave the old man hell, and we went back to Quesada.

Rolly was with me on the back seat. I asked him:

"Who is this Whidden? Why should Cotton pick on him?"

"Well, for one thing, Harve's got kind of a bad name, from being mixed up in the rum-running that used to go on here, and from being in trouble now and then."

"Yeah? And for another thing?"

The deputy sheriff frowned, hesitating, hunting for words; and before he had found them we were stopping in front of a vine-covered cottage on a dark street corner. The district attorney led the way to its front porch and rang the bell.

After a little while a woman's voice sounded overhead:

"Who's there?"

We had to retreat to the steps to see her—Mrs. Cotton at a second-story window.

"Dick got home yet?" Vernon asked.

"No, Mr. Vernon, he hasn't. I was getting worried. Wait a minute; I'll come down."

"Don't bother," he said. "We won't wait. I'll see him in the morning."

"No. Wait," she said urgently and vanished from the window.

A moment later she opened the front door. Her blue

eyes were dark and excited. She had on a rose bathrobe.

"You needn't have bothered," the district attorney said. "There was nothing special. We got separated from him a little while ago, and just wanted to know if he'd got back yet. He's all right."

"Was——?" Her hands worked folds of her bathrobe over her thin breasts. "Was he after——after Harvey——Harvey Whidden?"

Vernon didn't look at her when he said, "Yes;" and he said it without showing his teeth. Feeney and Rolly looked as uncomfortable as Vernon.

Mrs. Cotton's face turned pink. Her lower lip trembled, blurring her words.

"Don't believe him, Mr. Vernon. Don't believe a word he tells you. Harve didn't have anything to do with those Collinsons, with neither one of them. Don't let Dick tell you he did. He didn't."

Vernon looked at his feet and didn't say anything. Rolly and Feeney were looking intently out through the open door——we were standing just inside it——at the rain. Nobody seemed to have any intention of speaking.

I asked, "No?" putting more doubt in my voice than I actually felt.

"No, he didn't," she cried, turning her face to me. "He couldn't. He couldn't have had anything to do with it." The pink went out of her face, leaving it white and desperate. "He——he was here that night——all night——from before seven until daylight."

"Where was your husband?"

"Up in the city, at his mother's."

"What's her address?"

She gave it to me, a Noe Street number.

"Did anybody——?"

"Aw, come on," the sheriff protested, still staring at the rain. "Ain't that enough?"

Mrs. Cotton turned from me to the district attorney again, taking hold of one of his arms.

"Don't tell it on me, please, Mr. Vernon," she begged. "I don't know what I'd do if it came out. But I had to tell you. I couldn't let him put it on Harve. Please, you won't tell anybody else?"

The district attorney swore that under no circumstances would he, or any of us, repeat what she had told us to anybody; and the sheriff and his deputy agreed with vigorous red-faced nods.

But when we were in the Ford again, away from her, they forgot their embarrassment and became manhunters again. Within ten minutes they had decided that Cotton, instead of going to San Francisco to his mother's Friday night, had remained in Quesada, had killed Collinson, had gone to the city to phone Fitzstephan and mail the letter, and then had returned to Quesada in time to kidnap Mrs. Collinson; planning from the first to plant the evidence against Whidden, with whom he had long been on bad terms, having always suspected what everybody else knew —that Whidden was Mrs. Cotton's lover.

The sheriff—he whose chivalry had kept me from more thoroughly questioning the woman a few minutes ago— now laughed his belly up and down.

"That's rich," he gurgled. "Him out framing Harve, and Harve getting himself a alibi in *his* bed. Dick's face ought to be a picture for Puck when we spring that on him. Let's find him tonight."

"Better wait," I advised. "It won't hurt to check up his San Francisco trip before we put it to him. All we've got on him so far is that he tried to frame Whidden. If he's the murderer and kidnapper he seems to have gone to a lot of unnecessary foolishness."

Feeney scowled at me and defended their theory:

"Maybe he was more interested in framing Harve than anything else."

"Maybe," I said; "but it won't hurt to give him a little more rope and see what he does with it."

Feeney was against that. He wanted to grab the marshal *pronto;* but Vernon reluctantly backed me up. We dropped Rolly at his house and returned to the hotel.

In my room, I put in a phone-call for the agency in San Francisco. While I was waiting for the connection knuckles tapped my door. I opened it and let in Jack Santos, pajamaed, bathrobed, and slippered.

"Have a nice ride?" he asked, yawning.

"Swell."

"Anything break?"

"Not for publication, but—under the hat—the new angle is that our marshal is trying to hang the job on his wife's boy friend—with homemade evidence. The other big officials think Cotton turned the trick himself."

"That ought to get them all on the front page." Santos sat on the foot of my bed and lit a cigarette. "Ever happen to hear that Feeney was Cotton's rival for the telegraphing hand of the present Mrs. Cotton, until she picked the marshal—the triumph of dimples over mustachios?"

"No," I admitted. "What of it?"

"How do I know? I just happened to pick it up. A fellow in the garage told me."

"How long ago?"

"That they were rival suitors? Less than a couple of years."

I got my San Francisco call, and told Field—the agency night-man—to have somebody check up the marshal's Noe Street visit. Santos yawned and went out while I was talking. I went to bed when I had finished.

XVII : BELOW DULL POINT

The telephone bell brought me out of sleep a little before ten the following morning. Mickey Linehan, talking from

San Francisco, told me Cotton had arrived at his mother's house at between seven and seven-thirty Saturday morning. The marshal had slept for five or six hours—telling his mother he had been up all night laying for a burglar—and had left for home at six that evening.

Cotton was coming in from the street when I reached the lobby. He was red-eyed and weary, but still determined.

"Catch Whidden?" I asked.

"No, durn him, but I will. Say, I'm glad you jiggled my arm, even if it did let him get away. I—well, sometimes a fellow's enthusiasm gets the best of his judgment."

"Yeah. We stopped at your house on our way back, to see how you'd made out."

"I ain't been home yet," he said. "I put in the whole durned night hunting for that fellow. Where's Vern and Feeney?"

"Pounding their ears. Better get some sleep yourself," I suggested. "I'll ring you up if anything happens."

He set off for home. I went into the café for breakfast. I was half through when Vernon joined me there. He had telegrams from the San Francisco police department and the Marin County sheriff's office, confirming Fitzstephan's alibis.

"I got my report on Cotton," I said. "He reached his mother's at seven or a little after Saturday morning, and left at six that evening."

"Seven or a little after?" Vernon didn't like that. If the marshal had been in San Francisco at that time he could hardly have been abducting the girl. "Are you sure?"

"No, but that's the best we've been able to do so far. There's Fitzstephan now." Looking through the café door, I had seen the novelist's lanky back at the hotel desk. "Excuse me a moment."

I went over and got Fitzstephan, bringing him back to the table with me, and introducing him to Vernon. The district attorney stood up to shake hands with him, but was too busy with thoughts of Cotton to bother now with anything else. Fitzstephan said he had had breakfast before leaving the city, and ordered a cup of coffee. Just then I was called to the phone.

Cotton's voice, but excited almost beyond recognition:

"For God's sake get Vernon and Feeney and come up here."

"What's the matter?" I asked.

"Hurry! Something awful's happened. Hurry!" he cried, and hung up.

I went back to the table and told Vernon about it. He jumped up, upsetting Fitzstephan's coffee. Fitzstephan got up too, but hesitated, looking at me.

"Come on," I invited him. "Maybe this'll be one of the things you like."

Fitzstephan's car was in front of the hotel. The marshal's house was only seven blocks away. Its front door was open. Vernon knocked on the frame as we went in, but we didn't wait for an answer.

Cotton met us in the hall. His eyes were round and bloodshot in a face as hard-white as marble. He tried to say something, but couldn't get the words past his tight-set teeth. He gestured towards the door behind him with a fist that was clenched on a piece of brown paper.

Through the doorway we saw Mrs. Cotton. She was lying on the blue-carpeted floor. She had on a pale blue dress. Her throat was covered with dark bruises. Her lips and tongue—the tongue, swollen, hung out—were darker than the bruises. Her eyes were wide open, bulging, up-turned, and dead. Her hand, when I touched it, was still warm.

Cotton, following us into the room, held out the brown paper in his hand. It was an irregularly torn piece of wrapping paper, covered on both sides with writing—nervously, unevenly, hastily scribbled in pencil. A softer pencil had been used than on Fitzstephan's message, and the paper was a darker brown.

I was closest to Cotton. I took the paper, and read it aloud hurriedly, skipping unnecessary words:

"Whidden came last night . . . said husband after him

. . . frame him for Collinson trouble . . . I hid him in garret . . . he said only way to save him was to say he was here Friday night . . . said if I didn't they'd hang him . . . when Mr. Vernon came Harve said he'd kill me if I didn't . . . so I said it . . . but he wasn't here that night . . . I didn't know he was guilty then . . . told me afterwards . . . tried to kidnap her Thursday night . . . husband nearly caught him . . . came in office after Collinson sent telegram and saw it . . . followed him and killed him . . . went to San Francisco, drinking whiskey . . . decided to go through with kidnapping anyway . . . phoned man who knew her to try to learn who he could get money from . . . too drunk to talk good . . . wrote letter and came back . . . met her on road . . . took her to old bootleggers' hiding place somewhere below Dull Point . . . goes in boat . . . afraid he'll kill me . . . locked in garret . . . writing while he's down getting food . . . murderer . . . I won't help him . . . Daisy Cotton."

The sheriff and Rolly had arrived while I was reading it. Feeney's face was as white and set as Cotton's.

Vernon bared his teeth at the marshal, snarling:

"You wrote that."

Feeney grabbed it from my hands, looked at it, shook his head, and said hoarsely:

"No, that's her writing, all right."

Cotton was babbling:

"No, before God, I didn't. I planted that stuff on him, I'll admit that, but that was all. I come home and find her like this. I swear to God!"

"Where were you Friday night?" Vernon asked.

"Here, watching the house. I thought—I thought he might— But he wasn't here that night. I watched till daybreak and then went to the city. I didn't—"

The sheriff's bellow drowned the rest of Cotton's words. The sheriff was waving the dead woman's letter. He bellowed:

"Below Dull Point! What are we waiting for?"

He plunged out of the house, the rest of us following. Cotton and Rolly rode to the waterfront in the deputy's car. Vernon, the sheriff, and I rode with Fitzstephan. The sheriff cried throughout the short trip, tears splashing on the automatic pistol he held in his lap.

At the waterfront we changed from the cars to a green and white motor boat run by a pink-cheeked, tow-headed youngster called Tim. Tim said he didn't know anything about any bootleggers' hiding places below Dull Point, but if there was one there he could find it. In his hands the boat produced a lot of speed, but not enough for Feeney and Cotton. They stood together in the bow, guns in their fists, dividing their time between straining forward and yelling back for more speed.

Half an hour from the dock, we rounded a blunt promontory that the others called Dull Point, and Tim cut down our speed, putting the boat in closer to the rocks that jumped up high and sharp at the water's edge. We were now all eyes—eyes that soon ached from staring under the noon sun but kept on staring. Twice we saw clefts in the rock-walled shore, pushed hopefully in to them, saw that they were blind, leading nowhere, opening into no hiding-places.

The third cleft was even more hopeless-looking at first sight, but, now that Dull Point was some distance behind us, we couldn't pass up anything. We slid in to the cleft, got close enough to decide that it was another blind one, gave it up, and told Tim to go on. We were washed another couple of feet nearer before the tow-headed boy could bring the boat around.

Cotton, in the bow, bent forward from the waist and yelled:

"Here it is."

He pointed his gun at one side of the cleft. Tim let the boat drift in another foot or so. Craning our necks, we could see that what we had taken for the shore-line on that side was actually a high, thin, saw-toothed ledge of rock, separated from the cliff at this end by twenty feet of water.

"Put her in," Feeney ordered.

Tim frowned at the water, hesitated, said: "She can't make it."

The boat backed him up by shuddering suddenly under our feet, with an unpleasant rasping noise.

"That be damned!" the sheriff bawled. "Put her in."

Tim took a look at the sheriff's wild face, and put her in.

The boat shuddered under our feet again, more violently, and now there was a tearing sound in with the rasping, but we went through the opening and turned down behind the saw-tooth ledge.

We were in a v-shaped pocket, twenty feet wide where we had come in, say eighty feet long, high-walled, inaccessible by land, accessible by sea only as we had come. The water that floated us—and was coming in rapidly to sink us—ran a third of the way down the pocket. White sand paved the other two thirds. A small boat was resting its nose on the edge of the sand. It was empty. Nobody was in sight. There didn't seem to be anywhere for anybody to hide. There were footprints, large and small, in the sand, empty tin cans, and the remains of a fire.

"Harve's," Rolly said, nodding at the boat.

Our boat grounded beside it. We jumped, splashed, ashore—Cotton ahead, the others spread out behind him.

As suddenly as if he had sprung out of the air, Harvey Whidden appeared in the far end of the v, standing in the sand, a rifle in his hands. Anger and utter astonishment were mixed in his heavy face, and in his voice when he yelled:

"You God-damned double-crossing—" The noise his rifle made blotted out the rest of his words.

Cotton had thrown himself down sideways. The rifle bullet missed him by inches, sang between Fitzstephan and me, nicking his hat-brim, and splattered on the rocks behind. Four of our guns went off together, some more than once.

Whidden went over backwards, his feet flying in the air. He was dead when we got to him—three bullets in his chest, one in his head.

We found Gabrielle Collinson cowering back in the corner of a narrow-mouthed hole in the rock wall—a long triangular cave whose mouth had been hidden from our view by the slant at which it was set. There were blankets in there, spread over a pile of dried seaweed, some canned goods, a lantern, and another rifle.

The girl's small face was flushed and feverish, and her voice was hoarse: she had a cold in her chest. She was too frightened at first to tell us anything coherent, and apparently recognized neither Fitzstephan nor me.

The boat we had come in was out of commission. Whidden's boat couldn't be trusted to carry more than three with safety through the surf. Tim and Rolly set off for Quesada in it, to get us a larger vessel. It was an hour-and-a-half's round trip. While they were gone we worked on the girl, soothing her, assuring her that she was among friends, that there was nothing to be afraid of now. Her eyes gradually became less scary, her breathing easier, and her nails less tightly pressed into her palms. At the end of an hour she was answering our questions.

She said she knew nothing of Whidden's attempt to kidnap her Thursday night, nothing of the telegram Eric had sent me. She sat up all Friday night waiting for him to return from his walk, and at daylight, frantic at his failure to return, had gone to look for him. She found him—as I had. Then she went back to the house and tried to commit suicide—to put an end to the curse by shooting herself.

"I tried twice," she whispered; "but I couldn't. I couldn't. I was too much a coward. I couldn't keep the pistol pointing at myself while I did it. I tried the first time to shoot myself in the temple, and then in the breast; but I hadn't the courage. Each time I jerked it away just before I fired. And after the second time I couldn't even get courage to try again."

She changed her clothes then—evening clothes, now muddy and torn from her search—and drove away from the house. She didn't say where she had intended going. She didn't seem to know. Probably she hadn't had any destination—was simply going away from the place where the curse had settled on her husband.

She hadn't driven far when she had seen a machine

coming towards her, driven by the man who had brought her here. He had turned his car across the road in front of her, blocking the road. Trying to avoid hitting his car, she had run into a tree—and hadn't known anything else until she had awakened in the cave. She had been here since then. The man had left her here alone most of the time. She had neither strength nor courage to escape by swimming, and there was no other way out.

The man had told her nothing, had asked her nothing, had addressed no words to her except to say, "Here's some food," or, "Till I bring you some water, you'll have to get along on canned tomatoes when you're thirsty," or other things of that sort. She never remembered having seen him before. She didn't know his name. He was the only man she had seen since her husband's death.

"What did he call you?" I asked. "Mrs. Carter? Or Mrs. Collinson?"

She frowned thoughtfully, then shook her head, saying:

"I don't think he ever called me by name. He never spoke unless he had to, and he wasn't here very much. I was usually alone."

"How long had he been here this time?"

"Since before daylight. The noise of his boat woke me up."

"Sure? This is important. Are you sure he's been here since daylight?"

"Yes."

I was sitting on my heels in front of her. Cotton was standing on my left, beside the sheriff. I looked up at the marshal and said:

"That puts it up to you, Cotton. Your wife was still warm when we saw her—after eleven."

He goggled at me, stammering: "Wh-what's that you say?"

On the other side of me I heard Vernon's teeth click together sharply.

I said:

"Your wife was afraid Whidden would kill her, and wrote that statement. But he didn't kill her. He's been here since daylight. You found the statement, learned from it that they *had* been too friendly. Well, what did you do then?"

"That's a lie," he cried. "There ain't a word of truth in it. She was dead there when I found her. I never—"

"You killed her," Vernon barked at him over my head. "You choked her, counting on that statement to throw suspicion on Whidden."

"That's a lie," the marshal cried again, and made the mistake of trying to get his gun out.

Feeney slugged him, dropping him, and had handcuffs on his wrists before he could get up again.

XVIII : THE PINEAPPLE

"It doesn't make sense," I said. "It's dizzy. When we grab our man—or woman—we're going to find it's a goof, and Napa will get it instead of the gallows."

"That," Owen Fitzstephan said, "is characteristic of you. You're stumped, bewildered, flabbergasted. Do you admit you've met your master, have run into a criminal too wily for you? Not you. He's outwitted you: therefore he's an idiot or a lunatic. Now really. Of course there's a certain unexpected modesty to that attitude."

"But he's got to be goofy," I insisted. "Look: Mayenne marries—"

"Are you," he asked disgustedly, "going to recite that catalogue again?"

"You've got a flighty mind. That's no good in this business. You don't catch murderers by amusing yourself with interesting thoughts. You've got to sit down to all the facts you can get and turn them over and over till they click."

"If that's your technic, you'll have to put up with it," he said; "but I'm damned if I see why I should suffer. You recited the Mayenne-Leggett-Collinson history step by step last night at least half a dozen times. You've done nothing else since breakfast this morning. I'm getting enough of it. Nobody's mysteries ought to be as tiresome as you're making this one."

"Hell," I said; "I sat up half the night after you went to bed and recited it to myself. You got to turn them over and over, my boy, till they click."

"I like the Nick Carter school better. Aren't you even threatened with any of the conclusions that this turning-them-over-and-over is supposed to lead to?"

"Yeah, I've got one. It's that Vernon and Feeney are wrong in thinking that Cotton was working with Whidden on the kidnapping, and double-crossed him. According to them, Cotton thought up the plan and persuaded Whidden to do the rough stuff while the marshal used his official position to cover him up. Collinson stumbled on the plan and was killed. Then Cotton made his wife write that statement—it's phony, right enough, was dictated to her—killed her, and led us to Whidden. Cotton was the first man ashore when we got to the hiding place—to make sure Whidden was killed resisting arrest before he could talk."

Fitzstephan ran long fingers through his sorrel hair and asked:

"Don't you think jealousy would have given Cotton motive enough?"

"Yeah. But where's Whidden's motive for putting himself in Cotton's hands? Besides, where does that layout fit in with the Temple racket?"

"Are you sure," Fitzstephan asked, "that you're right in thinking there must be a connection?"

"Yeah. Gabrielle's father, step-mother, physician, and husband have been slaughtered in less than a handful of weeks—all the people closest to her. That's enough to tie it all together for me. If you want more links, I can point them out to you. Upton and Ruppert were the apparent instigators of the first trouble, and got killed. Haldorn of the second, and got killed. Whidden of the third, and got killed. Mrs. Leggett killed her husband; Cotton apparently killed his wife; and Haldorn would have killed his if I hadn't blocked him. Gabrielle, as a child, was made to kill her mother; Gabrielle's maid was made to kill Riese, and nearly me. Leggett left behind him a statement explaining —not altogether satisfactorily—everything, and was killed. So did and was Mrs. Cotton. Call any of these pairs coincidences. Call any couple of pairs coincidences. You'll still have enough left to point at somebody who's got a system he likes, and sticks to it."

Fitzstephan squinted thoughtfully at me, agreeing:

"There may be something in that. It does, as you put it, look like the work of one mind."

"And a goofy one."

"Be obstinate about it," he said. "But even your goof must have a motive."

"Why?"

"Damn your sort of mind," he said with good-natured impatience. "If he had no motive connected with Gabrielle, why should his crimes be connected with her?"

"We don't know that all of them are," I pointed out. "We only know of the ones that are."

He grinned and said:

"You'll go any distance to disagree, won't you?"

I said:

"Then again, maybe the goof's crimes are connected with Gabrielle because he is."

Fitzstephan let his gray eyes go sleepy over that, pursing his mouth, looking at the door closed between my room and Gabrielle's.

"All right," he said, looking at me again. "Who's your maniac close to Gabrielle?"

"The closest and goofiest person to Gabrielle is Gabrielle herself."

Fitzstephan got up and crossed the hotel room—I was sitting on the edge of the bed—to shake my hand with solemn enthusiasm.

"You're wonderful," he said. "You amaze me. Ever have night sweats? Put out your tongue and say, 'Ah.'"

"Suppose," I began, but was interrupted by a feeble tapping on the corridor door.

I went to the door and opened it. A thin man of my own age and height in wrinkled black clothes stood in the corridor. He was breathing heavily through a red-veined nose, and his small brown eyes were timid.

"You know me," he said apologetically.

"Yeah. Come in." I introduced him to Fitzstephan: "This is the Tom Fink who was one of Haldorn's helpers in the Temple of the Holy Grail."

Fink looked reproachfully at me, then dragged his crumpled hat from his head and crossed the room to shake Fitzstephan's hand. That done, he returned to me and said, almost whispering:

"I come down to tell you something."

"Yeah?"

He fidgeted, turning his hat around and around in his hands. I winked at Fitzstephan and went out with Fink. In the corridor, I closed the door and stopped, saying: "Let's have it."

Fink rubbed his lips with his tongue and then with the back of one scrawny hand. He said, in his half-whisper:

"I come down to tell you something I thought you ought to know."

"Yeah?"

"It's about this fellow Whidden that was killed."

"Yeah?"

"He was—"

The door to my room split open. Floors, walls, and ceiling wriggled under, around, and over us. There was too much noise to be heard—a roar that was felt bodily. Tom Fink was carried away from me, backward. I had sense enough to throw myself down as I was blown in the opposite direction, and got nothing worse out of it than a bruised shoulder when I hit the wall. A door-frame stopped Fink, wickedly, its edge catching the back of his head. He came forward again, folding over to lie face-down on the floor, still except for blood running from his head.

I got up and made for my room. Fitzstephan was a mangled pile of flesh and clothing in the center of the floor. My bed was burning. There was neither glass nor wire netting left in the window. I saw these things mechanically as I staggered toward Gabrielle's room. The connecting door was open—perhaps blown open.

She was crouching on all fours in bed, facing the foot, her feet on the pillows. Her nightdress was torn at one shoulder. Her green-brown eyes—glittering under brown curls that had tumbled down to hide her forehead—were the eyes of an animal gone trap-crazy. Saliva glistened on her pointed chin. There was nobody else in the room.

"Where's the nurse?" My voice was choked.

The girl said nothing. Her eyes kept their crazy terror focused on me.

"Get under the covers," I ordered. "Want to get pneumonia?"

She didn't move. I walked around to the side of the bed, lifting an end of the covers with one hand, reaching out the other to help her, saying:

"Come on, get inside."

She made a queer noise deep in her chest, dropped her head, and put her sharp teeth into the back of my hand. It hurt. I put her under the covers, returned to my room, and was pushing my burning mattress through the window when people began to arrive.

"Get a doctor," I called to the first of them; "and stay out of here."

I had got rid of the mattress by the time Mickey Linehan pushed through the crowd that was now filling the corridor. Mickey blinked at what was left of Fitzstephan, at me, and asked:

"What the hell?"

His big loose mouth sagged at the ends, looking like a grin turned upside down.

I licked burnt fingers and asked unpleasantly:

"What the hell does it look like?"

"More trouble, sure." The grin turned right side up on his red face. "Sure—you're here."

Ben Rolly came in. "Tch, tch, tch," he said, looking around. "What do you suppose happened?"

"Pineapple," I said.

"Tch, tch, tch."

Doctor George came in and knelt beside the wreck of Fitzstephan. George had been Gabrielle's physician since her return from the cave the previous day. He was a short, chunky, middle-aged man with a lot of black hair everywhere except on his lips, cheeks, chin, and nose-bridge. His hairy hands moved over Fitzstephan.

"What's Fink been doing?" I asked Mickey.

"Hardly any. I got on his tail when they sprung him yesterday noon. He went from the hoosegow to a hotel on Kearny Street and got himself a room. He spent most of the afternoon in the Public Library, reading the newspaper files on the girl's troubles, from beginning to date. He ate after that, and went back to the hotel. He could have back-doored me. If he didn't, he camped in his room all night. It was dark at midnight when I knocked off so I could be on the job at six A.M. He showed at seven something, got breakfast, and grabbed a rattler for Poston, changed to the stage for here, and came straight to the hotel, asking for you. That's the crop."

"Damn my soul!" the kneeling doctor exclaimed. "The man's not dead."

I didn't believe him. Fitzstephan's right arm was gone, and most of his right leg. His body was too twisted to see what was left of it, but there was only one side to his face. I said:

"There's another one out in the hall, with his head knocked in."

"Oh, he's all right," the doctor muttered without looking up. "But this one—well, damn my soul!"

He scrambled to his feet and began ordering this and that. He was excited. A couple of men came in from the corridor. The woman who had been nursing Gabrielle Collinson—a Mrs. Herman—joined them, and another man with a blanket. They took Fitzstephan away.

"That fellow out in the hall Fink?" Rolly asked.

"Yeah." I told him what Fink had told me, adding: "He hadn't finished when the blow-up came."

"Suppose the bomb was meant for him, meant to keep him from finishing?"

Mickey said: "Nobody followed him down from the city, except me."

"Maybe," I said. "Better see what they're doing with him, Mick."

Mickey went out.

"This window was closed," I told Rolly. "There was no noise as of something being thrown through the glass just before the explosion; and there's no broken window-glass inside the room. The screen was over it, too, so we can say the pineapple wasn't chucked in through the window."

Rolly nodded vaguely, looking at the door to Gabrielle's room.

"Fink and I were in the corridor talking," I went on. "I ran straight back through here to her room. Nobody could have got out of her room after the explosion without my seeing them—or hearing them. There wasn't finger-snapping time between my losing sight of her corridor-door from the outside, and seeing it again from the inside. The screen over her window is still O K."

"Mrs. Herman wasn't in there with her?" Rolly asked.

"She was supposed to be, but wasn't. We'll find out about that. There's no use thinking Mrs. Collinson chucked the bomb. She's been in bed since we brought her back from Dull Point yesterday. She couldn't have had the bomb planted there because she had no way of knowing that she was going to occupy the room. Nobody's been in there since except you, Feeney, Vernon, the doctor, the nurse, and me."

"I wasn't going to say she had anything to do with it," the deputy sheriff mumbled. "What does she say?"

"Nothing yet. We'll try her now, though I doubt if it'll get us much."

It didn't. Gabrielle lay in the middle of the bed, the covers gathered close to her chin as if she was prepared to duck down under them at the first alarm, and shook her head No to everything we asked, whether the answer fit or didn't.

The nurse came in, a big-breasted, red-haired woman of forty-something with a face that seemed honest because it was homely, freckled, and blue-eyed. She swore on the Gideon Bible that she had been out of the room for less than five minutes, just going downstairs for some stationery, intending to write a letter to her nephew in Vallejo while her patient was sleeping; and that was the only time she had been out of the room all day. She had met nobody in the corridor, she said.

"You left the door unlocked?" I asked.

"Yes, so I wouldn't be as likely to wake her when I came back."

"Where's the stationery you got?"

"I didn't get it. I heard the explosion and ran back upstairs." Fear came into her face, turning the freckles to ghastly spots. "You don't think—!"

"Better look after Mrs. Collinson," I said gruffly.

XIX : THE DEGENERATE

Rolly and I went back to my room, closing the connecting door. He said:

"Tch, tch, tch. I'd of thought Mrs. Herman was the last person in the world to—"

"You ought to've," I grumbled. "You recommended her. Who is she?"

"She's Tod Herman's wife. He's got the garage. She used to be a trained nurse before she married Tod. I thought she was all right."

"She got a nephew in Vallejo?"

"Uh-huh; that would be the Schultz kid that works at Mare Island. How do you suppose she come to get mixed up in—?"

"Probably didn't, or she would have had the writing paper she went after. Put somebody here to keep people out till we can borrow a San Francisco bomb-expert to look it over."

The deputy called one of the men in from the corridor, and we left him looking important in the room. Mickey Linehan was in the lobby when we got there.

"Fink's got a cracked skull. He's on his way to the county hospital with the other wreck."

"Fitzstephan dead yet?" I asked.

"Nope, and the doc thinks if they get him over where they got the right kind of implements they can keep him from dying. God knows what for—the shape he's in! But that's just the kind of stuff a croaker thinks is a lot of fun."

"Was Aaronia Haldorn sprung with Fink?" I asked.

"Yes. Al Mason's tailing her."

"Call up the Old Man and see if Al's reported anything on her. Tell the Old Man what's happened here, and see if they've found Andrews."

"Andrews?" Rolly asked as Mickey headed for the phone. "What's the matter with him?"

"Nothing that I know of; only we haven't been able to find him to tell him Mrs. Collinson has been rescued. His office hasn't seen him since yesterday morning, and nobody will say they know where he is."

"Tch, tch, tch. Is there any special reason for wanting him?"

"I don't want her on my hands the rest of my life," I said. "He's in charge of her affairs, he's responsible for her, and I want to turn her over to him."

Rolly nodded vaguely.

We went outside and asked all the people we could find all the questions we could think of. None of the answers led anywhere, except to repeated assurance that the bomb hadn't been chucked through the window. We found six people who had been in sight of that side of the hotel immediately before, and at the time of, the explosion; and none of them had seen anything that could be twisted into bearing on the bomb-throwing.

Mickey came away from the phone with the information that Aaronia Haldorn, when released from the city prison, had gone to the home of a family named Jeffries in San Mateo, and had been there ever since; and that Dick Foley, hunting for Andrews, had hopes of locating him in Sausalito.

District attorney Vernon and sheriff Feeney, with a horde of reporters and photographers close behind them, arrived from the county seat. They went through a lot of detecting motions that got them nowhere except on the front pages of all the San Francisco and Los Angeles papers —the place they liked best.

I had Gabrielle Collinson moved into another room in the hotel, and posted Mickey Linehan next door, with the connecting door unlocked. Gabrielle talked now, to Vernon, Feeney, Rolly, and me. What she said didn't help us much. She had been asleep, she said; had been awakened by a terrible noise and a terrible jarring of her bed; and then I had come in. That was all she knew.

Late in the afternoon McCracken, a San Francisco police department bomb-expert, arrived. After examining all the fragments of this and that which he could sweep up, he gave us a preliminary verdict that the bomb had been a small one, of aluminum, charged with a low-grade nitroglycerine, and exploded by a crude friction device.

"Amateur or professional job?" I asked.

McCracken spit out loose shreds of tobacco—he was one of the men who chew their cigarettes—and said:

"I'd say it was made by a guy that knew his stuff, but had to work with what he could get his hands on. I'll tell you more when I've worked this junk over in the lab."

"No timer on it?" I asked.

"No signs of one."

Doctor George returned from the county seat with the news that what was left of Fitzstephan still breathed. The doctor was tickled pink. I had to yell at him to make him hear my questions about Fink and Gabrielle. Then he told me Fink's life wasn't in danger, and the girl's cold was enough better that she might get out of bed if she wished. I asked about her nerves, but he was in too much of a hurry to get back to Fitzstephan to pay much attention to anything else.

"Hm-m-m, yes, certainly," he muttered, edging past me towards his car. "Quiet, rest, freedom from anxiety," and he was gone.

I ate dinner with Vernon and Feeney in the hotel café that evening. They didn't think I had told them all I knew about the bombing, and kept me on the witness stand throughout the meal, though neither of them accused me pointblank of holding out.

After dinner I went up to my new room. Mickey was sprawled on the bed reading a newspaper.

"Go feed yourself," I said. "How's our baby?"

"She's up. How do you figure her—only fifty cards to her deck?"

"Why?" I asked. "What's she been doing?"

"Nothing. I was just thinking."

"That's from having an empty stomach. Better go eat."

"Aye, aye, Mr. Continental," he said and went out.

The next room was quiet. I listened at the door and then tapped it. Mrs. Herman's voice said: "Come in."

She was sitting beside the bed making gaudy butterflies on a piece of yellowish cloth stretched on hoops. Gabrielle Collinson sat in a rocking chair on the other side of the room, frowning at hands clasped in her lap—clasped hard enough to whiten the knuckles and spread the finger-ends. She had on the tweed clothes in which she had been kidnapped. They were still rumpled, but had been brushed clean of mud. She didn't look up when I came in. The nurse did, pushing her freckles together in an uneasy smile.

"Good evening," I said, trying to make a cheerful entrance. "Looks like we're running out of invalids."

That brought no response from the girl, too much from the nurse.

"Yes, indeed," Mrs. Herman exclaimed with exaggerated enthusiasm. "We can't call Mrs. Collinson an invalid now—now that she's up and about—and I'm almost sorry that she is—he-he-he—because I certainly never did have such a nice patient in every way; but that's what we girls used to say at the hospital when we were in training: the nicer the patient was, the shorter the time we'd have him, while you take a disagreeable one and she'd live—I mean, be there—forever and a day, it seems like. I remember once when—"

I made a face at her and wagged my head at the door. She let the rest of her words die inside her open mouth. Her face turned red, then white. She dropped her embroidery and got up, saying idiotically: "Yes, yes, that's the way it always is. Well, I've got to go see about those—you know—what do you call them. Pardon me for a few minutes, please." She went out quickly, sidewise, as if afraid I'd sneak up behind her and kick her.

When the door had closed, Gabrielle looked up from her hands and said:

"Owen is dead."

She didn't ask, she said it; but there was no way of treating it except as a question.

"No." I sat down in the nurse's chair and fished out cigarettes. "He's alive."

"Will he live?" Her voice was still husky from her cold.

"The doctors think so," I exaggerated.

"If he lives, will he—?" She left the question unfinished, but her husky voice seemed impersonal enough.

"He'll be pretty badly maimed."

She spoke more to herself than to me:

"That should be even more satisfactory."

I grinned. If I was as good an actor as I thought, there was nothing in the grin but good-humored amusement.

"Laugh," she said gravely. "I wish you could laugh it away. But you can't. It's there. It will always be there." She looked down at her hands and whispered: "Cursed."

Spoken in any other tone, that last word would have been melodramatic, ridiculously stagey. But she said it automatically, without any feeling, as if saying it had become a habit. I could see her lying in bed in the dark, whispering it to herself hour after hour, whispering it to her body when she put on her clothes, to her face reflected in mirrors, day after day.

I squirmed in my chair and growled:

"Stop it. Just because a bad-tempered woman works off her hatred and rage in a ten-twenty-thirty speech about—"

"No, no; my step-mother merely put in words what I have always known. I hadn't known it was in the Dain blood, but I knew it was in mine. How could I help knowing? Hadn't I the physical marks of degeneracy?" She crossed the room to stand in front of me, turning her head sidewise, holding back her curls with both hands. "Look at my ears—without lobes, pointed tops. People don't have ears like that. Animals do." She turned her face to me again, still holding back her hair. "Look at my forehead—its smallness, its shape—animal. My teeth." She bared them —white, small, pointed. "The shape of my face." Her hands left her hair and slid down her cheeks, coming together under her oddly pointed small chin.

"Is that all?" I asked. "Haven't you got cloven hoofs? All right. Say these things are as peculiar as you seem to think they are. What of it? Your step-mother was a Dain, and she was poison, but where were her physical marks of degeneracy? Wasn't she as normal, as wholesome-looking as any woman you're likely to find?"

"But that's no answer." She shook her head impatiently.

"She didn't have the physical marks perhaps. I have, and the mental ones too. I—" She sat down on the side of the bed close to me, elbows on knees, tortured white face between hands. "I've not ever been able to think clearly, as other people do, even the simplest thoughts. Everything is always so confused in my mind. No matter what I try to think about, there's a fog that gets between me and it, and other thoughts get between us, so I barely catch a glimpse of the thought I want before I lose it again, and have to hunt through the fog, and at last find it, only to have the same thing happen again and again and again. Can you understand how horrible that can become: going through life like that—year after year—knowing you will always be like that—or worse?"

"I can't," I said. "It sounds normal as hell to me. Nobody thinks clearly, no matter what they pretend. Thinking's a dizzy business, a matter of catching as many of those foggy glimpses as you can and fitting them together the best you can. That's why people hang on so tight to their beliefs and opinions; because, compared to the haphazard way in which they're arrived at, even the goofiest opinion seems wonderfully clear, sane, and self-evident. And if you let it get away from you, then you've got to dive back into that foggy muddle to wangle yourself out another to take its place."

She took her face out of her hands and smiled shyly at me, saying:

"It's funny I didn't like you before." Her face became serious again. "But—"

"But nothing," I said. "You're old enough to know that everybody except very crazy people and very stupid people suspect themselves now and then—or whenever they happen to think about it—of not being exactly sane. Evidence of goofiness is easily found: the more you dig into yourself, the more you turn up. Nobody's mind could stand the sort of examination you've been giving yours. Going around trying to prove yourself cuckoo! It's a wonder you haven't driven yourself nuts."

"Perhaps I have."

"No. Take my word for it, you're sane. Or don't take my word for it. Look. You got a hell of a start in life. You got into bad hands at the very beginning. Your step-mother was plain poison, and did her best to ruin you, and in the end succeeded in convincing you that you were smeared with a very special family curse. In the past couple of months—the time I've known you—all the calamities known to man have been piled up on you, and your belief in your curse has made you hold yourself responsible for every item in the pile. All right. How's it affected you? You've been dazed a lot of the time, hysterical part of the time, and when your husband was killed you tried to kill yourself, but weren't unbalanced enough to face the shock of the bullet tearing through your flesh.

"Well, good God, sister! I'm only a hired man with only a hired man's interest in your troubles, and some of them have had me groggy. Didn't I try to bite a ghost back in that Temple? And I'm supposed to be old and toughened to crime. This morning—after all you'd been through—somebody touches off a package of nitroglycerine almost beside your bed. Here you are this evening, up and dressed, arguing with me about your sanity.

"If you aren't normal, it's because you're tougher, saner, cooler than normal. Stop thinking about your Dain blood and think about the Mayenne blood in you. Where do you suppose you got your toughness, except from him? It's the same toughness that carried him through Devil's Island, Central America, and Mexico, and kept him standing up till the end. You're more like him than like the one Dain I saw. Physically, you take after your father, and if you've got any physical marks of degeneracy—whatever that means—you got them from him."

She seemed to like that. Her eyes were almost happy. But I had talked myself out of words for the moment, and while I was hunting for more behind a cigarette the shine went out of her eyes.

"I'm glad—I'm grateful to you for what you've said, if you've meant it." Hopelessness was in her tone again, and her face was back between her hands. "But, whatever I am, she was right. You can't say she wasn't. You can't deny that my life has been cursed, blackened, and the lives of everyone who's touched me."

"I'm one answer to that," I said. "I've been around you a lot recently, and I've mixed into your affairs enough, and nothing's happened to me that a night's sleep wouldn't fix up."

"But in a different way," she protested slowly, wrinkling her forehead. "There's no personal relationship with you. It's professional with you—your work. That makes a difference."

I laughed and said:

"That won't do. There's Fitzstephan. He knew your family, of course, but he was here through me, on my account, and was actually, then, a step further removed from you than I. Why shouldn't I have gone down first? Maybe the bomb was meant for me? Maybe. But that brings us to a human mind behind it—one that can bungle —and not your infallible curse."

"You are mistaken," she said, staring at her knees. "Owen loved me."

I decided not to appear surprised. I asked:

"Had you—?"

"No, please! Please don't ask me to talk about it. Not now—after what happened this morning." She jerked her shoulders up high and straight, said crisply: "You said something about an infallible curse. I don't know whether you misunderstand me, or are pretending to, to make me seem foolish. But I don't believe in an infallible curse, one coming from the devil or God, like Job's, say." She was earnest now, no longer talking to change the conversation. "But can't there be—aren't there people who are so thoroughly—fundamentally—evil that they poison—bring out the worst in—everybody they touch? And can't that—?"

"There are people who can," I half-agreed, "when they want to."

"No, no! Whether they want to or not. When they desperately don't want to. It is so. It is. I loved Eric because he was clean and fine. You know he was. You knew him well enough, and you know men well enough, to know he was. I loved him that way, wanted him that way. And then, when we were married—"

She shuddered and gave me both of her hands. The palms were dry and hot, the ends of her fingers cold. I had to hold them tight to keep the nails out of my flesh. I asked:

"You were a virgin when you married him?"

"Yes, I was. I am. I—"

"It's nothing to get excited about," I said. "You are, and have the usual silly notions. And you use dope, don't you?"

She nodded. I went on:

"That would cut your own interest in sex to below normal, so that a perfectly natural interest in it on somebody else's part would seem abnormal. Eric was too young, too much in love with you, maybe too inexperienced, to keep from being clumsy. You can't make anything horrible out of that."

"But it wasn't only Eric," she explained. "Every man I've known. Don't think me conceited. I know I'm not beautiful. But I don't want to be evil. I don't. Why do men—? Why have all the men I've—?"

"Are you," I asked, "talking about me?"

"No—you know I'm not. Don't make fun of me, please."

"Then there are exceptions? Any others? Madison Andrews, for instance?"

"If you know him at all well, or have heard much about him, you don't have to ask that."

"No," I agreed. "But you can't blame the curse with him—it's habit. Was he very bad?"

"He was very funny," she said bitterly.

"How long ago was it?"

"Oh, possibly a year and a half. I didn't say anything to my father and step-mother. I was—I was ashamed that men were like that to me, and that—"

"How do you know," I grumbled, "that most men aren't like that to most women? What makes you think your case is so damned unique? If your ears were sharp enough, you could listen now and hear a thousand women in San Francisco making the same complaint, and—God knows—maybe half of them would be thinking themselves sincere."

She took her hands away from me and sat up straight on the bed. Some pink came into her face.

"Now you *have* made me feel silly," she said.

"Not much sillier than I do. I'm supposed to be a detective. Since this job began, I've been riding around on a merry-go-round, staying the same distance behind your curse, suspecting what it'd look like if I could get face to face with it, but never getting there. I will now. Can you stand another week or two?"

"You mean—?"

"I'm going to show you that your curse is a lot of hooey, but it'll take a few days, maybe a couple of weeks."

She was round-eyed and trembling, wanting to believe me, afraid to. I said:

"That's settled. What are you going to do now?"

"I—I don't know. Do you mean what you've said? That this can be ended? That I'll have no more—? That you can—?"

"Yeah. Could you go back to the house in the cove for a while? It might help things along, and you'll be safe enough there. We could take Mrs. Herman with us, and maybe an op or two."

"I'll go," she said.

I looked at my watch and stood up saying:

"Better go back to bed. We'll move down tomorrow. Good night."

She chewed her lower lip, wanting to say something, not wanting to say it, finally blurting it out:

"I'll have to have morphine down there."

"Sure. What's your day's ration?"

"Five—ten grains."

"That's mild enough," I said, and then, casually: "Do you like using the stuff?"

"I'm afraid it's too late for my liking or not liking it to matter."

"You've been reading the Hearst papers," I said. "If

you want to break off, and we've a few days to spare down there, we'll use them weaning you. It's not so tough."

She laughed shakily, with a queer twitching of her mouth.

"Go away," she cried. "Don't give me any more assurances, any more of your promises, please. I can't stand any more tonight. I'm drunk on them now. Please go away."

"All right. Night."

"Good night—and thanks."

I went into my room, closing the door. Mickey was unscrewing the top of a flask. His knees were dusty. He turned his half-wit's grin on me and said:

"What a swell dish you are. What are you trying to do? Win yourself a home?"

"Sh-h-h. Anything new?"

"The master minds have gone back to the county seat. The red-head nurse was getting a load at the keyhole when I came back from feeding. I chased her."

"And took her place?" I asked, nodding at his dusty knees.

You couldn't embarrass Mickey. He said:

"Hell, no. She was at the other door, in the hall."

XX : THE HOUSE IN THE COVE

I got Fitzstephan's car from the garage and drove Gabrielle and Mrs. Herman down to the house in the cove late the following morning. The girl was in low spirits. She made a poor job of smiling when spoken to, and had nothing to say on her own account. I thought she might be depressed by the thought of returning to the house she had shared with Collinson, but when we got there she went in with no appearance of reluctance, and being there didn't seem to increase her depression.

After luncheon—Mrs. Herman turned out to be a good cook—Gabrielle decided she wanted to go outdoors, so she and I walked over to the Mexican settlement to see Mary Nunez. The Mexican woman promised to come back to work the next day. She seemed fond of Gabrielle, but not of me.

We returned home by way of the shore, picking a path between scattered rocks. We walked slowly. The girl's forehead was puckered between her eyebrows. Neither of us said anything until we were within a quarter of a mile of the house. Then Gabrielle sat down on the rounded top of a boulder that was warm in the sun.

"Can you remember what you told me last night?" she asked, running her words together in her hurry to get them out. She looked frightened.

"Yeah."

"Tell me again," she begged, moving over to one end of her boulder. "Sit down and tell me again—all of it."

I did. According to me, it was as foolish to try to read character from the shape of ears as from the position of stars, tea-leaves, or spit in the sand; anybody who started hunting for evidence of insanity in himself would certainly find plenty, because all but stupid minds were jumbled affairs; she was, as far as I could see, too much like her father to have much Dain blood in her, or to have been softened much by what she had, even if you wanted to believe that things like that could be handed down; there was nothing to show that her influence on people was any worse than anybody else's, it being doubtful that many people had a very good influence on those of the opposite sex, and, anyway, she was too young, inexperienced, and self-centered to judge how she varied from the normal in this respect; I would show her in a few days that there was for her difficulties a much more tangible, logical, and jailable answer than any curse; and she wouldn't have much trouble breaking away from morphine, since she was a fairly light user of the stuff and had a temperament favorable to a cure.

I spent three-quarters of an hour working these ideas over for her, and didn't make such a lousy job of it. The fear went out of her eyes as I talked. Toward the last she smiled to herself. When I had finished she jumped up, laughing, working her fingers together.

"Thank you. Thank you," she babbled. "Please don't let me ever stop believing you. Make me believe you even if— No. It *is* true. Make me believe it always. Come on. Let's walk some more."

She almost ran me the rest of the way to the house, chattering all the way. Mickey Linehan was on the porch. I stopped there with him while the girl went in.

"Tch, tch, tch, as Mr. Rolly says." He shook his grinning face at me. "I ought to tell her what happened to that poor girl up in Poisonville that got so she thought she could trust you."

"Bring any news down from the village with you?" I asked.

"Andrews has turned up. He was at the Jeffries' place in San Mateo, where Aaronia Haldorn's staying. She's still there. Andrews was there from Tuesday afternoon till last night. Al was watching the place and saw him go in, but didn't peg him till he came out. The Jeffries are away— San Diego. Dick's tailing Andrews now. Al says the Haldorn broad hasn't been off the place. Rolly tells me Fink's awake, but don't know anything about the bomb. Fitzstephan's still hanging on to life."

"I think I'll run over and talk to Fink this afternoon," I said. "Stick around here. And—oh, yeah—you'll have to act respectful to me when Mrs. Collinson's around. It's important that she keep on thinking I'm hot stuff."

"Bring back some booze," Mickey said. "I can't do it sober."

Fink was propped up in bed when I got to him, looking out under bandages. He insisted that he knew nothing about the bomb, that all he had come down for was to tell me that Harvey Whidden was his step-son, the missing village-blacksmith's son by a former marriage.

"Well, what of it?" I asked.

"I don't know what of it, except that he was, and I thought you'd want to know about it."

"Why should I?"

"The papers said you said there was some kind of connection between what happened here and what happened up there, and that heavy-set detective said you said I knew more about it than I let on. And I don't want any more trouble, so I thought I'd just come down and tell you, so you couldn't say I hadn't told all I knew."

"Yeah? Then tell me what you know about Madison Andrews."

"I don't know anything about him. I don't know him. He's her guardian or something, ain't he? I read that in the newspapers. But I don't know him."

"Aaronia Haldorn does."

"Maybe she does, mister, but I don't. I just worked for the Haldorns. It wasn't anything to me but a job."

"What was it to your wife?"

"The same thing, a job."

"Where is she?"

"I don't know."

"Why'd she run away from the Temple?"

"I told you before, I don't know. Didn't want to get in trouble, I— Who wouldn't of run away if they got a chance?"

The nurse who had been fluttering around became a nuisance by this time, so I left the hospital for the district attorney's office in the court house. Vernon pushed aside a stack of papers with a the-world-can-wait gesture, and said, "Glad to see you; sit down," nodding vigorously, showing me all his teeth.

I sat down and said:

"Been talking to Fink. I couldn't get anything out of him, but he's our meat. The bomb couldn't have got in there except by him."

Vernon frowned for a moment, then shook his chin at me, and snapped:

"What was his motive? And you were there. You say you were looking at him all the time he was in the room. You say you saw nothing."

"What of that?" I asked. "He could outsmart me there. He was a magician's mechanic. He'd know how to make a bomb, and how to put it down without my seeing it. That's his game. We don't know what Fitzstephan saw. They tell me he'll pull through. Let's hang on to Fink till he does."

Vernon clicked his teeth together and said: "Very well, we'll hold him."

I went down the corridor to the sheriff's office. Feeney wasn't in, but his chief deputy—a lanky, pockmarked man named Sweet—said he knew from the way Feeney had spoken of me that he—Feeney—would want me to be given all the help I asked for.

"That's fine," I said. "What I'm interested in now is picking up a couple of bottles of—well, gin, Scotch—whatever happens to be best in this part of the country."

Sweet scratched his Adam's apple and said:

"I wouldn't know about that. Maybe the elevator boy. I guess his gin would be safest. Say, Dick Cotton's crying his head off wanting to see you. Want to talk to him?"

"Yeah, though I don't know what for."

"Well, come back in a couple of minutes."

I went out and rang for the elevator. The boy—he had an age-bent back and a long yellow-gray mustache—was alone in it.

"Sweet said maybe you'd know where I could get a gallon of the white," I said.

"He's crazy," the boy grumbled, and then, when I kept quiet: "You'll be going out this way?"

"Yeah, in a little while."

He closed the door. I went back to Sweet. He took me down an inclosed walk that connected the court house with the prison behind, and left me alone with Cotton in a small boiler-plate cell. Two days in jail hadn't done the marshal of Quesada any good. He was gray-faced and jumpy, and the dimple in his chin kept squirming as he talked. He hadn't anything to tell me except that he was innocent.

All I could think of to say to him was: "Maybe, but you brought it on yourself. What evidence there is is against you. I don't know whether it's enough to convict you or not—depends on your lawyer."

"What did he want?" Sweet asked when I had gone back to him.

"To tell me that he's innocent."

The deputy scratched his Adam's apple again and asked:

"It's supposed to make any difference to you?"

"Yeah, it's been keeping me awake at night. See you later."

I went out to the elevator. The boy pushed a newspaper-wrapped gallon jug at me and said: "Ten bucks." I paid him, stowed the jug in Fitzstephan's car, found the local telephone office, and put in a call for Vic Dallas's drug-store in San Francisco's Mission district.

"I want," I told Vic, "fifty grains of M. and eight of those calomel-ipecac-atropine-strychnine-cascara shots. I'll have somebody from the agency pick up the package tonight or in the morning. Right?"

"If you say so, but if you kill anybody with it don't tell them where you got the stuff."

"Yeah," I said; "they'll die just because I haven't got a lousy pill-roller's diploma."

I put in another San Francisco call, for the agency, talking to the Old Man.

"Can you spare me another op?" I asked.

"MacMan is available, or he can relieve Drake. Whichever you prefer."

"MacMan'll do. Have him stop at Dallas's drug-store for a package on the way down. He knows where it is."

The Old Man said he had no new reports on Aaronia Haldorn and Andrews.

I drove back to the house in the cove. We had company. Three strange cars were standing empty in the driveway, and half a dozen newshounds were sitting and standing around Mickey on the porch. They turned their questions on me.

"Mrs. Collinson's here for a rest," I said. "No interviews, no posing for pictures. Let her alone. If anything breaks here I'll see that you get it, those of you who lay off her. The only thing I can tell you now is that Fink's being held for the bombing."

"What did Andrews come down for?" Jack Santos asked.

That wasn't a surprise to me: I had expected him to turn up now that he had come out of seclusion.

"Ask him," I suggested. "He's administering Mrs. Collinson's estate. You can't make a mystery out of his coming down to see her."

"Is it true that they're on bad terms?"

"No."

"Then why didn't he show up before this—yesterday, or the day before?"

"Ask him."

"Is it true that he's up to his tonsils in debt, or was before the Leggett estate got into his hands?"

"Ask him."

Santos smiled with thinned lips and said:

"We don't have to: we asked some of his creditors. Is there anything to the report that Mrs. Collinson and her husband had quarreled over her being too friendly with Whidden, a couple of days before her husband was killed?"

"Anything but the truth," I said. "Tough. You could do a lot with a story like that."

"Maybe we will," Santos said. "Is it true that she and her husband's family are on the outs, that old Hubert has said he's willing to spend all he's got to see that she pays for any part she had in his son's death?"

I didn't know. I said:

"Don't be a chump. We're working for Hubert now, taking care of her."

"Is it true that Mrs. Haldorn and Tom Fink were released because they had threatened to tell all they knew if they were held for trial?"

"Now you're kidding me, Jack," I said. "Is Andrews still here?"

"Yes."

I went indoors and called Mickey in, asking him: "Seen Dick?"

"He drove past a couple of minutes after Andrews came."

"Sneak away and find him. Tell him not to let the newspaper gang make him, even if he has to risk losing Andrews for a while. They'd go crazy all over their front pages if they learned we were shadowing him, and I don't want them to go that crazy."

Mrs. Herman was coming down the stairs. I asked her where Andrews was.

"Up in the front room."

I went up there. Gabrielle, in a low-cut dark silk gown, was sitting stiff and straight on the edge of a leather rocker. Her face was white and sullen. She was looking at a handkerchief stretched between her hands. She looked up at me as if glad I had come in. Andrews stood with his back to the fireplace. His white hair, eyebrows, and mustache stood out every which way from his bony pink face. He shifted his scowl from the girl to me, and didn't seem glad I had come in.

I said, "Hullo," and found a table-corner to prop myself on.

He said: "I've come to take Mrs. Collinson back to San Francisco."

She didn't say anything. I said:

"Not to San Mateo?"

"What do you mean by that?" The white tangles of his brows came down to hide all but the bottom halves of his blue eyes.

"God knows. Maybe my mind's been corrupted by the questions the newspapers have been asking me."

He didn't quite wince. He said, slowly, deliberately:

"Mrs. Haldorn sent for me professionally. I went to see her to explain how impossible it would be, in the circumstances, for me to advise or represent her."

"That's all right with me," I said. "And if it took you thirty hours to explain that to her, it's nobody's business."

"Precisely."

"But—I'd be careful how I told the reporters waiting downstairs that. You know how suspicious they are—for no reason at all."

He turned to Gabrielle again, speaking quietly, but with some impatience:

"Well, Gabrielle, are you going with me?"

"Should I?" she asked me.

"Not unless you especially want to."

"I—I don't."

"Then that's settled," I said.

Andrews nodded and went forward to take her hand, saying:

"I'm sorry, but I must get back to the city now, my dear. You should have a phone put in, so you can reach me in case you need to."

He declined her invitation to stay to dinner, said, "Good evening," not unpleasantly, to me, and went out. Through a window I could see him presently getting into his car, giving as little attention as possible to the newspaper men gathered around him.

Gabrielle was frowning at me when I turned away from the window.

"What did you mean by what you said about San Mateo?" she asked.

"How friendly are he and Aaronia Haldorn?" I asked.

"I haven't any idea. Why? Why did you talk to him as you did?"

"Detective business. For one thing, there's a rumor that getting control of the estate may have helped him keep his own head above water. Maybe there's nothing in it. But it won't hurt to give him a little scare, so he'll get busy straightening things out—if he has done any juggling—between now and clean-up day. No use of you losing money along with the rest of your troubles."

"Then he—?" she began.

"He's got a week—several days at least—to unjuggle in. That ought to be enough."

"But—"

Mrs. Herman, calling us to dinner, ended the conversation.

Gabrielle ate very little. She and I had to do most of the talking until I got Mickey started telling about a job he had been on up in Eureka, where he posed as a foreigner who knew no English. Since English was the only language he did know, and Eureka normally held at least one specimen of every nationality there is, he'd had a hell of a time keeping people from finding out just what he was supposed to be. He made a long and laughable story of it. Maybe some of it was the truth: he always got a lot of fun out of acting like the other half of a half-wit.

After the meal he and I strolled around outside while the spring night darkened the grounds.

"MacMan will be down in the morning," I told him. "You and he will have to do the watchdog. Divide it between you anyway you want, but one will have to be on the job all the time."

"Don't give yourself any of the worst of it," he complained. "What's this supposed to be down here—a trap?"

"Maybe."

"Maybe. Uh-huh. You don't know what the hell you're doing. You're stalling around waiting for the horseshoe in your pocket to work."

"The outcome of successful planning always looks like luck to saps. Did Dick have any news?"

"No. He tailed Andrews straight here from his house."

The front door opened, throwing yellow light across the porch. Gabrielle, a dark cape on her shoulders, came into the yellow light, shut the door, and came down the gravel walk.

"Take a nap now if you want," I told Mickey. "I'll call

you when I turn in. You'll have to stand guard till morning."

"You're a darb." He laughed in the dark. "By God, you're a darb."

"There's a gallon of gin in the car."

"Huh? Why didn't you say so instead of wasting my time just talking?" The lawn grass swished against his shoes as he walked away.

I moved towards the gravel walk, meeting the girl.

"Isn't it a lovely night?" she said.

"Yeah. But you're not supposed to go roaming around alone in the dark, even if your troubles are practically over."

"I didn't intend to," she said, taking my arm. "And what does practically over mean?"

"That there are a few details to be taken care of—the morphine, for instance."

She shivered and said:

"I've only enough left for tonight. You promised to—"

"Fifty grains coming in the morning."

She kept quiet, as if waiting for me to say something else. I didn't say anything else. Her fingers wriggled on my sleeve.

"You said it wouldn't be hard to cure me." She spoke half-questioningly, as if expecting me to deny having said anything of the sort.

"It wouldn't."

"You said, perhaps . . ." letting the words fade off.

"We'd do it while we were here?"

"Yes."

"Want to?" I asked. "It's no go if you don't."

"Do I want to?" She stood still in the road, facing me. "I'd give—" A sob ended that sentence. Her voice came again, high-pitched, thin: "Are you being honest with me? Are you? Is what you've told me—all you told me last night and this afternoon—as true as you made it sound? Do I believe in you because you're sincere? Or because you've learned how—as a trick of your business—to make people believe in you?"

She might have been crazy, but she wasn't so stupid. I gave her the answer that seemed best at the time:

"Your belief in me is built on mine in you. If mine's unjustified, so is yours. So let me ask you a question first: were you lying when you said, 'I don't want to be evil'?"

"Oh, I don't. I don't."

"Well, then," I said with an air of finality, as if that settled it. "Now if you want to get off the junk, off we'll get you."

"How—how long will it take?"

"Say a week, to be safe. Maybe less."

"Do you mean that? No longer than that?"

"That's all for the part that counts. You'll have to take care of yourself for some time after, till your system's hitting on all eight again, but you'll be off the junk."

"Will I suffer—much?"

"A couple of bad days; but they won't be as bad as you'll think they are, and your father's toughness will carry you through them."

"If," she said slowly, "I should find out in the middle of it that I can't go through with it, can I—?"

"There'll be nothing you can do about it," I promised cheerfully. "You'll stay in till you come out the other end."

She shivered again and asked:

"When shall we start?"

"Day after tomorrow. Take your usual snort tomorrow, but don't try to stock up. And don't worry about it. It'll be tougher on me than on you: I'll have to put up with you."

"And you'll make allowances—you'll understand—if I'm not always nice while I'm going through it? Even if I'm nasty?"

"I don't know." I didn't want to encourage her to cut up on me. "I don't think so much of niceness that can be turned into nastiness by a little grief."

"Oh, but—" She stopped, wrinkled her forehead, said: "Can't we send Mrs. Herman away? I don't want to—I don't want her looking at me."

"I'll get rid of her in the morning."

"And if I'm—you won't let anybody else see me—if I'm not—if I'm too terrible?"

"No," I promised. "But look here: you're preparing to put on a show for me. Stop thinking about that end of it. You're going to behave. I don't want a lot of monkey-business out of you."

She laughed suddenly, asking:

"Will you beat me if I'm bad?"

I said she might still be young enough for a spanking to do her good.

XXI : AARONIA HALDORN

Mary Nunez arrived at half-past seven the next morning. Mickey Linehan drove Mrs. Herman to Quesada, leaving her there, returning with MacMan and a load of groceries.

MacMan was a square-built, stiff-backed ex-soldier. Ten years of the island had baked his tight-mouthed, solid-jawed, grim face a dark oak. He was the perfect soldier: he went where you sent him, stayed where you put him, and had no ideas of his own to keep him from doing exactly what you told him.

He gave me the druggist's package. I took ten grains of morphine up to Gabrielle. She was eating breakfast in bed. Her eyes were watery, her face damp and grayish. When she saw the bindles in my hand she pushed her tray aside and held her hands out eagerly, wriggling her shoulders.

"Come back in five minutes?" she asked.

"You can take your jolt in front of me. I won't blush."

"But I would," she said, and did.

I went out, shut the door, and leaned against it, hearing the crackle of paper and the clink of a spoon on the water-glass. Presently she called:

"All right."

I went in again. A crumpled ball of white paper in the tray was all that remained of one bindle. The others weren't in sight. She was leaning back against her pillows, eyes half closed, as comfortable as a cat full of goldfish. She smiled lazily at me and said:

"You're a dear. Know what I'd like to do today? Take some lunch and go out on the water—spend the whole day floating in the sun."

"That ought to be good for you. Take either Linehan or MacMan with you. You're not to go out alone."

"What are you going to do?"

"Ride up to Quesada, over to the county seat, maybe as far as the city."

"Mayn't I go with you?"

I shook my head, saying: "I've got work to do, and you're supposed to be resting."

She said, "Oh," and reached for her coffee. I turned to the door. "The rest of the morphine." She spoke over the edge of her cup. "You've put it in a safe place, where nobody will find it?"

"Yeah," I said, grinning at her, patting my coat-pocket.

In Quesada I spent half an hour talking to Rolly and reading the San Francisco papers. They were beginning to poke at Andrews with hints and questions that stopped just short of libel. That was so much to the good. The deputy sheriff hadn't anything to tell me.

I went over to the county seat. Vernon was in court. Twenty minutes of the sheriff's conversation didn't add anything to my education. I called up the agency and talked to the Old Man. He said Hubert Collinson, our client, had expressed some surprise at our continuing the operation, having supposed that Whidden's death had cleared up the mystery of his son's murder.

"Tell him it didn't," I said. "Eric's murder was tied up with Gabrielle's troubles, and we can't get to the bottom of one except through the other. It'll probably take another week. Collinson's all right," I assured the Old Man. "He'll stand for it when it's explained to him."

The Old Man said, "I certainly hope so," rather coldly, not enthusiastic over having five operatives at work on a job that the supposed client might not want to pay for.

I drove up to San Francisco, had dinner at the St. Germain, stopped at my rooms to collect another suit and a bagful of clean shirts and the like, and got back to the house in the cove a little after midnight. MacMan came out of the darkness while I was tucking the car—we were still using Fitzstephan's—under the shed. He said nothing had happened in my absence. We went into the house together. Mickey was in the kitchen, yawning and mixing himself a drink before relieving MacMan on sentry duty.

"Mrs. Collinson gone to bed?" I asked.

"Her light's still on. She's been in her room all day."

MacMan and I had a drink with Mickey and then went upstairs. I knocked at the girl's door.

"Who is it?" she asked. I told her. She said: "Yes?"

"No breakfast in the morning."

"Really?" Then, as if it were something she had almost forgotten: "Oh, I've decided not to put you to all the trouble of curing me." She opened the door and stood in the opening, smiling too pleasantly at me, a finger holding her place in a book. "Did you have a nice ride?"

"All right," I said, taking the rest of the morphine from my pocket and holding it out to her. "There's no use of my carrying this around."

She didn't take it. She laughed in my face and said:

"You *are* a brute, aren't you?"

"Well, it's your cure, not mine." I put the stuff back in my pocket. "If you—" I broke off to listen. A board had creaked down the hall. Now there was a soft sound, as of a bare foot dragging across the floor.

"That's Mary watching over me," Gabrielle whispered gaily. "She made a bed in the attic and refused to go home. She doesn't think I'm safe with you and your friends. She warned me against you, said you were—what was it? —oh, yes—wolves. Are you?"

"Practically. Don't forget—no breakfast in the morning."

The following afternoon I gave her the first dose of Vic Dallas's mixture, and three more at two-hour intervals. She spent that day in her room. That was Saturday.

On Sunday she had ten grains of morphine and was in high spirits all day, considering herself as good as cured already.

On Monday she had the remainder of Vic's concoction, and the day was pretty much like Saturday. Mickey Linehan returned from the county seat with the news that Fitzstephan was conscious, but too weak and too bandaged to have talked if the doctors had let him; that Andrews had been to San Mateo to see Aaronia Haldorn again; and that she had been to the hospital to see Fink, but had been refused permission by the sheriff's office.

Tuesday was a more exciting day.

Gabrielle was up and dressed when I carried her orange-juice breakfast in. She was bright-eyed, restless, talkative, and laughed easily and often until I mentioned— off-hand—that she was to have no more morphine.

"Ever, you mean?" Her face and voice were panicky. "No, you don't mean that?"

"Yeah."

"But I'll die." Tears filled her eyes, ran down her small white face, and she wrung her hands. It was childishly pathetic. I had to remind myself that tears were one of the symptoms of morphine withdrawal. "You know that's not the way. I don't expect as much as usual. I know I'll get less and less each day. But you can't stop it like this. You're joking. That would kill me." She cried some more at the thought of being killed.

I made myself laugh as if I were sympathetic but amused.

"Nonsense," I said cheerfully. "The chief trouble you're

going to have is in being too alive. A couple of days of that, and you'll be all set."

She bit her lips, finally managed a smile, holding out both hands to me.

"I'm going to believe you," she said. "I do believe you. I'm going to believe you no matter what you say."

Her hands were clammy. I squeezed them and said:

"That'll be swell. Now back to bed. I'll look in every now and then, and if you want anything in between, sing out."

"You're not going off today?"

"No," I promised.

She stood the gaff pretty well all afternoon. Of course, there wasn't much heartiness in the way she laughed at herself between attacks when the sneezing and yawning hit her, but the thing was that she tried to laugh.

Madison Andrews came between five and half-past. Having seen him drive in, I met him on the porch. The ruddiness of his face had been washed out to a weak orange.

"Good evening," he said politely. "I wish to see Mrs. Collinson."

"I'll deliver any message to her," I offered.

He pulled his white eyebrows down and some of his normal ruddiness came back.

"I wish to see her." It was a command.

"She doesn't wish to see you. Is there any message?"

All of his ruddiness was back now. His eyes were hot. I was standing between him and the door. He couldn't go in while I stood there. For a moment he seemed about to push me out of the way. That didn't worry me: he was carrying a handicap of twenty pounds and twenty years.

He pulled his jaw into his neck and spoke in the voice of authority:

"Mrs. Collinson must return to San Francisco with me. She cannot stay here. This is a preposterous arrangement."

"She's not going to San Francisco," I said. "If necessary, the district attorney can hold her here as a material witness. Try upsetting that with any of your court orders, and we'll give you something else to worry about. I'm telling you this so you'll know how we stand. We'll prove that she might be in danger from you. How do we know you haven't played marbles with the estate? How do we know you don't mean to take advantage of her present upset condition to shield yourself from trouble over the estate? Why, man, you might even be planning to send her to an insane-asylum so the estate will stay under your control."

He was sick behind his eyes, though the rest of him stood up well enough under this broadside. When he had got his breath and had swallowed, he demanded:

"Does Gabrielle believe this?" His face was magenta.

"Who said anybody believed it?" I was trying to be bland. "I'm just telling you what we'll go into court with. You're a lawyer. You know there's not necessarily any connection between what's true and what you go into court with—or into the newspapers."

The sickness spread from behind his eyes, pushing the color from his face, the stiffness from his bones; but he held himself tall and he found a level voice.

"You may tell Mrs. Collinson," he said, "that I shall return my letters testamentary to the court this week, with an accounting of the estate, and a request that I be relieved."

"That'll be swell," I said, but I felt sorry for the old boy shuffling down to his car, climbing slowly into it.

I didn't tell Gabrielle he had been there.

She was whining a little now between her yawning and sneezing, and her eyes were running water. Face, body, and hands were damp with sweat. She couldn't eat. I kept her full of orange juice. Noises and odors—no matter how faint, how pleasant—were becoming painful to her, and she twitched and jerked continually in her bed.

"Will it get much worse than this?" she asked.

"Not much. There'll be nothing you can't stand."

Mickey Linehan was waiting for me when I got downstairs.

"The spick's got herself a chive," he said pleasantly.

"Yeah?"

"Yeah. It's the one I've been using to shuck lemons to take the stink out of that bargain-counter gin you bought—or did you just borrow it, the owner knowing you'd return it because nobody could drink it? It's a paring knife—four or five inches of stainless steel blade—so you won't get rust-marks on your undershirt when she sticks it in your back. I couldn't find it, and asked her about it, and she didn't look at me like I was a well-poisoner when she said she didn't know anything about it, and that's the first time she never looked at me that way, so I knew she had it."

"Smart of you," I said. "Well, keep an eye on her. She don't like us much."

"I'm to do that?" Mickey grinned. "My idea would be for everybody to look out for himself, seeing that you're the lad she dog-eyes most, and it's most likely you that'll get whittled on. What'd you ever do to her? You haven't been dumb enough to fool with a Mex lady's affections, have you?"

I didn't think he was funny, though he may have been.

Aaronia Haldorn arrived just before dark, in a Lincoln limousine driven by a Negro who turned the siren loose when he brought the car into the drive. I was in Gabrielle's room when the thing howled. She all but jumped out of bed, utterly terrorized by what must have been an ungodly racket to her too sensitive ears.

"What was it? What was it?" she kept crying between rattling teeth, her body shaking the bed.

"Sh-h-h," I soothed her. I was acquiring a pretty fair bedside manner. "Just an automobile horn. Visitors. I'll go down and head them off."

"You won't let anybody see me?" she begged.

"No. Be a good girl till I get back."

Aaronia Haldorn was standing beside the limousine talking to MacMan when I came out. In the dim light, her face was a dusky oval mask between black hat and black fur coat—but her luminous eyes were real enough.

"How do you do?" she said, holding out a hand. Her voice was a thing to make warm waves run up your back.

"I'm glad for Mrs. Collinson's sake that you're here. She and I have had excellent proof of your protective ability, both owing our lives to it."

That was all right, but it had been said before. I made a gesture that was supposed to indicate modest distaste for the subject, and beat her to the first tap with:

"I'm sorry she can't see you. She isn't well."

"Oh, but I should so like to see her, if only for a moment. Don't you think it might be good for her?"

I said I was sorry. She seemed to accept that as final, though she said: "I came all the way from the city to see her."

I tried that opening with:

"Didn't Mr. Andrews tell you . . . ?" letting it ravel out.

She didn't say whether he had. She turned and began walking slowly across the grass. There was nothing for me to do but walk along beside her. Full darkness was only a few minutes away. Presently, when we had gone thirty or forty feet from the car, she said:

"Mr. Andrews thinks you suspect him."

"He's right."

"Of what do you suspect him?"

"Juggling the estate. Mind, I don't know, but I do suspect him."

"Really?"

"Really," I said; "and not of anything else."

"Oh, I should suppose that was quite enough."

"It's enough for me. I didn't think it was enough for you."

"I beg your pardon?"

I didn't like the ground I was on with this woman. I was afraid of her. I piled up what facts I had, put some guesses on them, and took a jump from the top of the heap into space:

"When you got out of prison, you sent for Andrews, pumped him for all he knew, and then, when you learned he was playing with the girl's pennies, you saw what looked to you like a chance to confuse things by throwing suspicion on him. The old boy's woman-crazy: he'd be duck-soup for a woman like you. I don't know what you're planning to do with him, but you've got him started, and have got the papers started after him. I take it you gave them the tip-off on his high financing? It's no good, Mrs. Haldorn. Chuck it. It won't work. You can stir him up, all right, and make him do something criminal, get him into a swell jam: he's desperate enough now that he's being poked at. But whatever he does now won't hide what somebody else did in the past. He's promised to get the estate in order and hand it over. Let him alone. It won't work."

She didn't say anything while we took another dozen steps. A path came under our feet. I said:

"This is the path that runs up the cliff, the one Eric Collinson was pushed from. Did you know him?"

She drew in her breath sharply, with almost a sob in her throat, but her voice was steady, quiet and musical, when she replied:

"You know I did. Why should you ask?"

"Detectives like questions they already know the answers to. Why did you come down here, Mrs. Haldorn?"

"Is that another whose answer you know?"

"I know you came for one or both of two reasons."

"Yes?"

"First, to learn how close we were to our riddle's answer. Right?"

"I've my share of curiosity, naturally," she confessed.

"I don't mind making that much of your trip a success. I know the answer."

She stopped in the path, facing me, her eyes phosphorescent in the deep twilight. She put a hand on my shoulder: she was taller than I. The other hand was in her coatpocket. She put her face nearer mine. She spoke very slowly, as if taking great pains to be understood:

"Tell me truthfully. Don't pretend. I don't want to do an unnecessary wrong. Wait, wait—think before you speak

—and believe me when I say this isn't the time for pretending, for lying, for bluffing. Now tell me the truth: do you know the answer?"

"Yeah."

She smiled faintly, taking her hand from my shoulder, saying:

"Then there's no use of our fencing."

I jumped at her. If she had fired from her pocket she might have plugged me. But she tried to get the gun out. By then I had a hand on her wrist. The bullet went into the ground between our feet. The nails of her free hand put three red ribbons down the side of my face. I tucked my head under her chin, turned my hip to her before her knee came up, brought her body hard against mine with one arm around her, and bent her gun-hand behind her. She dropped the gun as we fell. I was on top. I stayed there until I had found the gun. I was getting up when MacMan arrived.

"Everything's eggs in the coffee," I told him, having trouble with my voice.

"Have to plug her?" he asked, looking at the woman lying still on the ground.

"No, she's all right. See that the chauffeur's behaving."

MacMan went away. The woman sat up, tucked her legs under her, and rubbed her wrist. I said:

"That's the second reason for your coming, though I thought you meant it for Mrs. Collinson."

She got up, not saying anything. I didn't help her up, not wanting her to know how shaky I was. I said:

"Since we've gone this far, it won't do any harm and it might do some good to talk."

"I don't think anything will do any good now." She set her hat straight. "You say you know. Then lies are worthless, and only lies would help." She shrugged. "Well, what now?"

"Nothing now, if you'll promise to remember that the time for being desperate is past. This kind of thing splits up in three parts—being caught, being convicted, and being punished. Admit it's too late to do anything about the first, and—well, you know what California courts and prison boards are."

She looked curiously at me and asked: "Why do you tell me this?"

"Because being shot at's no treat to me, and because when a job's done I like to get it cleaned up and over with. I'm not interested in trying to convict you for your part in the racket, and it's a nuisance having you horning in now, trying to muddy things up. Go home and behave."

Neither of us said anything more until we had walked back to the limousine. Then she turned, put out her hand to me, and said:

"I think—I don't know yet—I think I owe you even more now than before."

I didn't say anything and I didn't take her hand. Perhaps it was because she was holding her hand out that she asked:

"May I have my pistol now?"

"No."

"Will you give my best wishes to Mrs. Collinson, and tell her I'm so sorry I couldn't see her?"

"Yeah."

She said, "Goodbye," and got into the car; I took off my hat and she rode away.

XXII : CONFESSIONAL

Mickey Linehan opened the front door for me. He looked at my scratched face and laughed:

"You do have one hell of a time with your women.

Why don't you ask them instead of trying to take it away from them? It'd save you a lot of skin." He poked a thumb at the ceiling. "Better go up and negotiate with that one. She's been raising hell."

I went up to Gabrielle's room. She was sitting in the middle of the wallowed-up bed. Her hands were in her hair, tugging at it. Her soggy face was thirty-five years old. She was making hurt-animal noises in her throat.

"It's a fight, huh?" I said from the door.

She took her hands out of her hair.

"I won't die?" The question was a whimper between edge-to-edge teeth.

"Not a chance."

She sobbed and lay down. I straightened the covers over her. She complained that there was a lump in her throat, that her jaws and the hollows behind her knees ached.

"Regular symptoms," I assured her. "They won't bother you much, and you'll miss the cramps."

Fingernails scratched the door. Gabrielle jumped up in bed, crying:

"Don't go away again."

"No farther than the door," I promised, and went to it. MacMan was there.

"That Mexican Mary," he whispered, "was hiding in the bushes watching you and the woman. I spotted her when she came out, and tailed her across to the road below. She stopped the limousine and talked with the woman— five-ten minutes. I couldn't get near enough to hear any of it."

"Where is she now?"

"In the kitchen. She came back. The woman in the heap went on. Mickey says the Mex is packing a knife and is going to make grief for us. Reckon he's right?"

"He generally is," I said. "She's strong for Mrs. Collinson, and doesn't think we mean her any good. Why in hell can't she mind her own business? It adds up that she peeped and saw Mrs. Haldorn wasn't for us, figured she was for Mrs. Collinson, and braced her. I hope Mrs. Haldorn had sense enough to tell her to behave. Anyway, there's nothing we can do but watch her. No use giving her the gate: we've got to have a cook."

When MacMan had gone Gabrielle remembered we had had a visitor, and asked me about it, and about the shot she had heard and my scratched face.

"It was Aaronia Haldorn," I told her; "and she lost her head. No harm done. She's gone now."

"She came here to kill me," the girl said, not excitedly, but as if she knew certainly.

"Maybe. She wouldn't admit anything. Why should she kill you?"

I didn't get an answer to that.

It was a long bad night. I spent most of it in the girl's room, in a leather rocker dragged in from the front room. She got perhaps an hour and a half of sleep, in three instalments. Nightmares brought her screaming out of all three. I dozed when she let me. Off and on through the night I heard stealthy sounds in the hall—Mary Nunez watching over her mistress, I supposed.

Wednesday was a longer and worse day. By noon my jaws were as sore as Gabrielle's, from going around holding my back teeth together. She was getting the works now. Light was positive, active pain to her eyes, sound to her ears, odors of any sort to her nostrils. The weight of her silk nightgown, the touch of sheets over and under her, tortured her skin. Every nerve she had yanked every muscle she had, continually. Promises that she wasn't going to die were no good now: life wasn't nice enough.

"Stop fighting it, if you want," I said. "Let yourself go. I'll take care of you."

She took me at my word, and I had a maniac on my hands. Once her shrieks brought Mary Nunez to the door, snarling and spitting at me in Mex-Spanish. I was holding Gabrielle down in bed by the shoulders, sweating as much as she was.

"Get out of here," I snarled back at the Mexican woman.

She put a brown hand into the bosom of her dress and

came a step into the room. Mickey Linehan came up behind her, pulled her back into the hall, and shut the door.

Between the high spots, Gabrielle lay on her back, panting, twitching, staring at the ceiling with hopeless suffering eyes. Sometimes her eyes closed, but the jerking of her body didn't stop.

Rolly came down from Quesada that afternoon with word that Fitzstephan had come sufficiently alive to be questioned by Vernon. Fitzstephan had told the district attorney that he had not seen the bomb, had seen nothing to show when, where, and how it came into the room; but that he had an indistinct memory of hearing a tinkling, as of broken glass falling, and a thud on the floor close to him just after Fink and I had left the room.

I told Rolly to tell Vernon I'd try to get over to see him the next day, and to hang on to Fink. The deputy sheriff promised to deliver the message, and left. Mickey and I were standing on the porch. We didn't have anything to say to each other, hadn't all day. I was lighting a cigarette when the girl's voice came from indoors. Mickey turned away, saying something with the name of God in it.

I scowled at him and asked angrily:

"Well, am I right or wrong?"

He glared back at me, said, "I'd a damned sight rather be wrong," and walked away.

I cursed him and went inside. Mary Nunez, starting up the front stairs, retreated towards the kitchen when she saw me, walking backwards, her eyes watching me crazily. I cursed her and went upstairs to where I had left MacMan at the girl's door. He wouldn't look at me, so I made it unanimous by cursing him.

Gabrielle spent the balance of the afternoon shrieking, begging, and crying for morphine. That evening she made a complete confession:

"I told you I didn't want to be evil," she said, wadding the bedclothes in feverish hands. "That was a lie. I did. I've always wanted to, always have been. I wanted to do to you what I did to the others; but now I don't want you: I want morphine. They won't hang me: I know that. And I don't care what else they do to me, if I get morphine."

She laughed viciously and went on:

"You were right when you said I brought out the worst in men because I wanted to. I did want to; and I did—except, I failed with Doctor Riese, and with Eric. I don't know what was the matter with them. But I failed with both of them, and in failing let them learn too much about me. And that's why they were killed. Joseph drugged Doctor Riese, and I killed him myself, and then we made Minnie think she had. And I persuaded Joseph to kill Aaronia, and he would have done it—he would have done anything I asked—if you hadn't interfered. I got Harvey to kill Eric for me. I was tied to Eric—legally—a good man who wanted to make a good woman of me."

She laughed again, licking her lips.

"Harvey and I had to have money, and I couldn't—I was too afraid of being suspected—get enough from Andrews; so we pretended I had been kidnapped, to get it that way. It was a shame you killed Harvey: he was a glorious beast. I had that bomb, had had it for months. I took it from father's laboratory, when he was making some experiments for a moving picture company. It wasn't very large, and I always carried it with me—just in case. I meant it for you in the hotel room. There was nothing between Owen and me—that was another lie—he didn't love me. I meant it for you, because you were—because I was afraid you were getting at the truth. I was feverish, and when I heard two men go out, leaving one in your room, I was sure the one was you. I didn't see that it was Owen till too late—till I had opened the door a little and thrown the bomb in. Now you've got what you want. Give me morphine. There's no reason for your playing with me any longer. Give me morphine. You've succeeded. Have what I've told you written out: I'll sign it. You can't pretend now I'm worth curing, worth saving. Give me morphine."

Now it was my turn to laugh, asking:

"And aren't you going to confess to kidnapping Charlie Ross and blowing up the *Maine?*"

We had some more hell—a solid hour of it—before she exhausted herself again. The night dragged through. She got a little more than two hours' sleep, a half-hour gain over the previous night. I dozed in the chair when I could.

Sometime before daylight I woke to the feel of a hand on my coat. Keeping my breathing regular, I pushed my eyelids far enough apart to squint through the lashes. We had a very dim light in the room, but I thought Gabrielle was in bed, though I couldn't see whether she was asleep or awake. My head was tilted back to rest on the back of the chair. I couldn't see the hand that was exploring my inside coat-pocket, nor the arm that came down over my shoulder; but they smelled of the kitchen, so I knew they were brown.

The Mexican woman was standing behind me. Mickey had told me she had a knife. Imagination told me she was holding it in her other hand. Good judgment told me to let her alone. I did that, closing my eyes again. Paper rustled between her fingers, and her hand left my pocket.

I moved my head sleepily then, and changed a foot's position. When I heard the door close quietly behind me, I sat up and looked around. Gabrielle was sleeping. I counted the bindles in my pocket and found that eight of them had been taken.

Presently Gabrielle opened her eyes. This was the first time since the cure started that she had awakened quietly. Her face was haggard, but not wild-eyed. She looked at the window and asked:

"Isn't day coming yet?"

"It's getting light." I gave her some orange juice. "We'll get some solid food in you today."

"I don't want food. I want morphine."

"Don't be silly. You'll get food. You won't get morphine. Today won't be like yesterday. You're over the hump, and the rest of it's down-hill going, though you may hit a couple of rough spots. It's silly to ask for morphine now. What do you want to do? Have nothing to show for the hell you've been through? You've got it licked now: stay with it."

"Have I—have I really got it licked?"

"Yeah. All you've got to buck now is nervousness, and the memory of how nice it felt to have a skinful of hop."

"I can do it," she said. "I can do it because you say I can."

She got along fine till late in the morning, when she blew up for an hour or two. But it wasn't so bad, and I got her straightened out again. When Mary brought up her luncheon I left them together and went downstairs for my own.

Mickey and MacMan were already at the dining room table. Neither of them spoke a word—to one another or to me—during the meal. Since they kept quiet, I did.

When I went back upstairs, Gabrielle, in a green bathrobe, was sitting in the leather rocker that had been my bed for two nights. She had brushed her hair and powdered her face. Her eyes were mostly green, with a lift to the lower lids as if she was hiding a joke. She said with mock solemnity:

"Sit down. I want to talk seriously to you."

I sat down.

"Why did you go through all this with—for me?" She was really serious now. "You didn't have to, and it couldn't have been pleasant. I was—I don't know how bad I was." She turned red from forehead to chest. "I know I was revolting, disgusting. I know how I must seem to you now. Why—why did you?"

I said:

"I'm twice your age, sister; an old man. I'm damned if I'll make a chump of myself by telling you why I did it, why it was neither revolting nor disgusting, why I'd do it again and be glad of the chance."

She jumped out of her chair, her eyes round and dark, her mouth trembling.

"You mean—?"

"I don't mean anything that I'll admit," I said; "and if you're going to parade around with that robe hanging open you're going to get yourself some bronchitis. You ex-hop-heads have to be careful about catching cold."

She sat down again, put her hands over her face, and began crying. I let her cry. Presently she giggled through her fingers and asked:

"Will you go out and let me be alone all afternoon?"

"Yeah, if you'll keep warm."

I drove over to the county seat, went to the county hospital, and argued with people until they let me into Fitzstephan's room.

He was ninety per cent bandages, with only an eye, an ear, and one side of his mouth peeping out. The eye and the half-mouth smiled through linen at me, and a voice came through:

"No more of your hotel rooms for me." It wasn't a clear voice because it had to come out sidewise, and he couldn't move his jaw; but there was plenty of vitality in it. It was the voice of a man who meant to keep on living.

I smiled at him and said:

"No hotel rooms this time, unless you think San Quentin's a hotel. Strong enough to stand up under a third-degree, or shall we wait a day or two?"

"I ought to be at my best now," he said. "Facial expressions won't betray me."

"Good. Now here's the first point: Fink handed you that bomb when he shook hands with you. That's the only way it could have got in without my seeing it. His back was to me then. You didn't know what he was handing you, but you had to take it, just as you have to deny it now, or tip us off that you were tied up with the Holy Grail mob, and that Fink had reasons for killing you."

Fitzstephan said: "You say the most remarkable things. I'm glad he had reasons, though."

"You engineered Riese's murder. The others were your accomplices. When Joseph died the blame was put all on him, the supposed madman. That's enough to let the others

200

out, or ought to be. But here you are killing Collinson and planning God knows what else. Fink knows that if you keep it up you're going to let the truth out about the Temple murder, and he'll swing with you. So, scared panicky, he tries to stop you."

Fitzstephan said: "Better and better. So I killed Collinson?"

"You had him killed—hired Whidden and then didn't pay him. He kidnapped the girl then, holding her for his money, knowing she was what you wanted. It was you his bullet came closest to when we cornered him."

Fitzstephan said: "I'm running out of exclamatory phrases. So I was after her? I wondered about my motive."

"You must have been pretty rotten with her. She'd had a bad time with Andrews, and even with Eric, but she didn't mind talking about them. But when I tried to learn the details of your wooing she shuddered and shut up. I suppose she slammed you down so hard you bounced, and you're the sort of egoist to be driven to anything by that."

Fitzstephan said: "I suppose. You know, I've had more than half an idea at times that you were secretly nursing some exceptionally idiotic theory."

"Well, why shouldn't I? You were standing beside Mrs. Leggett when she suddenly got that gun. Where'd she get it? Chasing her out of the laboratory and down the stairs wasn't in character—not for you. Your hand was on her gun when that bullet hit her neck. Was I supposed to be deaf, dumb, and blind? There was, as you agreed, one mind behind all Gabrielle's troubles. You're the one person who has that sort of a mind, whose connection with each episode can be traced, and who has the necessary motive. The motive held me up: I couldn't be sure of it till I'd had my first fair chance to pump Gabrielle—after the explosion. And another thing that held me up was my not being able to tie you to the Temple crowd till Fink and Aaronia Haldorn did it for me."

Fitzstephan said: "Ah, Aaronia helped tie me? What

has she been up to?" He said it absent-mindedly, and his one visible gray eye was small, as if he was busy with other thoughts behind it.

"She's done her best to cover you up by gumming the works, creating confusion, setting us after Andrews, even trying to shoot me. I mentioned Collinson just after she'd learned that the Andrews false-trail was no good. She gave me a half-concealed gasp and sob, just on the off-chance that it'd lead me astray, overlooking no bets. I like her: she's shifty."

"She's so headstrong," Fitzstephan said lightly, not having listened to half I had said, busy with his own thoughts. He turned his head on the pillow so that his eye looked at the ceiling, narrow and brooding.

I said: "And so ends the Great Dain Curse."

He laughed then, as well as he could with one eye and a fraction of a mouth, and said:

"Suppose, my boy, I were to tell you I'm a Dain?"

I said: "Huh?"

He said: "My mother and Gabrielle's maternal grandfather were brother and sister."

I said: "I'll be damned."

"You'll have to go away and let me think," he said. "I don't know yet what I shall do. Understand, at present I admit nothing. But the chances are I shall insist on the curse, shall use it to save my dear neck. In that event, my son, you're going to see a most remarkable defense, a circus that will send the nation's newspapers into happy convulsions. I shall be a Dain, with the cursed Dain blood in me, and the crimes of Cousin Alice and Cousin Lily and Second-cousin Gabrielle and the Lord knows how many other criminal Dains shall be evidence in my behalf. The number of my own crimes will be to my advantage, on the theory that nobody but a lunatic could have committed so many. And won't they be many? I'll produce crimes and crimes, dating from the cradle.

"Even literature shall help me. Didn't most reviewers agree that *The Pale Egyptian* was the work of a sub-Mongolian? And, as I remember, the consensus was that my

Eighteen Inches bore all the better known indications of authorial degeneracy. Evidence, son, to save my sweet neck. And I shall wave my mangled body at them—an arm gone, a leg gone, parts of my torso and face—a ruin whose crimes and high Heaven have surely brought sufficient punishment upon him. And perhaps the bomb shocked me into sanity again, or, at least, out of criminal insanity. Perhaps I'll even have become religious. It'll be a splendid circus. It tempts me. But I must think before I commit myself."

He panted through the uncovered half of his mouth, exhausted by his speech, looking at me with a gray eye that held triumphant mirth.

"You'll probably make a go of it," I said as I prepared to leave. "And I'm satisfied if you do. You've taken enough of a licking. And, legally, you're entitled to beat the jump if ever anybody was."

"Legally entitled?" he repeated, the mirth going out of his eye. He looked away, and then at me again, uneasily. "Tell me the truth. Am I?"

I nodded.

"But, damn it, that spoils it," he complained, fighting to keep the uneasiness out of his eye, fighting to retain his usual lazily amused manner, and not making such a poor job of it. "It's no fun if I'm really cracked."

When I got back to the house in the cove, Mickey and MacMan were sitting on the front steps. MacMan said, "Hello," and Mickey said: "Get any fresh woman-scars while you were away? Your little playmate's been asking for you." I supposed from this—from my being readmitted to the white race—that Gabrielle had had a good afternoon.

She was sitting up in bed with pillows behind her back, her face still—or again—powdered, her eyes shining happily.

"I didn't mean for you to go away forever," she scolded. "It was nasty of you. I've got a surprise for you and I've nearly burst waiting."

"Well, here I am. What is it?"

"Shut your eyes."

I shut them.

"Open your eyes."

I opened them. She was holding out to me the eight bindles that Mary Nunez had picked my pocket for.

"I've had them since noon," she said proudly; "and they've got finger-marks and tear-marks on them, but not one of them has been opened. It—honestly—it wasn't so hard not to."

"I knew it wouldn't be, for you," I said. "That's why I didn't take them away from Mary."

"You knew? You trusted me that much—to go away and leave me with them?"

Nobody but an idiot would have confessed that for two days the folded papers had held powdered sugar instead of the original morphine.

"You're the nicest man in the world." She caught one of my hands and rubbed her cheek into it, then dropped it quickly, frowned her face out of shape, and said: "Except! You sat there this noon and deliberately tried to make me think you were in love with me."

"Well?" I asked, trying to keep my face straight.

"You hypocrite. You deceiver of young girls. It would serve you right if I made you marry me—or sued you for breach of promise. I honestly believed you all afternoon—and it *did* help me. I believed you until you came in just now, and then I saw—" She stopped.

"Saw what?"

"A monster. A nice one, an especially nice one to have around when you're in trouble, but a monster just the same, without any human foolishness like love in him, and —— What's the matter? Have I said something I shouldn't?"

"I don't think you should have," I said. "I'm not sure I wouldn't trade places with Fitzstephan now—if that big-eyed woman with the voice was part of the bargain."

"Oh, dear!" she said.

XXIII : THE CIRCUS

Owen Fitzstephan never spoke to me again. He refused to see me, and when, as a prisoner, he couldn't help himself there, he shut his mouth and kept it shut. This sudden hatred of me—for it amounted to that—had grown, I supposed, out of his knowing I thought him insane. He wanted the rest of the world, or at least the dozen who would represent the world on his jury, to think he had been crazy —and did make them think so—but he didn't want me to agree with them. As a sane man who, by pretending to be a lunatic, had done as he pleased and escaped punishment, he had a joke—if you wanted to call it that—on the world. But if he was a lunatic who, ignorant of his craziness, thought he was pretending to be a lunatic, then the joke— if you wanted to call it that—was on him. And my having such a joke on him was more that his egotism could stomach, even though it's not likely he ever admitted to himself that he was, or might be, actually crazy. Whatever he thought, he never spoke to me after the hospital interview in which I had said he was legally entitled to escape hanging.

His trial, when he was well enough to appear in court some months later, was every bit of the circus he had promised, and the newspapers had their happy convulsions. He was tried in the county court house for Mrs. Cotton's murder. Two new witnesses had been found, who had seen him walking away from the rear of the Cotton house that morning, and a third who identified his car as the one that had been parked four blocks away all—or all the latter part of—the previous night. The city and county district attorneys agreed that this evidence made the Cotton case the strongest against him.

Fitzstephan's plea was *Not guilty by reason of insanity,* or whatever the legal wording was. Since Mrs. Cotton's murder had been the last of his crimes, his lawyers could, and did, introduce, as proof of his insanity, all that he had done in the others. They made a high, wide, and handsome job of it, carrying out his original idea that the best way to prove him crazy was to show he had committed more crimes than any sane man could have. Well, it was plain enough that he had.

He had known Alice Dain, his cousin, in New York when she and Gabrielle, then a child, were living there. Gabrielle couldn't corroborate this: we had only Fitzstephan's word for it; but it may have been so. He said they concealed his relationship from the others because they did not want the girl's father—for whom Alice was then searching—to know that she was bringing with her any links with the dangerous past. Fitzstephan said Alice had been his mistress in New York: that could have been true, but didn't matter.

After Alice and Gabrielle left New York for San Francisco, Fitzstephan and the woman exchanged letters occasionally, but with no definite purpose. Fitzstephan then met the Haldorns. The cult was his idea: he organized it, financed it, and brought it to San Francisco, though he kept his connection with it a secret, since everyone who knew him knew his skepticism; and his interest in it would have advertised it as the fake it was. To him, he said, the cult was a combination of toy and meal-ticket: he liked influencing people, especially in obscure ways, and people didn't seem to like buying his books.

Aaronia Haldorn was his mistress. Joseph was a puppet, in the family as in the Temple.

In San Francisco Fitzstephan and Alice arranged so that he became acquainted with her husband and Gabrielle through other friends of the family. Gabrielle was now a young woman. Her physical peculiarities, which he interpreted pretty much as she had, fascinated him; and he tried his luck with her. He didn't have any. That made him doubly determined to land her: he was that way. Alice was his ally. She knew him and she hated the girl—so she wanted him to have her. Alice had told Fitzstephan the family history. The girl's father did not know at this time that she had been taught to think him her mother's murderer. He knew she had a deep aversion to him, but did not know on what it was based. He thought that what he had gone through in prison and since had marked him with a hardness naturally enough repellant to a young girl who was, in spite of their relationship, actually only a recent acquaintance.

He learned the truth about it when, surprising Fitzstephan in further attempts to make Gabrielle—as Fitzstephan put it—listen to reason, he had got into a three-cornered row with the pair of them. Leggett now began to understand what sort of a woman he was married to. Fitzstephan was no longer invited to the Leggett house, but kept in touch with Alice and waited his time.

His time came when Upton arrived with his demand for blackmail. Alice went to Fitzstephan for advice. He gave it to her—poisonously. He urged her to handle Upton herself, concealing his demand—his knowledge of the Leggett past—from Leggett. He told her she should above all else continue to keep her knowledge of Leggett's Central American and Mexican history concealed from him—a valuable hold on him now that he hated her because of what she'd taught the girl. Giving Upton the diamonds, and faking the burglary evidence, were Fitzstephan's ideas. Poor Alice didn't mean anything to him: he didn't care what happened to her so long as he could ruin Leggett and get Gabrielle.

He succeeded in the first of those aims: guided by him, Alice completely demolished the Leggett household, thinking, until the very last, when he pursued her after giving her the pistol in the laboratory, that he had a clever plan by which they would be saved; that is, she and he would:

her husband didn't count with her any more than she with Fitzstephan. Fitzstephan had had to kill her, of course, to keep her from exposing him when she found that his clever plan was a trap for her.

Fitzstephan said he killed Leggett himself. When Gabrielle left the house after seeing Ruppert's murder, she left a note saying she had gone for good. That broke up the arrangement as far as Leggett was concerned. He told Alice he was through, was going away, and offered of his own accord to write a statement assuming responsibility for what she had done. Fitzstephan tried to persuade Alice to kill him, but she wouldn't. He did. He wanted Gabrielle, and he didn't think a live Leggett, even though a fugitive from justice, would let him have her.

Fitzstephan's success in getting rid of Leggett, and in escaping detection by killing Alice, encouraged him. He went blithely on with his plan to get the girl. The Haldorns had been introduced to the Leggetts some months before, and already had her nibbling at their hook. She had gone to them when she ran away from home. Now they persuaded her to come to the Temple again. The Haldorns didn't know what Fitzstephan was up to, what he had done to the Leggetts: they thought that the girl was only another of the likely prospects he fed them. But Doctor Riese, hunting for Joseph in Joseph's part of the Temple the day I got there, opened a door that should have been locked, and saw Fitzstephan and the Haldorns in conference.

That was dangerous: Riese couldn't be kept quiet, and, once Fitzstephan's connection with the Temple was known, as likely as not the truth about his part in the Leggett riot would come out. He had two easily handled tools—Joseph and Minnie. He had Riese killed. But that woke Aaronia up to his true interest in Gabrielle. Aaronia, jealous, could and would either make him give up the girl or ruin him. He persuaded Joseph that none of them was safe from the gallows while Aaronia lived. When I saved Aaronia by killing her husband, I also saved Fitzstephan for the time: Aaronia and Fink had to keep quiet about Riese's death if they wanted to save themselves from being charged with complicity in it.

By this time Fitzstephan had hit his stride. He looked on Gabrielle now as his property, bought with the deaths he had caused. Each death had increased her price, her value to him. When Eric carried her off and married her, Fitzstephan hadn't hesitated. Eric was to be killed.

Nearly a year before, Fitzstephan had wanted a quiet place where he could go to finish a novel. Mrs. Fink, my village-blacksmith, had recommended Quesada. She was a native of the village, and her son by a former marriage, Harvey Whidden, was living there. Fitzstephan went to Quesada for a couple of months, and became fairly well acquainted with Whidden. Now that there was another murder to be done, Fitzstephan remembered Whidden as a man who might do it, for a price.

When Fitzstephan heard that Collinson wanted a quiet place where his wife could rest and recuperate while they were waiting for the Haldorns' trial, he suggested Quesada. Well, it was a quiet place, probably the quietest in California. Then Fitzstephan went to Whidden with an offer of a thousand dollars for Eric's murder. Whidden refused at first, but he wasn't nimble-witted, and Fitzstephan could be persuasive enough, so the bargain had been made.

Whidden bungled a try at it Thursday night, frightening Collinson into wiring me, saw the wire in the telegraph office, and thought he had to go through with it then to save himself. So he fortified himself with whiskey, followed Collinson Friday night, and shoved him off the cliff. Then he took some more whiskey and came to San Francisco, considering himself by this time a hell of a desperate guy. He phoned his employer, saying: "Well, I killed him easy enough and dead enough. Now I want my money."

Fitzstephan's phone came through the house switchboard: he didn't know who might have heard Whidden talking. He decided to play safe. He pretended he didn't know who was talking nor what he was talking about. Thinking Fitzstephan was double-crossing him, knowing what the novelist wanted, Whidden decided to take the girl and hold her for, not his original thousand dollars, but ten thousand. He had enough drunken cunning to disguise his handwriting when he wrote his note to Fitzstephan, not to sign it, and to so word it that Fitzstephan couldn't tell the police who had sent it without explaining how he knew who had sent it.

Fitzstephan wasn't sitting any too pretty. When he got Whidden's note, he decided to play his hand boldly, pushing his thus-far-solid luck. He told me about the phone-call and gave me the letter. That entitled him to show himself in Quesada with an excellent reason for being there. But he came down ahead of time, the night before he joined me, and went to the marshal's house to ask Mrs. Cotton—whose relation to Whidden he knew—where he could find the man. Whidden was there, hiding from the marshal. Whidden wasn't nimble-witted, and Fitzstephan was persuasive enough when he wanted to be: Fitzstephan explained how Whidden's recklessness had forced him to pretend to not understand the phone-call. Fitzstephan had a scheme by which Whidden could now collect his ten thousand dollars in safety, or so he made Whidden think.

Whidden went back to his hiding-place. Fitzstephan remained with Mrs. Cotton. She, poor woman, now knew too much, and didn't like what she knew. She was doomed: killing people was the one sure and safe way of keeping them quiet: his whole recent experience proved it. His experience with Leggett told him that if he could get her to leave behind a statement in which various mysterious points were satisfactorily—and not too truthfully—explained, his situation would be still further improved. She suspected his intentions, and didn't want to help him carry them out. She finally wrote the statement he dictated, but not until late in the morning. His description of how he finally got it from her wasn't pleasant; but he got it, and then strangled her, barely finishing when her husband arrived home from his all-night hunt.

Fitzstephan escaped by the back door—the witnesses who had seen him go away from the house didn't come forward until his photograph in the papers jogged their memories—and joined Vernon and me at the hotel. He went with us to Whidden's hiding-place below Dull Point. He knew Whidden, knew the dull man's probable reaction to this second betrayal. He knew that neither Cotton nor Feeney would be sorry to have to shoot Whidden. Fitzstephan believed he could trust to his luck and what gamblers call the percentage of the situation. That failing, he meant to stumble when he stepped from the boat, accidentally shooting Whidden with the gun in his hand. (He remembered how neatly he had disposed of Mrs. Leggett.) He might have been blamed for that, might even have been suspected, but he could hardly have been convicted of anything.

Once again his luck held. Whidden, seeing Fitzstephan with us, had flared up and tried to shoot him, and we had killed Whidden.

That was the story with which this crazy man, thinking himself sane, tried to establish his insanity, and succeeded. The other charges against him were dropped. He was sent to the state asylum at Napa. A year later he was discharged. I don't suppose the asylum officials thought him cured: they thought he was too badly crippled ever to be dangerous again.

Aaronia Haldorn carried him off to an island in Puget Sound, I've heard.

She testified at his trial, as one of his witnesses, but was not herself tried for anything. The attempt of her husband and Fitzstephan to kill her had, for all practical purposes, removed her from among the guilty.

We never found Mrs. Fink.

Tom Fink drew a five-to-fifteen-years jolt in San Quentin for what he had done to Fitzstephan. Neither of them seemed to blame the other now, and each tried to cover the other up on the witness stand. Fink's professed motive for the bombing was to avenge his step-son's death, but nobody swallowed that. He had tried to check Fitzstephan's activities before Fitzstephan brought the whole works down on their ears.

Released from prison, finding himself shadowed, Fink had seen both reason for fear and a means to safety in that shadow. He *had* back-doored Mickey that night, slipping out to get the material for his bomb, and then in again, working all night on the bomb. The news he had brought me was supposed to account for his presence in Quesada. The bomb wasn't large—its outer cover was an aluminum soap container wrapped in white paper—and neither he nor Fitzstephan had had any difficulty in concealing it from me when it passed between them during their handshaking. Fitzstephan had thought it something Aaronia was sending him, something important enough to justify the risk in sending it. He couldn't have refused to take it without attracting my attention, without giving away the connection between him and Fink. He had concealed it until we had left the room, and then had opened it—to wake up in the hospital. Tom Fink had thought himself safe, with Mickey to testify that he had shadowed him from the time he had left the prison, and me to account for his behavior on the scene of the bombing.

Fitzstephan said that he did not think Alice Leggett's account of the killing of her sister Lily was the truth, that he thought she—Alice—had done the killing herself and had lied to hurt Gabrielle. Everybody took it for granted that he was right—everybody, including Gabrielle—though he didn't have any evidence to support what was after all only his guess. I was tempted to have the agency's Paris correspondent see what he could dig up on that early affair, but decided not to. It was nobody's business except Gabrielle's, and she seemed happy enough with what had already been dug up.

She was in the Collinsons' hands now. They had come to Quesada for her as soon as the newspapers put out their first extra accusing Fitzstephan of Eric's murder. The Collinsons hadn't had to be crude about it—to admit that they'd ever suspected her of anything: when Andrews had surrendered his letters testamentary, and another administrator—Walter Fielding—had been appointed, the Collinsons had simply seemed to pick her up, as was their right as her closest relations, where Andrews had put her down. Two months in the mountains topped off her cure, and she came back to the city looking like nothing that she had been. The difference was not only in appearance.

"I can't really make myself believe that all that actually happened to me," she told me one noon when she, Laurence Collinson, and I were lunching together between morning and afternoon court-sessions. "Is it, do you think, because there was so much of it that I became callous?"

"No. Remember you were going around coked up most of the time. That saved you from the sharp edge. Lucky for you you were. Stay away from the morphine now and it'll always be a hazy sort of dream. Any time you want to bring it back clear and vivid, take a jolt."

"I won't, I won't, ever," she said; "not even to give you the—the fun of bullying me through a cure again. He enjoyed himself awfully," she told Laurence Collinson. "He used to curse me, ridicule me, threaten me with the most terrible things, and then, at the last, I think he tried to seduce me. And if I'm uncouth at times, Laurence, you'll have to blame him: he positively hadn't a refining influence."

She seemed to have come back far enough.

Laurence Collinson laughed with us, but not from any farther down than his chin. I had an idea he thought I hadn't a refining influence.

DASHIELL HAMMETT was born in St. Mary's County, Maryland, in 1894. He grew up in Philadelphia and Baltimore. He left school at fourteen and held all kinds of jobs thereafter—messenger boy, newsboy, clerk, timekeeper, yardman, machine operator, and stevedore. He finally became an operative for Pinkerton's Detective Agency.

World War I, in which he served as a sergeant, interrupted his sleuthing and injured his health. When he was finally discharged from the last of several hospitals, he resumed detective work. Subsequently he turned to writing, and in the late 1920's he became the unquestioned master of detective-story fiction in America. During World War II, Mr. Hammett again served as a sergeant in the Army, this time for over two years, most of which was spent in the Aleutians. He died in 1961.